WHITE LIGHT
A Paranormal Mystery

Anna Simpson

White Light by Anna Simpson Published by Faux Publishing, PO Box 399, Grand Forks, BC, Canada, V0H 1H0

Book ISBN: 978-0-9950744-1-5

Dedication

Bossman880

I'm shouting three words for all the world to hear.

Mum

Chapter 1

To stay free, I perform a ritual every morning. It begins with stepping outside, where dawn streams through the leafy branches of my maple tree, landing, shifting, and dancing on the flowerbeds at my bare feet. A steaming cup of coffee warms my hands. The fragrant air fills my lungs. I sip, leaving the liquid on my tongue to capture a moment of rich goodness.

My name is Emma, and I need to stay grounded and calm. It's important for my health, so I walk along the fence and let the cool blades of grass tickle my toes and dewdrops cling to my skin. For fun, I kick a ball of dandelion fluff. Little parachutes take flight catching the same breeze moving the leaves above my head. The seeds float up, and up, over the fence to land on Mrs. Perkins' perfectly tended lawn. Not a dandelion or mat of moss to be seen.

In a half acre of green sits one flowerbed, brimming with Lily of the Valley. I remember the first time I saw them over fifteen years ago. The delicate white bells could only be fairy hats. Today, the round base of cemented river stone is still full of waxy green spear tips. I don't see fairy hats anymore. No, now I enjoy the effects of nature—its simple perfection.

Mrs. Perkins does it best. In fact, everything around Mrs. Perkins is perfectly cared for—her home, her yard, her car—all perfect.

But not today. A dark line sits between the jamb and the edge of the door.

A few inches of shadow drives my calm away and prickles the long blonde hairs at the nape of my neck. Butterflies in my stomach tell, no scratch that, *demand* I find my phone and go next door.

Don't get the wrong idea. I'm not a snoop.

Mrs. Perkins, a wiry old bird, did everything herself. I'm not sure if it is because she's the independent sort or if she has no one else to help her. Either way, when she suggested we watch out for one another, I agreed.

I'm also alone. It doesn't bother me unless I catch the flu or something. Then I wonder if I will die and no one will notice. It's a thought, or fear, I can't shake. Mrs. Perkins' house has my full attention, and within it sits the same worry. I'll check on her because she would do the same for me.

I crash into my kitchen, slopping my coffee onto the

counter as I slam the mug down. My phone could be anywhere. My gaze travels from the pine tabletop to the gray marble counter. It's not here. I push through the swinging door to the living area, run my fingertips between the couch and chair cushions, scan the smoked-glass coffee table through my veil of long blonde hair, and sneak a peek under my overturned book on the throw rug. Desperate, I check around the bowl by the door where I toss my keys as I pass the spiral staircase to the loft. Still nothing.

Down the short hallway, I rush to my bedroom. I tug the midnight blue duvet off the bed and shake it. My pulse speeds up as something thuds on to the carpet. I pick up my smartphone and check the battery. Half power.

Excellent. I dash through my front door, across the lawn and unlatch Mrs. Perkins' white picket gate. Her shiny yellow front door looks as solid as stone. I follow her path to the back wondering if danger lurks.

I gasp as I near the door. It's like living a moment in a crime drama. I mimic what I have watched on television and bring up my phone to take a picture. Inching forward, heart pounding, I wonder if poor Mrs. Perkins is sprawled out on the bathroom floor, from a stroke, heart attack, or a butcher knife.

Don't worry, Mrs. Perkins. I'm coming.

I pull my cotton sleeve over my hand and push the door wider. Her kitchen looks untouched as if it's sterilized or newly installed. Tiles cool my bare feet with each step. Fear scratches at my nerves, "Mrs. Perkins? It's Emma from next door. Are you okay?"

Silence.

I raise the phone to call for help.

A small sound carries from deeper in the house. I should stop, leave, and make the call. Following the sound might be dangerous or, worse, plain stupid. And I'm scared. So scared, my breathing is all I hear over the pounding of my heart.

I'd look stupid if I'm wrong. Ravenglass Lake is so small-townsville, and Benny the bully is like no cop I've ever met. He would be no help. Worst of all, they'd call me crazy for sure. I slip the phone back into my denim pocket, quietly open her knife drawer, and pull out a meat cleaver. Armed, I creep forward.

Thank goodness Mrs. Perkins likes an open airy room. Evil housebreakers have nowhere to hide in the dining room.

A small thump like a cat landing on carpet makes me jump. But Mrs. Perkins doesn't have a cat...or carpet— only allergies.

I tighten my grip on the cleaver as I stick my head into the living room. All is quiet and undisturbed. I enter the corridor to the front door. To my right are stairs to the upper floor. Farther ahead is a hall closet and nook where she keeps a desk and a small bookcase. Nothing seems touched.

I glance up at the glittery ceiling, swallow, and pull my phone from my pocket. The sensible thing is to dial 911. I sidestep for the front door, but in my mind's eye Mrs. Perkins, wiry but frail, shakes her head. Her arm outstretched urging me not to leave.

Thump, I freeze. The noise is right beside me coming from the hall closet.

Without thinking, I open the door and find Mrs. Perkins tied up with duct tape across her lips. Her green eyes, round and unblinking, grow wide, and her usual perfect curls are mussed. I drop the cleaver. It clatters on the floor, and I pull the tape free.

"Are you okay?" My voice is a loud whisper.

"Finally," she mutters. Her lined face pales against the pink patches on her cheeks.

"The door was open. What—"

"You took long enough." Mrs. Perkins raises her arms bound at the wrist with plastic ties. "Don't just stare.

Cut me free."

"Hold still." I grab the cleaver.

"Are you mad?"

I blink at her.

"Oh, all right, but be careful. I'm out of time. Another minute and I'd've soiled myself."

I bite my lip to stop my smile, gently tuck the blade under the strapping, and drag the blade against the plastic. She pulls her wrists down on the blade, and in moments, she half-runs half-walks toward her guest bathroom.

I turn on my heel and take the cleaver back to the kitchen. I'm not sure if putting it back where I found it is a good idea. Would Mrs. Perkins prefer to wash it before it is put away? As I'm mulling this over, Mrs. Perkins enters the kitchen still tucking her blouse into her slacks.

Her slippers slap the floor tiles as she heads for the coffeepot. "I still don't understand what took you so long. I should've had a plan B, apparently you are unreliable."

"Unreliable? Me? What were you doing all tied up in the hall closet anyway?" I drop the cleaver in the drawer.

"Oh, didn't I tell you? I have taken up the fine art of writing fiction."

My dark blonde eyebrows come together. "You said you were retired. Is that supposed to explain tying yourself up and locking yourself in a closet?"

"Well, I'm writing a murder mystery, and I want to describe the experience. My readers will want to live the events as I describe them."

"I understand." But I didn't really. Maybe my old doctor should check her out. "Was there no other way?"

Mrs. Perkins turns to face me. "Do you take cream or sugar?"

"You want to play coy? Fine, but you know I'll figure it out sooner or later." I take in the bare counters again. On every other occasion Mrs. Perkins left plates full of goodies sitting out. "Where did you stash your snacks? I'm starved. I haven't had breakfast yet."

"Check my freezer. Just pop what you choose into the gillibebop."

"Gilly-be-bop?" I look around, but I have no idea what she means.

Her smile widens. "What do you want? I have pie—apple, blueberry, strawberry-rhubarb—or chocolate chip cookies." Mrs. Perkins lifts a packet from the freezer drawer and waves it at me. "Oh, I have birthday cake. Better toss that."

"I like birthday cake." I try to catch the waving packet. "If you hold still for a moment."

A packet in each hand, Mrs. Perkins rests a wrist on her hips. "I'm tossing the birthday cake. I can't remember when it went in. Emma, promise me you'll eat nothing out of the fridge when you don't remember when it went in." She taps her foot, waiting.

I say nothing. What's there to say?

"Well, I'm waiting." Her foot stops.

"Oh, you mean right now. Okay, I promise. Just hand over something, anything. I can't wait another minute."

She gives me a sharp nod and hands me both packages. Grabs the coffeepot and fills it with water. Humming, she transfers the water to the coffeemaker.

I place the frozen packages on her table. I'd defrost them if I knew what the gillibebop was. Realizing frozen cookies are almost as good as frozen cookie dough, I tear open the wrappings and try to break a chunk off. It's impossible. I gnaw on the cookie clump. Not bad.

Mrs. Perkins loads a tray with cups and saucers, cream and sugar, and a small plate for the solid mass of six cookies with the chewed corner.

"Oh, Emma really." She tsks me when she glances my way. "Were you raised by wolves? Manners young lady."

"I said I was starving. I was on my way to breakfast when I spotted your door. My heart is still pounding out of control." I place my palm to my chest to make my point. "I'm supposed to stay calm you know."

"You're such a dramatic young woman. Is it your blood sugar? Your aunt had the same thing."

I don't have blood sugar problems, but that answer is as good as any. "She was my great aunt, and you were closer than I ever was." I twist my hair into a rope and throw it over my shoulder.

"Emma," says Mrs. Perkins. "You two are from the same cloth. Get the tray will you and follow me upstairs. I have something to show you."

The heavy tray rattles and clatters as I try to keep up with Mrs. Perkins quick steps. She moves with such a straight back that I wonder if she was ever in the military. The way she keeps house, her manners, strict regimen make it a possibility.

I follow her through an open door and stop in my tracks. I have read of rooms like this. She must have spent years collecting odds and ends from across the globe. One wall is filled with bookshelves stuffed with knickknacks, awards, and books—not one hardcover in the lot. Pocket books shoved in all directions crammed into two shelves.

Photo albums, from the old fashioned cardboard antique variety to modern new ones with plastic sheets over sticky pages, stand tall along the next shelf. A 2-inch thick scrapbook lays open on the floor. The pages visible show a tribute to my aunt's funeral.

By the window stands a coat rack with wigs, clothing, and such. I get an inkling Mrs. Perkins plays dress-up when writing her scenes. I spot a brilliant blue feather boa among the clutter. An old writing desk angles away from the wall, a closed laptop on the work surface and a modern office chair behind it. The chair has so many levers and buttons, I can only guess their uses.

A guest chair, a straight-back wooden job, sits in a corner. Mrs. Perkins removes a packing box from its seat and slides the sturdy box beside her wastebasket.

"Just put the tray there." Her long fingers point in the general direction of the desk.

I do what I'm told, then sit on the chair in the corner. The chair sways slightly, squeaking as I shift my weight.

Mrs. Perkins glares at me, and I glare back, stretching to pick up my frozen mass of cookies. I find a soft spot and break a chunk free.

The chair complains as I shift uncomfortably.

"Emma maybe you should sit on the couch."

There is no couch. "Are you referring to the one next door?"

"You are such a card." Mrs. Perkins snorts then sidesteps around me to the costumes and moves the feather boa aside. "Here it is."

If that's a couch, I'm a walking talking beanbag. "Guess again." I rise from the chair, and slide the box to the side of the desk, push down on its folded top, and find it solid enough to sit on. I smile sweetly at my old family friend, grab the cushion off of the chair, square it on the box top, and sit again.

Mrs. Perkins eyebrows almost disappear into her wild gray hair. I widen my smile and lift the cookies to my mouth. "Emma Leigh Johnston. Stop right there."

I don't stop. I stare into her shining green eyes, pull back my lips, and attempt to gnaw free a chunk of chocolate.

She tries to stare me down, but Mrs. Perkins hasn't met my mother.

The thought of Mom stops me cold. "Okay, you said you had something to show me. What is it?"

She spreads her arms out as if ready to take a bow.

"Please just tell me what you want me to see. I

haven't even had a whole cup of coffee yet today." I try looking harder at the room. Over Mrs. Perkins left shoulder hanging on the wall rests a bulletin board. I read some of the notes: grocery list, a to-do list; several scraps of paper with names and phone numbers. Behind her head, a group of photos flare in a bouquet. I recognize no one.

She doesn't move or answer me.

What's she waiting for?

My gaze follows her arms, and I wonder if she is trying to give me a clue. Her right fingertips almost touch a silk Japanese lily while her left hand aims at the empty wooden chair. Still confused, I meet her eyes.

"You don't have the gift, do you?"

"The gift?" I drop the cookies on the tray.

She tries to find the words. While she slowly sips her coffee, I hope for a proper explanation and force myself to relax, not believing for one moment she was ever experimenting or writing a book.

I stand up and walk over to the scrapbook. "Do you mind?" Expecting no reply, I pick it up and flip to the front. "Is this you and my aunt in jail?"

"Yes, we always seemed to find our share of trouble." She smiles and color brightens her pale cheeks. "Alice was such fun."

An internal warning alarm goes off. "What do you mean?"

"Well, I've known your great aunt most of my adult life." She stops talking tapping a fingertip on the desk. "The question is how well did you know your aunt?"

"Me, I met her only once." Bringing the large book back to my box, I sit, resting it on my knees. My fingertip slides between the thick pages as I flip through. "I do feel bad about that. When I was sixteen she sent me a tarot deck, then, this year, she willed me her house."

I glance up at her, and she glares hard at me. "I think you'd have liked her."

"Tell me about that." This time I meet and hold her gaze. Something important looms in the air, and I stare above the old woman's perfectly plucked brows.

"I tied myself up to test you. I was sure you'd sense I was in trouble and come over, but you didn't. You had to see the door ajar before you sought me out."

"Test me for what? Please, just say it straight out. What is on your mind? Mrs. Perkins…Millie, talk to me."

"Alice was my best friend. My world, my life, was different—better—with her in. I miss that. I miss her." She relaxes her arms. "I was hoping you had the same outlook."

"I don't understand."

"And that's the problem."

"I'll tell you what, you tell me what's on your mind and I promise to help you anyway I can."

"Thank you, but I don't think you have her ability."

"Oh, you're not talking about her psychic abilities are you?"

She falls back in her chair. "Yes." She exhales slowly. "I need help, and you're my last hope."

"Sorry?" I almost laugh but purse my lips at the last moment when I take in her expression. Millie Perkins has tears in her eyes. My voice softens. "I understand. What do you need me to do?"

Chapter 2

We enter my house through the front door, and it reminds me of the first time I walked in the door after Aunt Alice died. Emptiness hangs in the air, and the place seems hollow…and too quiet.

"Do you want coffee or tea?" I don't expect Mrs. Perkins to choose either. She finished a cup of whatever at her place but asking seems the polite thing to do, and I suddenly realize being polite may be the only way to get through the next half hour.

"No, but I know you do. May I go up to the loft?"

"Sure, go on up."

Mrs. Perkins hasn't visited the loft for at least six months, and I haven't been at all. I just couldn't get past the first step.

I pause at the kitchen door until her singsong voice drifts down the hallway as she speaks to the empty room. My heart breaks for the old gal.

I trudge into the kitchen and close the back door. Next, I wipe away my spilled coffee and dump out the cup. It takes time to find a thermal mug in cluttered cupboards, and when I do, I fill it to the top with my wonderful brew.

I hope the coffee keeps me grounded—something has to. Inside a kitchen drawer await my cards fully protected and wrapped in silk. I sigh and gently pick them up.

These tarot cards are supposed to speak to me like old friends might, guiding me, offering sound advice. My sweet-sixteen gift from Aunt Alice because she saw something in me no one else did. For a while I hoped she was right, but in high school my predictions proved too far off. I soon gave up reading for anyone but myself.

At the foot of the stairs I take a few deep breaths. After two tries I make it to the second step. The rest seem easier, and, in moments, I enter the psychic world of Alice Bontaine. She was a worldwide celebrity in psychic circles and very, very good at what she did.

The cards tremble in my hand. "Do you mind if I get acquainted with the room before we get started?"

Mrs. Perkins rests in a wingback chair. In front of her sits a small table large enough for a spread of cards, a candle, and a cup. I carefully place my cards on the round table in the center of the room. All the things I had dreamt of and read about as a teenager boldly displayed. A crystal ball the size of an apple sits with a whole host of other paraphernalia, a glass bowl for water gazing, a large collection of tiny bottles full of essential oils, candles of every possible color for grounding, protection, energy, focus, etc. I recognize almost everything.

I choose a fat white candle, wiping away the dust on it as I bring it to the table. Mrs. Perkins' elbows rest on the table edge as I mutter a blessing and light the candlewick. Not ready to do what I must, I go through the collection of incense and light a stick each of sandalwood and lavender. I circle the room once more, wondering if I forgot anything.

I meet Mrs. Perkins' eyes. A small smile tugs at her lightly painted lips. Her green eyes sparkle with something akin to excitement. She sits on the edge of her chair, and I wonder momentarily if I'm humoring an old woman or if I'm able to do as she asks.

Electricity dances along my skin. The nape of my neck tingles, and I can almost sense another presence in the room.

Ready or not, I sit and unwrap my deck silently asking each card to help my aunt's last friend. A tingling sensation travels up from my fingertips, and images flash through my mind: flapping white fabric, a young face of a woman, and rows of dark windows.

I offer Mrs. Perkins the deck. "Please cut the cards

and concentrate on a question."

A moment later I open my eyes and find myself on the living room couch, looking up at the ceiling. The room bathed in twilight, and my head throbs.

"What happened?" I croak it out, clear my throat, and try again. "Mrs. Perkins, what's going on?"

"What do you mean?"

She acts as if nothing has happened. She looks happy, her eyes still sparkling with life.

"Is there something wrong with the tea, dear?"

She rarely calls me dear, and when she does I've learned bad news follows. "No. Nothing. I feel like I just woke up."

"Oh, you're tired. I should get going."

I sit up straighter. "No. Stay." My aunt's tea set is spread out on the coffee table. She liked pansies, and their little blue-yellow faces decorate each piece of china. *Okay, Emma, you can do this.* "I'm a bit foggy. I know this sounds stupid, but remind me what we did today."

"Well, you read my cards. You're better than Alice, do you know that? Right after you finished, you leaned back and closed your eyes. You took so long I was ready to go home and let you rest, but just as I got up to leave, you suggested a walk in the park."

So no doctors, no hospital. Unless she is lying.
"You're sure that's all?"

"I would like to remind you of who you are talking to." She brings her arched brows together. Mrs. Perkins places a cup of sweet tea in my hand, holding on until I grasp it. Two little tablets rest on the coffee table. "Drink your tea."

She means, take your pills.

Two windows are open in the living room. Birdsong rides in with the honeysuckle breeze fluttering the curtains. "What time is it?"

"Oh, about seven. The six o'clock news just finished up."

She knows about my meds but not my stay in the hospital or why I take them. Today, I walked and talked as if I was fine, but I'm not. How fine can I be? I blacked out.

Maybe I forgot to take my morning pills. That must be it. I pick up the tablets, pop them into my mouth, and take a sip of tea.

"Are you ready?" Mrs. Perkins sits perched on the edge of the glider.

"Ready? Ready for what?" My voice doesn't sound right, and I clear my throat.

"To talk about what to do next. I checked the paper

while you made up the tea tray. There wasn't much there. What do you think? Take a look at back issues?"

I bite my inner lip. "Um…I don't know—"

She raises a hand palm toward my chest. "You promised to help me."

"What? Oh, I will." She doesn't have a clue, and I need to keep it that way. The delicate cup shakes in my grasp. I sip, long and slow. This simple act calms me, and I let the stillness I desperately need take over. "I was okay all day, right? I didn't act weird or scary?"

Mrs. Perkins puts her teacup down. "Why would you say a thing like that? You acted like you've always done."

I stare at her not sure if I should be frightened or relieved.

"Emma?"

"I'd like to make a doctor's appointment for tomorrow."

"What's the matter?" Mrs. Perkins reaches for my forehead resting her palm on my brow. "You're flushed but no fever."

My thumb squeaks along the golden edge of my cup. "Something's off. Can you recommend somebody?" I barely hear my whisper.

"Yes. Dr. Logan." She smiles, glancing down at her delicate gold wristwatch. "Oh, is that the time? I have things to do at home before bed. I'll call first thing and get you in tomorrow."

"Thanks." I let out a breath full of relief.

"They'll ask why."

"Yes, yes, of course." I shake my head. "I've been light headed today."

"And you didn't say a word 'til now?" Mrs. Perkins stands and shakes out her skirt. "I understand. We had such a nice day."

I almost hear the ending to her sentence—until you started acting like this. "Promise to come in and get me if I don't answer the door." The thought of being too ill to let her in makes me shiver.

"You're not feeling well at all, but don't worry you can count on me. I'll make the appointment and come over for coffee. Shall I drive us in?"

I nod and silently follow her to the door. She steps out, and I lockup after her.

Even with Mrs. Perkins gone, I don't feel alone.

Chapter 3

"Focus on the light." Dr. Logan holds a small flashlight within inches of my eye. "Okay…good…now follow it. Great." He sits back on his stool and wheels to his computer. "I'll send your blood work to the lab, but from what I can see, you are a healthy young woman."

Good. *Okay, I'm fine as far as a physician can tell.*

I sit on the exam table and glance out the window. His office, and three others like it, take up a wing within the Dunster General Hospital, the only place in the tri-town area for medical care.

He looks at my file and pulls a face. He knows. I know he knows about me. I swallow to steady my voice. "Should I see a specialist?"

He smiles and nods his understanding. His yellow teeth tell me they must have come with the original package. No dentures would be that bad. "Don't jump ahead. We'll get your results from the lab first."

My grip eases on the examination table. "I'm done?" My gut reaction is beyond my control. A lone wave of fear hits. It ebbs slowly away leaving my skin clammy.

Was I let out too soon? What if I shouldn't be running around loose?

"Emma, don't worry and trust me. I have over forty years of experience. I'm sure I've seen everything there is to see. You're fine." He puts the keyboard down, reaches out, and pats my hand. "I promise to call you if anything is amiss."

I take a deep breath, exhale, and slide closer to the edge of the table, wanting to believe him.

"For you my dear, I'll put a rush on it." He leans back again to pick up his wireless keyboard and pecks away to make a note. "Now, if you find the stress of waiting too much, I can give you a tablet for tonight."

"No, no thank you." I gather my things and pile them on my lap. "Do you think I might hear sometime tomorrow?"

He smiles. "Think of it as no news is good news."

I can do this. It's only twenty-four, maybe forty-eight hours. I just need to keep busy. "Okay. Thanks for seeing me on such short notice." I offer him my hand.

The doctor holds it for a moment looking at it. *What's this about?* "When I heard that Alice had a grandniece, I jumped at the chance to help. She was my patient too. You remind me of her. She had long fingers like yours." He gives me a gentle squeeze, let's go, and opens the door. "Take care, young lady." He pulls the door closed behind him. It seals with a click.

How did he do it? I fumble with my clothes and dress. I'm fine. With one touch, my fear is gone.

The four doctor's offices share a central waiting area. Several rows of chairs with a small bookcase on each end are grouped around a cozy play area. As I follow the hallway from the examination room to the waiting area, I scan the large space for Mrs. Perkins.

She waves me over, while speaking with two older-looking women near the street entrance. I join them. They glance at me, at each other, and back at me.

Blushing to the roots, I check for an exposed seam.

"Alice, this is Gladys and Jaylynne. They go by Glady and Jay. And this is Ali...oh, excuse me, what am I saying?" Mrs. Perkins laughs, shaking her head. "This is Emma."

Blue-haired Glady's smile widens. False teeth click together as she offers me her delicate hand. "Nice to meet you Emma."

I smile back, taking it. She's nice.

Jay, the frail one with the cane and a chicken neck, whacks me away when I offer her a shake. "Don't give me any lip chickadee, and we'll get along just fine."

I step back giving Jay space, sensing something in the wind.

"How are you feeling? Any better?" Mrs. Perkins smiles one of her more sympathetic smiles, then winks at me.

Wondering what the wink means, I ignore it. "Ah, well…yes. Just a checkup."

Mrs. Perkins frowns, curling her bottom lip. *Right, I told her I wasn't feeling well.*

The two women speak together.

"Really." Glady beams, her blue hair bobbing.

Cane lady, Jay, pipes up, "I'll call then. You're still using Alice's number, aren't you?"

Like stepping into ice water, it's all shock and alarms. Before I find out more about it, Glady and Jay chorus, "I'll call to set something up."

Mrs. Perkins waves a little hanky at the women walking away chattering like squirrels. They glance back at us and wave, then giggle as they make their way out the double doors to the parking lot.

"What just happened?" My hands go to my hips. I shift my weight to stop myself from tapping my foot.

"Well, I ran into Glady and Jay while I was waiting

for you." Mrs. Perkins gazes up at me. "They were worried that I was ill. Then one thing led to another, and I was talking about you and your reading for me—"

"Oh, no. You didn't…I mean, you didn't tell them." I take a few steps and turn back to her. "That was between you and me. I'm not going to read for anyone else. Most of what I said was probably crap."

"Emma, really. You are making a scene." I notice many of the people around us staring our way.

She takes my arm encouraging me to walk out the automatic doors. "I'll tell you right now, Glady and Jay will have this all over town. Your shouting about it backs up their story. So.Settle.Down."

As we leave the building, I bring a hand up to shade my eyes from the sun. It's coming up on high noon. The sunshine glares off the windshields in the parking lot and the windows across the street. Neat little houses surround the hospital like soldiers. Between the houses and the hospital is a narrow parking lot, a grassy patch and narrow road with gravelly edges.

We approach Mrs. Perkins' old sixty-something car. It's bigger than a boat. "I can't read for just anyone. How could you tell them? I trusted you."

Opening the car door without unlocking it, Mrs.

Perkins gets in and adjusts the rearview mirror. "Oh, you try talking to those two. They teamed up on me when I dropped my guard. Glady moved in for the kill, and before I knew it, I spilled my guts to Jay."

I climb into the car, trying to find a comfortable position on the bench seat as I reach for the seatbelt—a single strap that secures my hips. "Well, not much we can do about that now. But next time…just clam up. I mean it."

Mrs. Perkins pumps the gas pedal and starts the car. "Shall we go for lunch? There is this lovely place Alice and I used to go to. If we hurry, we can beat the rush."

The car's front seat is as forward as it will go, forcing my knees close to my ears and her toes still barely touch the pedals. A perfect example of why bucket seats were invented. All strapped in, Mrs. Perkins easily sees over the steering wheel. She has the shortest legs ever made. I shift over with my knees between us and lean on the door. Its sharp armrest bruises my back. The bench seat, as wide as my couch at home, allows me to stretch out my legs a little more.

Mrs. Perkins nods. "I hope you like Pie 'n' All?"

"Actually, I don't like pie at all."

She signals right as we leave the parking lot. "It's the name of the restaurant. It used to be a tearoom, but now they serve breakfast and lunch too. I like knowing I can have High Tea anytime of the day."

She signals left and turns onto Main Street. "What did the doctor say?"

I try to ignore the signal indicator still blinking long after the turn is complete. "He thinks I'm fine, but he took blood."

"Alice and I always liked him."

"Was there something going on between the two of them?"

"Oh…Alice was fond of him. They got together after hours, but a lady doesn't talk about that sort of thing."

Good to know. "Is that why you called him instead of another doctor?"

"We used him, and I still do. He is the best GP in town."

Ah, the stud-muffin of geriatrics? "He also looks like the oldest in town."

She smiles. "Experience counts, young lady."

He sure knew how to calm me down. "I guess so. I felt safe with him. Most of the time I'm nervous around doctors. Like they know something I don't."

Her pink lips pull back exposing perfect teeth. "They do. They know how a body works or should work at any rate."

Mrs. Perkins parks in front of a two-story brownstone with forest-green awnings above the windows and door. 'Pie 'n' All' is stenciled along the fabric's hem in gold. A tiny bell above the door on the corner of the building catches and rings as we enter.

Little round tables sit snug under the tall windows with four squares of tables in the center. A counter reminding me of a bakery case stands parallel with the back wall. All kinds of pastry and finger sandwiches await behind its glass. Old photos of a time before motor vehicles were commonplace hang on the back wall.

We settle by the wall at a table large enough to accommodate tea for two, a couple of small plates slightly larger than saucers and a tiered tray. The top and smallest tier has the desserts, and the bottom two larger tiers hold assorted finger sandwiches. We eat in a comfortable silence. To be honest, I don't want to talk about anything. I want to consider what has happened over the last twenty-four hours. It's all a jumble, but one thing sticks out.

"Mrs. Perkins, I'd like to thank you for bringing me to the doctor." I raise my hand to stop her from butting in. "I have to ask you about yesterday. Was I acting unusual?"

"You seemed different after the reading."

"Really? Go on." I take a small bite and chew.

"Well, you invited me to spend the day with you," she stirs her tea for a while and sighs, "you've never done that before."

I almost choke. I didn't think my avoidance was obvious. Our age difference pretty much told me we wouldn't have much in common. "Did I say anything? Do anything else odd?"

Mrs. Perkins gently huffs. "You were so easy to get along with. It was nice. I haven't had that type of connection since…since Alice."

"Hey, I'm easy to get along with." I pop the rest of the cake into my mouth.

"Of course you are…dear." She picks up the teapot and pours us another round.

I decide on another cake.

"Since we are in Dunster, why don't we drop by the morgue?"

I drop my new selection on my plate. Say what? "Morgue? What do they have a tour or something?" I inwardly gag at the thought, but it doesn't stop me from undoing the top button on my pants in preparation to eat the bottom tier of sandwiches.

"You crack me up." Mrs. Perkins purses her lips. "I

mean the newspaper morgue at the Dunster Dispatch."

"Why? What are you looking for?"

"Did the doctor test your memory?"

I blink at her.

"We need to look at back issues for two weddings and a funeral."

I roll my eyes. "Is this one of those things you and Aunt Alice used to do?"

"I have to go, but you can do whatever you want." Mrs. Perkins stares me down.

"Okay, okay, I'll go." I don't have a ride home unless I stick with her. Ravenglass Lake is a fifteen minute drive down the highway.

"I'm glad that's settled. Should I get Maggie to box up the rest?" Mrs. Perkins smiles at a woman about ten years older than I am. Her short black hair is tucked behind her ears. As she gets closer her nametag reads Maggie. She wipes her hand on her apron and checks her pocket for our bill.

So, on a glorious day of blue skies and light breezes, we leave the cafe and make for the basement of the Dunster Dispatch. Where everywhere else on the planet uses computers, here we find microfiche and gray metal file cabinets. Oh, and dust, lots and lots of dust. Mrs. Perkins walks over to a cabinet like she owns the place and pulls reels from a drawer. She has both machines ready before I select a chair.

"Were you a librarian? Newspaper woman?"

"No, why?" She pulls a hanky from her sleeve and wipes her nose.

I mull over what she said. Mrs. Perkins' skills are wasted on a retired person. "I've never seen anyone set up microfiche that fast before."

"Yes. I have some experience with this machine. Don't hand me a computer to work with though. I don't know one end from the other."

She's lying. I've seen her spanking new laptop in her office, and I note her tell for the first time. Her smile stiffens.

"Oh, of course, women from different generations have different skills." I let the lie go, for now.

She pulls a chair out and settles in. "Come on. The sooner we begin the better."

"What are we looking for, and where should I begin?" I square my chair in front of my screen.

"Look through the announcements in the same calendar year."

The reading again. "So, do you know anyone that

has had two weddings this year?"

"No, not that I could remember and neither did Jay or Glady." She pulls two notebooks from her purse, handing me one. "Here take it. Tuck your copies in here and make notes of anything suspicious."

I see it now. Mrs. Perkins always planned to visit the morgue this afternoon. We took her car, so I'd be forced to go along with her plan. "How do you know the ceremonies are here?"

"I'm guessing, but where else should we start?" She wipes her nose again. "Try not to stir up the dust, Emma. Remember my allergies."

Here or at home I'd be sitting around waiting for a phone call that may never come. I pull my phone from my purse to double check the battery and bars. As long as I have bars, it doesn't matter what I'm doing.

To keep busy, I work my way through the back issues from most recent to the deeper past until I read an item mentioning a second Schmidt wedding. I find the announcement, print it, stuff the copy into my notebook, then search for the first Schmidt wedding announcement and repeat my process.

I pace myself, but slower this time. I find Aunt Alice's funeral announcement and read: "It is with great sorrow that I, Millie Perkins, announce the unexpected death of Alison Bontaine on March 27. An open service will be held at the Dunster Funeral Home Tuesday, April 2, at eleven a.m., and she will be laid to rest at Evergreen City Cemetery." I can't help thinking of Millie Perkins facing her best friend's death alone. I glance over as her eyes scan the screen, and, for a moment, I see the goodness and determination my Aunt Alice must have known.

With a sigh, I put a copy of Aunt Alice's announcement with the Schmidt printout.

When I come across a story about Aunt Alice's funeral, I'm shocked by the accompanying photo. A large group attended, pushed together like kids around an ice-cream truck. All except one woman leaning on a tree. She faces the group, looking like the odd man out with her collar up and her hat down. I fold the printout in half and tuck it away with my growing collection inside the notebook.

My papers slide, aligning one wedding photo with the other. Peter Schmidt is an ordinary balding man, with a crooked smile and light eyes and about four inches taller than both women beside him. Grace, the current wife, at least ten years his junior in a pale suit holds a small bouquet of daisies. The grainy black and white photo leaves me a little sad as I realign the pages and realize I've already forgotten what Peter Schmidt looks like.

I reorganize my pen and book, moving on to the next reel. It took until 2010 to find the Sanderson/Maars events. Soon after, Mrs. Perkins printed the McPherson/Henderson wedding/funeral 2008.

"Okay we found three. Can we quit now?" The voice coming out of my mouth prompts me to glance over my shoulder for a whining child, but I find nothing except my shadow.

"Well, the snacks are gone, and we uncovered some leads. Yes, let's stop. Like you said, we can always come back if we hit a dead end."

I don't remember saying that. "Great." I fiddle with my last reel.

"Let me do that before you break something."

Funny how I was fine until now. I surrender and step away giving her some room. "Hey, I worked on my own all afternoon and is anything broken?"

"Let me do it anyway. Why don't you pack up our things?"

I do as I'm asked and wait to hand them over. "Would you take me to the drive-thru before we head back? I'm starved."

"You've been eating all afternoon." She slips the last reel away.

"I eat when I'm nervous."

"Fine, but we need to hurry."

I stop in my tracks. "Why?"

Mrs. Perkins smiles brightly. "I have an appointment I can't miss."

Wow, she has more of a life than I do. I have a date with a burger, and she has a date with…It better not be with Dr. Logan. "Sure. What are you doing?" Hands still full, I follow after her using my elbow to turn off the lights.

"Bridge tourney. Glady and Jay need a fourth tonight."

Somewhere deep inside me I'm envious. I don't play bridge, but I could learn. I could be a fourth. Geesh. I need to find playmates my own age.

Chapter 4

I wake up blurry eyed after what should have been a restful night's sleep, yet I'm dragging myself to the shower. I make my coffee extra thick and step into the backyard to enjoy my early morning routine.

A blazing sun overhead suggests a warm summer's day. Mrs. Perkins tends her Lily of the Valley with a small purple watering can. "Oh, good you're up. Stay right there." She puts the can down and pulls off her gloves, pointing a forefinger skyward which I'm interpreting as hold on for a moment. She smiles and goes in her back door.

I rub my eyes and take in the deep blue sky through the high leaves. The wonderful drone of a lawn mower in the distance soothes me.

I sit on a patio chair, put my feet up on a planter, sip my coffee, and am almost asleep again when Mrs. Perkins calls from her yard.

"Here's a handful of messages for you." She waves little slips of paper at me. "Make sure you call each one of them back. They made me promise."

I carefully put my mug down on the cement and join her at the fence, scanning the top message. "This is asking for a reading. We talked about this."

"Yes, but it isn't up to me to tell them. That's up to you."

I didn't start this. She made this mess. "This is getting out of hand."

"I didn't start this."

I slap my forehead. "Yes you did."

"Well, I didn't mean to."

Now that I believe. I read a few more messages, and, when I glance up, she's gone back to her flowerbed. "Oh, no, you're not getting out of this that easy. Come back here. Put the can down and talk to me." My gaze drops down to my toes. I'm wearing neon green nail polish.

Omigod! I didn't do that.

Now, I need her for a different reason. "Mrs. Perkins…Millie…I've had another episode."

Mrs. Perkins slowly turns, face blank. "Episode? What episode? You were fine when you showed up at the tourney last night to play Bridge." She cleared her throat. "You kept coaching us. Jay almost called the police."

At the tourney? How did I know where to go? I've never played Bridge in my life. How did I coach anyone? I grab the fence for balance as the cold realization spreads. There's no way around it. I need someone to watch over me and make sure I don't hurt myself. Or anyone else.

There is only one person who's been with me while I'm blacked out.

I rush into the kitchen, fill a travel mug with some decent coffee, and storm over to Mrs. Perkins' place. My coffee sloshes around inside my mug as I march. By the time I arrive in her backyard, she's gone.

I walk into her kitchen without knocking.

Mrs. Perkins is at the coffeemaker spooning in loose tealeaves. "Are you all right?" Her voice more high pitched than usual.

"No, I'm not all right." I almost fall into a kitchen chair at the dinette set. "We need to talk. It's more like I need to tell you something." I close my eyes as if praying and take a deep breath. "I don't remember being at the tourney."

"Don't be ridiculous. I saw you. Jay chased you away from our table several times." Mrs. Perkins opens the fridge and pulls out an egg carton. "Want some breakfast?"

I stop and blink. "All this time you've been using your coffeemaker to make tea?" I shudder and cover my stomach. "Eggs? Yes, that sounds good."

Mrs. Perkins pulls a pan from a drawer. While the pan warms she drops a dab of butter in. "Scrambled okay, dear?" She's smiling.

Dear. She said dear. She knows something. "Okay." I take a long pull from my coffee reminding myself I'm brave enough to pursue the answers to the ugly truth. Inwardly, I cringe seeing one path, and it leads back to doctors, drugs, and group and one-on-one therapy.

Well, this is it. Everything counts on what I do now.

I try smiling, fighting my tears.

A strange expression comes over Mrs. Perkins' face.

I wipe the smile away, take another sip, and close my eyes, letting the coffee bring me into focus. The cooking eggs fragrance the kitchen. Mrs. Perkins' shoes click on the tile as she works on breakfast.

I imagine myself sitting there with pure white light entering the top of my head, flowing outward carrying with it black specks of negativity through and out of my chakras. The sunlight fills me with a healthy stillness. I push the light away and with it my fear.

China tinkles across from me, and the spell holds. I open my eyes.

"I need you to understand this wasn't my idea,"

Mrs. Perkins begins.

What?

She places a plate at my elbow and slips a napkin and a fork beside the plate. As Mrs. Perkins sits down, she straightens her napkin. She seems smaller in her large kitchen. Even the cup in front of her seems overly large for her fidgety hands.

"I don't understand." I don't dare smile and plan to share my news immediately after she has her say.

"It's just that I miss Alice so very much." Mrs. Perkins gazes into her cup rimmed with yellow rosebuds.

No surprise there. They were best friends for years. "Oh, that I get."

"Well." She sips her tea. Her hand trembles as she replaces the cup in its matching saucer. "Well…"

I nod, waiting.

She shakes her head. "Well. Here it is." Mrs. Perkins swallows hard, as if the words choke her, and continues. "You can channel Alice." She leans back in her chair adjusting her sweater like there is nothing left to say. When she looks up at me some expression I don't understand crosses her face. "She's back."

"Sorry." I shake my head slowly trying to comprehend her words. "Channel? That doesn't knock you out, doesn't it?"

"Alice said it was channeling, but she doesn't know everything. Maybe, it's possession."

"Possession? Channeling? Are you saying when I'm gone Aunt Alice is there? Like inside me? She's wearing me like a suit." This time my alter is named Alice. Poor Mrs. Perkins wants to believe it's Aunt Alice. I pierce a clump of scrambled eggs and have a taste.

"Yes. Well, right after I cut the cards day before yesterday she was there. It seemed like a cruel joke. I got quite upset and behaved rather badly at first." Mrs. Perkins blushes and waves to fan her face.

I inch forward on my chair leaning across the table. "No, this isn't your fault. This is a horrible misunderstanding. It's not channeling or even possession. My doctors call it something else entirely. You see—" My hand goes to my chest as if to protect my heart. "It's not a spirit."

"I'm only repeating what Alice told me." She sips again, hands shaking.

"Mrs. Perkins, Aunt Alice died months ago." The tears come. Slow fat droplets slide down my cheeks. I can barely face her never mind meet her eyes. "How long as this been going on?"

"The last few days. I don't understand it actually. It's addled me, I'm sorry, but I was at a loss as to what to do."

"It's okay." I finish my eggs. The tears keep falling onto my plate. I try to process it all, but I can't avoid it. I must tell her the truth. It's not possession or channeling. No, I'm not that lucky. It's Dissociative Identity Disorder aka Multiple Personality Syndrome. My mother noticed my trouble early, and I've been in treatment most of my life. "You spent all day with Alice. What did she tell you?"

"Nothing really, we simply visited like in the old days."

How can that be? What's going on? "Mrs. Perkins, tell me what happened in the old days."

"I'm not sure I want to. I can barely get you to help me now." Her voice cracks.

"Tell me, and I'll do anything you ask." I mean it.

"I'm the last of us, you see. There's no one else."

I understand what it is like to feel alone, but in my case, no one understood the depths of what was happening to me.

"What was it? Snooping?"

"Don't be rude. Your aunt was…is sensitive, and she would get feelings…or sometimes visitations. When she did, we would investigate."

What? Oh, boy. My alter, Alice, thinks she's psychic. If Mrs. Perkins thinks Alice is my aunt, then she'll expect us to snoop into other people's business. I'm not a snoop. I hate gossip and walk away when anyone starts. Is there a way to turn this into a positive? "I'll do it, but you have to promise if Alice comes back you tell her to leave. She can't visit anymore."

"No!" Her lips shape an O in disbelief. "Send her away? We need her. You see it's not just snooping. It's important. It's not always crime. Sometimes it's an action left undone, a message unsaid, or a lost object or person. And there is murder."

Murder. Whoa. "You can't be serious. This town is too small for murder." I'm way over my head. What is she saying? "Did Alice tell you she was murdered? Or because someone married twice in a year they're a murderer?"

"Don't you see? We need Alice because she knows what we need to do next."

Alice is a figment of my mind. A fractured chunk of my personality. Alice doesn't exist. It's impossible for her to be the driving force of the team. I'd be like a sidekick's sidekick of a—this is nuts. "So, you want it all. I help you, and you keep Alice. Tell me something. What do I get?" I slam my cup on the table harder than I mean to.

"You, you get a life with some fun in it."

The chill comes back again. My throat tightens. "What did she tell you?"

"Enough."

What does that mean? "So I've had it rough. So what? If anyone finds out about this, they'll lock me away…forever."

"Don't be selfish." She firms her jaw, readying for an argument."Everyone of us needs a purpose. A reason to wake up every day. To carry on." She looks into her lap for long moment. Softly she murmurs, "We are talking about helping others, and it could just as easily be saving a life."

"Helping is good…but murder. Well, murder. How does anyone deal with that?" *Someone hurting another, killing another. Omigod.* Did someone murder Aunt Alice? What am I saying? It's bad enough I've been playing bridge and hanging with Millie Perkins like we're best friends. "You said we need her. But what if it isn't Aunt Alice?"

"Dammit." Her frail fist hits the tabletop. "Alice is my best friend. I haven't seen or heard from her in almost a year, but I know her." She glares at me as if I didn't understand. "I missed her, and I thought having her back for a few days wouldn't hurt anyone, wouldn't hurt you." She palms her face. "I didn't consider you, and for that I'm so, so sorry."

No you didn't. "Mrs. Perkins, I need you to convince me Aunt Alice is real. Tell me how you know this Alice is my Great-Aunt Alice."

"Very well." Mrs. Perkins drops her hands into her lap and sits quiet for a long time.

Is she saying I haven't been ill all my life? No blocked trauma existed, shattering my psyche. How I'd like to believe. Is the answer this simple? But everything I've learned from the hospital screams that Mrs. Perkins is a desperately lonely woman and wishing for the impossible.

"...was Alice, your Great-Aunt Alice because when she first showed herself to me, she had to prove it. Like I said before, I thought you were playing a cruel trick. We argued and debated. I asked her questions only she could have answered. It was her. I have no doubt."

So, this is it. I either accept my Aunt Alice is occasionally taking over my body or accept fragmenting again and another alter takes over my body. Does it really matter? Either way, I will have blackouts. But one way, I stay where I am. One way, I become part of society, and I'm accepted as the local psychic.

I finger the little pieces of paper with appointment requests. I'm not ready for one-on-one readings, but trying to help someone else, just one someone with Mrs. Perkins beside me is doable.

"Mrs. Perkins, I want to believe you." I put my empty cup on the table, holding it tight to steady my nerves. "Let's do this thing."

"Thank you." She picks up her napkin, folds it, and straightens her shoulders as she meets my eyes. A sparkle of excitement shines out. I see vibrance and purpose. She clears her throat. "Someone's in danger."

"That's why we went to the morgue!"

"Yes." Sighing, she looks around. "The notebooks, where are they?"

"Where are the notebooks?" I pace. "I'm not sure. Where are they?"

"You had them last." Mrs. Perkins pales. "I'll check the car. Give me a minute."

Sitting at the dinette set and holding the table edge, I make myself calm down. I knew it wasn't going to be easy. I need to give it time, and I'll adjust. I will.

Mrs. Perkins returns empty handed. "They're not there."

"No problem. I don't have Alice's skills but I have

mine. I know how to use a computer and check the Internet from home." Seeing Mrs. Perkins' face, I add, "We can still go back to the morgue later if you like."

"So you'll help us?" She slowly walks to the chair and slides onto its seat.

"Us? You don't have to worry about me helping with this investigation. I do need a life and some fun." Then the realization hits me, sometimes the unexpected, almost unbelievable news can be exactly what the doctor ordered.

Chapter 5

Paper bags rattle below my fists as we rush through my front door. When Mrs. Perkins passes me, I kick the door closed. We hurry to the loft making a ruckus of shopping bags and food cartons.

"I'll go find my computer." I run down stairs looking around the house for my laptop bag. It's on the back of the kitchen chair. Lifting the bag, gauging its weight, I smile and hurry back to Mrs. Perkins.

She's in her chair, the cards cut in front of her, incense burning in its holder, and the white candle lit. I set up the laptop and wait for it to boot up.

I take a sip of pop and stuff a French fry in my mouth. "Okay, what is our first question?"

We stare at each other waiting for the other to say something brilliant.

"Is it the Schmidts, Sandersons, or McPhersons that are in danger?"

"Oh, that's good." Mrs. Perkins nibbles on a chicken nugget. "How about, what should we do to help them?"

"Now we're rolling." With the computer balancing on my knees, I type in the question and take another drink. What do we need to know? "And is someone gonna die?"

"Yes, but how would she know?"

How can she know anything? I still have shadowy doubts about Alice being Aunt Alice—never mind psychic. "No idea. Us following through should prove or disprove what she knows." I wipe my fingers on a paper napkin before I rest my fingertips on the keyboard. "What else should we know about the weddings and funeral? And…who's the victim?"

"They might be with her. You know, talking to her. Telling her what she needs to know." Mrs. Perkins suddenly raises her hand. "Wait! Wait, we need some kind of proof. We need to ask about motivation, means, opportunity, and where to find the evidence."

"That's what I'm saying." I shake my head, not wanting to admit I'm having fun. "And the whole reason we bought a digital audio recorder. Where are the notebooks? I'd rather not go back to that dusty hell hole."

"Emma." Mrs. Perkins tsks. "Anything else you want to ask?"

I stop. Mrs. Perkins doesn't understand. "Mrs. Perkins, I won't be asking the questions."

"What do you mean?" The yellow straw an inch from her lips.

Let's hope she isn't as computer shy as she pretends. "Well, I'll be busy. I black out when Aunt Alice uses my body. I won't be there to help."

She blinks at me. "You don't mean I have to learn how to use that." Mrs. Perkins points her forefinger in my computer's direction, her other hand brings the paper cup down to the table, dangerously close to my knees.

"Is that a problem?"

She blinks back some tears. "I don't know how to use one of those things. Until now, I never needed to."

What a load!

Mrs. Perkins is a computerphobe. I can do this. "It won't bite." I smile. "May I show you one thing and that's all?" I bring the computer to her and gently place it on her lap. "See this? It's a scroll bar. Try using these two fingers to move the arrowhead up or down. The page moves, so you can read all the questions."

"That's it." Mrs. Perkins relaxes.

"That's it." I watch her play a bit and wonder what she does with the one at home. "Think you can ask our questions now?"

"Of course, it's just a computer for crying out

loud." Mrs. Perkins' eyes shine.

Well, that was close one. "Good. Let's get started." I sit across from her and pick up the cards.

This time it's different. I wake up slowly. As I break the surface, something or someone ducks into the grayness. I drag my eyes open and find myself in my chair leaning on the right wing. I smile. Mrs. Perkins stops slapping my hand.

"Emma," she squeaks. "It worked, and there is more. So much more."

I try to move, but the stiffness in my back doesn't allow for more than forcing my eyes to stay open.

"I'll put some tea on. Rest. I won't be a moment." Mrs. Perkins rushes away. Her knuckles white as she tightly grasps the handrail round the stairs.

Gladly, I lean back and let my eyes close.

Below a cupboard door opens, closes, then another, and another. The fridge door opens with a rattle of half-full bottles in the door. After a moment of silence, the front door opens and closes with a solid click.

I close my eyes again enjoying the silence. So calm in the shadows of twilight, I stretch in the warmth, not remembering ever being this comfortable or relaxed before today. Time rides waves of vanilla and lavender. I float in a place where I'm not deeply asleep or completely awake.

Somewhere off in the distance brilliant white curtains catch gusts of air, flapping like laundry in the sun. I like it here in the white light.

The front door slams shut snapping me back to the loft. Mrs. Perkins mutters under her breath, and a regular thumping comes up the stairs to the loft. Around the chair back, she steps up the spiral staircase. Each step is accompanied by the thump of a cooler on wheels.

She never ceases to surprise me.

"What are you doing?" I stretch, a long slow one, reminding me of a cat before a catnap.

"I had to get it here, didn't I? Your kitchen is a disgrace. If Alice ever sees it, she'll give you nightmares."

I smile. She's already trying to give me nightmares.

Once the cooler rests beside me Mrs. Perkins removes its lid. A thermos full of what might be tea from her coffeemaker, some teacups, saucers, a china plate, and a baggie of my favorite cookies waited to be unpacked.

"It looks great."

"Thankfully my kitchen is fully stocked."

I snort and pull the baggie free. Mrs. Perkins unloads the rest. Once she pours the tea, she takes the cookies from me and places them on the plate.

"Emma, you need to bone up on your manners. We'll have to visit some people, and I won't tolerate this…relaxed behavior."

I think I understand what Mrs. Perkins means and don't care. "So she spilled."

Mrs. Perkins smiles from across the table, teacup held delicately with pinky out. "Not spilled so much as gave us a heading."

She did ask the questions, didn't she? "Was there trouble with the questions? Talk to me."

She slowly shakes her head, pushes the play button on the recorder, and leans back with her cup after dropping the notebooks on the table between us.

I close my eyes, waiting, leaning back to listen to Mrs. Perkins nervous voice ask the first question. "Alice. Thanks for coming. We were wondering, Emma and I were wondering, is it the Schmidts, Sandersons, or McPhersons that are in danger?"

I expect to hear my voice, but the old woman borrowing my body sounds like no one I've ever met. "Millie, you talked to her. How is she? Living up to her potential? Done any readings?"

"No, I can't get her to try."

"I see. Look at you. Your eyes are blazing again." A

rustle of fabric. "I've missed you so. How long was it this time?"

"Just days. Please, Alice, answer the question."

"What question?"

"You know exactly what question. Don't be coy."

"I will but first I need to talk to Emma. The doctors didn't understand. And that woman, your mother, she should have stood beside you instead of letting them send you away. Don't worry, my darling girl. All will become clear with time. Help Millie and you'll help yourself. You and Millie can stop her. It's so gray. I can't see it clearly but have my body checked for clues. I'm the clue. It's me."

"Omigod! They killed her," I croak.

"…where was I?" Alice's voice pauses and begins on a different track all together. "Right, you were still being scolded when I answered the door, but you stopped your mother in her tracks. You said something like, 'Mother, you're making a scene.' You sounded like your grandmother. It was perfect. I thought she was going to slap you, but she glanced up at me. I saw it in her eyes. Fear. Not knowing what to do, she ran to the car. I liked you right away, and that has never changed."

My first tea party with china cups.

"I left everything to you because I had…No, that's

not right. If I had a thousand people to choose from, I'd still left you everything. I understand you don't want to be sensitive. I understand, but it doesn't change a thing."

The voice clears its throat, and a rustle of fabric whispers in the background. Then she begins again:

"Her plan is not working out as she had first expected. Things are getting complicated. Time is running out. She'll get him. And if she finds out you're on to her she'll try to get you too."

Click. The voice stops.

What the hell? What happened? Where did the questions go? "Mrs. Perkins it's late afternoon."

"Yes it is."

I keep my voice level and plow forward. "What did you do for the rest of the afternoon?"

"Alice wanted to enjoy the sun on her face. We took a walk to the park near the beach. We watched the water, and she told me about the other side of the veil. Before you ask, I'm sworn to secrecy." Mrs. Perkins' cheeks glow. "She probably told me more—"

I raise a hand. When am I going to learn? "Stop, just stop."

"I thought—"

"Mrs. Perkins." I start but am not sure quite how to

phrase—I'm not your personal telephone to the other side—politely. I take a moment searching for the right words, before saying, "This is ridiculous. How many times are you going to break your word? I've kept mine. Aren't I helping you?" I stare at my hands. Once I'm calm, I try again. "I think I understand how much you miss my aunt, but how am I supposed to believe you? Believe in you? Can you keep the socializing down to a bare minimum, please?"

"Of course, dear." Mrs. Perkins smile stiffens.

My shoulders inch skyward as my muscles and her smile both tighten further. Her little telling smile telegraphing she's lying to me, again. I'm grateful for being alerted that she'll do as she pleases and make a personal note to keep the channeling to a minimum.

My eyes grow wider. "Does she have any idea how long ago she passed?"

Mrs. Perkins shakes her head and breaks eye contact. "I couldn't tell her."

Getting the clue from Aunt Alice means we need to exhume her body? Aunt Alice thinks we still have easy access to her. "Exhumed." The word aloud makes it much more horrible. "Mrs. Perkins, did someone kill my aunt?"

"I'll call Dr. Logan. He'll help us." Mrs. Perkins

offers me her open hand expecting me to hand over my phone.

I stand, check my empty pockets. I don't see my phone anywhere nearby.

As I walk around checking the different surfaces round the loft, I force out the words, almost choking on them. "He'll know what to do?"

"Don't worry, Emma. He's helped us before." Mrs. Perkins drops her hand into her lap. "Where's your phone?"

Something else is missing. "Where's my laptop?"

"At the bottom of the stairs." Mrs. Perkins sniffs and pulls her hanky from her sleeve.

I step over to the rod-iron railing and gaze down. Yep, she's right. "Did someone drop it or was it thrown?"

Mrs. Perkins shifts in her seat flattening her skirt. "Well, you could say you did it yourself."

I turn to take in the whole picture of an older woman in a pleated plaid skirt and simple cotton top. Her back is as straight as I've ever seen it. A woman ready for battle.

"I did it?" Stunned, I wait for more.

"Yes, I made the mistake of arguing with Alice about answering the questions, and she…was frustrated with us. So, she tossed it down stairs before I could stop her."

She's not a little kid throwing a tantrum. No, she's a grown woman. A dead, but grown woman. I bring a hand to my lips. "I had stuff on there. Important stuff."

"Please, Emma, get a hold of yourself." Mrs. Perkins reaches for a cookie and breaks it in half.

"You don't understand." I wave an arm. "I can't afford to buy another one."

"Of course you can. Alice left you fists full of money." Mrs. Perkins refills her cup.

"I'm on an allowance until I'm forty." Sitting down at the table, I palm my face. "I don't get fists full of anything. It's in trust."

"I see. Well then I'll lend you mine. A Christmas gift from my son. All I've managed to do with it is unpack it from the box and put it on my desk." She nibbles her cookie and sips.

"Oh." Wait! What does her stiff smile mean then? *Focus, Emma.*

"Arguing with her when she was my age and size wasn't intimidating? I'm sorry, but it turns out I'm quite cowardly when facing a raving lunatic of your age."

"Lunatic? Coward?" This isn't going well. "I'm sure you did the best you could, but you could've told me."

"Yes, maybe I should have." Her face overly serious, Mrs. Perkins places what's left of her cookie on her saucer, then places her cup and saucer on the table.

"Are you okay?" I don't like the teary eyes.

"Yes. I'm more than fine." She breaks into a wet smile, her hand over her heart. "I've not felt so alive."

Well, that would be one of us.

There's no point in trying to remember where I saw my phone last, so I begin a methodical search, starting with the key bowl downstairs and feel pretty lucky when it's there until I pull it free and hold it up to the light.

I step around my broken laptop and shout, "Tell Aunt Alice not to put my phone near my keys. They scratch the screen up, and, right now, I'm saving up for a new computer."

A snicker floats down from the loft. "I'll tell her. I can't promise she'll listen."

When I return to the table upstairs I hand over my phone. "Call our dear Dr. Logan and see if he will help us with Aunt Alice."

"Oh, he'll help. He's never let us down yet."

I sit down and take a cookie. "Was he part of the team?"

"In a way. He helped when necessary." She

stretches out her arm and punches in a number on my phone, then puts it to her ear. "Hello Doctor. This is Millie Perkins I need a favor."

At this point, I pick up the teacup again and almost drink from it. Cringing, I put it down and go downstairs. In the kitchen, I start a proper cup of coffee in my wonderful coffeemaker which is used just for making coffee and search my fridge. Nothing but several glass jars in the door, and they are all condiments. I don't cook much. As the coffee gurgles, I splash some cold water on my face. It feels good against my skin.

Done, I head back upstairs, coffee in hand. Settling into my chair, I notice Mrs. Perkins is frowning. "What's the matter?"

"He won't do it."

Not as under her thumb as she thought. "Is that right?" I sip, mulling this over. "Did he say why not?"

"We must follow proper procedure and go through the Police Department."

"Not Benny the bully." I've only heard of him and that was enough. This isn't good.

"I'm afraid so." No sign of Mrs. Perkins' soppy wet smile. It's as if it never existed. Her frown deepens.

I've seen this expression before and ready myself to

be thrown under the nearest bus. "So you called Benny?"

"Yes, and he wants a formal request explaining why we need to do such a thing."

"How do we explain Aunt Alice told us to, or that we suspect there are clues to be found?" I cross my fingers. "Is there anyone else?"

"No, but don't worry. If you sign them and fill in a few statistics. Dr. Logan will do the rest."

"Good, that's settled then." I take a sip of coffee, feeling better immediately. Leaning back in the chair, I select a cookie. "Have you looked at the notebooks since you found them?"

"You go ahead." She pushes back as far as her short legs will let her and closes her eyes. "I need to think."

"Let me fetch you a couple of cushions." I take them from the couch downstairs and tuck them behind her back and head. "Better?"

"Yes, thank you." She closes her eyes as if meditating and exhales.

Apparently it's not settled. She's pouting. "What did I do this time?" I wait, hoping for answer, but not expecting one.

"If you must know, it's not you. It's Alice." She slowly rubs the arms of the chair then clenches her fists. "I thought we were friends."

Here we go. "From where I sit you still are." How many friends come back from the dead to hang at the park? Zero. That's how many.

"Well, she remembered you in her will after meeting her once." Mrs. Perkins blushes. "And me, well, me she forgets completely."

"But you handled all the funeral arrangements. Took care of the house until I could move." I blink away some tears. "Are you saying she never left you anything?"

"Exactly. Not even a thank you, and I hinted at some nice pieces of jewelry." Her hand suddenly comes up to her trembling chin. "I have nothing but my memories."

"I had no idea. Let me make amends." I scan the loft for something personal. "Take something. Anything. Anything at all."

"You're missing the point." She clasps her hands together. "It should be her doing this."

"Aunt Alice must have had her reasons. Talk to her about it and no hinting, just say it straight out. Until then, take something." I walk over to the shelf and pick up the apple-shaped crystal ball. "How about this?"

"Oh, I shouldn't." A beautiful pink graces her face. "It's outrageously expensive."

More than you expected, huh? "And it's yours." I walk it over to her and gently place it by her teacup.

She picks it up and strokes it with a fingertip. "You're very kind."

"You did what I couldn't."

Glancing up, she meets my eyes. "What do you mean?"

"You were here for her." I sip my coffee and watch Mrs. Perkins with her gift. "Shall we unite forces?" I open a notebook and find the photocopy of the microfiche wedding photo. It's a bit blurred, but clear enough for me to see an older man in his best clothes standing beside an older woman with flowers in her hair and a bouquet of spring flowers held near her chest.

I check the note under it. A picture from his first wedding. The two women might have been sisters. "I've always loved black and white photos. They tend to bring out character and warmth a color pic doesn't always capture. Here Peter and Claire Schmidt seem very happy, so why did they annul the marriage?"

"I heard a rumor she became seriously ill and wanted out of the relationship." Mrs. Perkins exhales on the crystal and rubs it on her cuff.

"Make yourself useful." I try to hand her the pages

of the Schmidts' weddings, giving up I drop them on her teacup. "Was it the sickness, or is there more to it?"

"They were married for two months. The scandal made the papers." Mrs. Perkins sniffs and slides the ball into her skirt pocket.

"This couldn't've been that long ago. Why the gossip?"

"It's just what people do." Mrs. Perkins picks up the printouts. "Thanks."

"You're welcome." I drop the rest on the table. "I'm done. In my gut I know Peter Schmidt is the man we need to protect."

She throws her paper on the pile. "Tell me why. Was it Alice?"

"No, I'm not sure why. I said it's my gut talking, but when we ask him, maybe he'll be able to explain."

The doorbell rings. I don't bother moving. Door-to-door salesmen or someone trying to save my soul, I didn't care and wasn't interested.

"Don't just sit there. Answer it."

I lean back in my winged chair and stretch, making it clear I'm not moving. "Why? I'm not expecting anyone."

"That's your date." Mrs. Perkins mutters.

"My what?"

Chapter 6

"When we went to the park, Alice met a man named Henry…or Archie." Mrs. Perkins pinches her cheeks and glances up at me.

I blink. The bell goes again.

"Aunt Alice set me up with a man." I want to scream until the rafters fall and kill me. Mrs. Perkins has called me overly dramatic. Should I live up to the claim?

"Emma, answer the door." She stands, slips her hand into the pocket with the crystal ball, and checks it's secure.

No! You answer the door. "Right." I glance up at Mrs. Perkins while I go down the stairs. Looking in the mirror above the key bowl, I see smudges under my eyes and pale cheeks. I run my fingers through my hair and offer myself a wobbly smile. *Here it goes.*

I take a deep breath and exhale as I turn the knob.

My first impression is he played football…or should. He's a very tall and broad shouldered man. I look up into his scruffy face and smile. He smiles back. A warmth about him makes my smile widen. He is comfortable in his own skin, and it shows.

"Are you ready?" His voice is musical, a pleasant baritone.

"Ah, well it depends on where we go?"

He laughs aloud. "Now you let me make a decision." He smiles, but it appears more smirk. "I wanted to take you to the pub, remember? They have folk singers in and sometimes they lead the pub in a sing along."

"What did I say?" How weird is this date going to get?

He stares at me.

It dawns on me I should know and push on. "Would you like to come in? I need a moment to grab my purse."

"Sure." His hair brushes the inside of the doorjamb. "Whoa. What happened to your poor computer?"

"Please don't remind me." I glance at the cracked case as I pass and step over the hard drive. "It's a dead soldier in the battle of life."

Mrs. Perkins comes down the steps. She smiles at my date. "Ken, or is it Derrick?" She offers her hand to shake.

"Tom actually." He takes her hand in two of his mitts and winks at her. "I know. It's my good looks. No one bothers to learn my name."

"Oh, you are a rogue." Mrs. Perkins blushes batting her eyes as they release hands.

"That's me. Lock up your virgins."

I wait for it and Mrs. Perkins doesn't disappoint.

"Well, I guess Emma isn't in any danger then." She giggles, intending her comment to be funny.

It's not.

Scowling, I drop my keys into my purse. "Thanks, would you two rather go out?"

Tom raises his hands as if under arrest. "Oh, no. She is way too much woman for me."

I try not to be offended, but then what the hell am I? I swallow all the things I'd like to say and loudly whisper in her general direction, "Lock up when you leave."

"Feel like walking? It's not far." Tom presses my back with his palm as we make our way across the lawn to the sidewalk.

"Sure."

We leave his car, a rather ordinary silver sedan, parked in my driveway and stroll down the street. The air has a sweetness about it, and a breeze ruffles his golden brown hair.

Awkward and not knowing quite what to say to him, I become acutely aware of my hand swinging at my side. At thirteen, it would be an invitation to hold, but at twenty-one, what did it mean? I slip my thumb into my jean pocket, immediately transform into a country hick and pull it free again. I fumble with my purse strap, folding and unfolding the dark leather to give my hands something to do.

This will be the longest date ever. I'm trying to recall if I gave up dating because of my lack of people skills or something else. Like stress, discomfort, chronic silence.

"Alice—"

"No, it's Emma."

"Weird. I usually have a good memory for names."

She used her name? You'd think an old woman would use her brains. "Sorry, I don't ever remember calling myself Alice. Where did that come from?" I don't dare raise my head and meet his eyes as I flat out lie to him.

Down the block, a bright yellow awning catches my attention. Stenciled in black, a row of ducks silhouetted together march on each side of the word Quackers. A heritage building, like several other buildings around the area, constructed from large rough gray blocks of what may be solid rock, Quackers Pub takes up the majority of the main floor of the Ravenglass Hotel. A squeeze of my elbow snaps my attention back to my date. We step closer together to allow an approaching couple room to pass.

A strong spicy scent travels with them. I resist putting a hand to my nose and smile.

The man mumbles, "Tom."

The woman, a shapely brunette, nods at us.

Tom smiles and taps his forehead. "Milt. And Joanne, as beautiful as always."

We keep our momentum, and a moment later, it's as if we didn't see them at all.

"You were saying?" I coax.

"Oh, right. How long have you lived in town? I don't remember meeting you before." He grins, blushing a little. "On the other hand, I didn't remember your name so I might be slipping."

Unsure of myself, I say nothing as another couple round the corner under the awning. As they walk closer, we repeat the greetings again, but this time it's Jack and Nancy.

Under the awning, we turn the corner following the sidewalk. The lake laps along the beach across the road from us. Half way down the building, double doors open and a blast of music escapes. Someone plays a Rover's song about unicorns inside. I anticipate the atmosphere and perk up as we step through the door.

A cozy place. Quackers, a traditional pub, with golden wood lacquered as if coated in honey. The tables are clean, the stage small, and the wallpaper needs replacing. Everyone gathered around the stage looks like a wild and festive choir practicing folk songs.

We take our places at an empty table ordering pints and burgers, and sit close together on one side of the table. On a platform two men, armed with acoustic guitars, lead the small group in song. One puts his instrument down and walks among the tables. He points at people, and they sing a line or two into the microphone.

I swallow hard. *Don't pick me. Don't pick me.*

As the man gets closer, Tom stands beside him and drops an arm around his shoulders angling them away from the table. They sing together, swaying with the music until the end.

The whole place roars with approval and applauds the effort while I try to disappear into my chair.

What a horrible match. Everyone knows him, and he remembers everyone's name. He carries a tune and is quick to smile. And well, I know no one but Mrs. Perkins and haven't made much of an effort to meet anyone else.

He soaks up the camaraderie, enjoying the attention.

Attention I'm unable to handle. It's then I see his glow within. There is no ego, nor fluffed feathers, not even conceit in the fine edges of his face. It's in his eyes, a joy, a happiness I've never known. I stare in wonder.

What does he possibly see in me?

"Too much?" Tom drapes an arm on the back of my chair as he sits down.

"Too much?" My face burns as I realize he thinks I'm not having fun.

He glances up at the musicians strumming away.

"I didn't expect it to be like this. I figured it was like karaoke and the spotlight would be on the stage." My explanation hangs there like the wet rag I'm turning out to be.

"Well, try it and if you want to go after we eat. We'll leave."

"You don't mind." My face grows warmer with the added pressure of him knowing I'm not a good sport.

"Are you kidding? I come down here a couple of times a month. Anymore and they'd be spoiled."

I smile. What a nice man. I suspect even if he knows tonight is a mistake he'll be too much of a gentleman to end it before I'm ready to go home. I just won't see him again except to say hello on the street.

Chapter 7

I'm dreaming a wonderful dream of soft white light glowing on the horizon, glowing as if many small suns sit in a thick hazy mist. A breeze blows of evergreens, lavender and something foreign. It reminds me of Tom. Long white gauzy curtains flutter towards me. So many windows. So many curtains. Centered in a room of white stands a high platform. Its soft padding invites me to stretch out, and I do.

Then a weight shifts on the platform, and Aunt Alice sits beside me in her favorite housedress, a loose cotton print. Her white blonde hair is loosely knotted on the crown of her head. She's younger than I remember, with a slender figure and wide mouth tipped up at the edges in a constant smile. This is Aunt Alice and not a memory of her or one of my alters.

"Emma, finally in a state where I can visit you."

"What do you mean?" I stretch out on the soft padding and enjoy the sensation of floating.

"I mean I've being trying to contact you since you moved into the house and almost gave up. Then one breakthrough after another. And down came the walls." She smiles showing her straight white teeth. "Now, the three of us will get some work done."

"Well, not right now. Millie Perkins keeps claiming we've teamed up and then does as she pleases. Both of you do."

"Don't give up on us yet. The world still needs us." Tiny dimples appear as Aunt Alice smiles wider.

"Us? Needs us? You're not including me. How can I help anyone? Shall I burst in and announce I've had a vision and tell all *she* will try to kill Peter. When I don't even know who *she* is." I try to be logical. I can't help fighting this.

The air in the room becomes still, the curtains fall, and the walls fade slightly, dimmer. I gasp and as I exhale, the wind explodes bringing the curtains up with a snap. This room depends on me. Somehow it reflects my connection to Aunt Alice.

"Please settle down, or you will wake up and we'll lose the advantage."

For the first time, the windows are bare and matte blackness presses upon the panes. I sit up on the soft padding and glare at pale wisps. "Spirit or alter, you understand what I'm afraid of. If I say or do the wrong thing, I'll land up back where I started. I won't jeopardize my freedom for you or Millie Perkins. I take my pills and do my morning ritual religiously to maintain my calm. And if I do these things, I stay free."

"Oh, Emma, it's an illusion. I'm sorry Millie gives you trouble. This has been hardest on her. I'll talk to her. I promise." She reaches out as if to stroke my hair or straighten my collar, but doesn't touch me. "You are who you believe you are. It's that simple. You are already free."

"You don't understand." I pull away and glance at the dark windows hoping for a glimpse at what is hidden beyond.

"Millie is a wonderful woman and excellent friend." Her dimples are as cute as her bright blue eyes. "You could do much worse."

"But she's my only friend." As I share the truth, I blame myself for not going out more and being more social. I did this to myself.

"You went out with Tom," Aunt Alice chimes. "That's something."

Right. "Yes, thanks. He's great, but I doubt he likes me as much as I like him."

"Oh, he might surprise you." Her eyes sparkle with a fire akin to starlight.

From the expression on her face, I'm not the one surprised. I like the idea of having a man around.

"Let's talk about why I'm here," says Aunt Alice.

I nod and focus on her powdered face.

"By the hospital, you'll find a fine Tudor house with yellow shutters and door. It has the bright red mailbox in front."

I recall coming out of the waiting room's double doors, bright light searing my eyes. "I remember seeing it when I visited Dr. Logan."

"Good, Peter Schmidt and his wife, Grace, are having a barbeque tomorrow evening at that very house. It will be a big family event and *she* will be there. You go, too. Both of you go."

"Who is it? What does she look like?" I need a clue. Butterflies flutter in my middle and try to escape. To face a mysterious and dangerous woman set on hurting Peter Schmidt asks too much, especially when I have no idea who she might be.

"That's what's so silly. I get an impression, an alarm in my gut, but I don't see her face. I don't have any idea what she looks like, but she'll be there." Aunt Alice cups my cheek with her cool dry hand. "I'm hoping I'm right about her being female."

"Come on. Give me more than that." Pushing her hand away, I scrub my face with my palms. "There has to be something."

"Knock down the rest of your brick walls, let yourself feel, and you'll know her when you see her," Aunt Alice says. "It's their anniversary. Make sure you bring a gift."

I grind my teeth. "Sure. You're like a walking talking fortune cookie. What parts should I believe?"

"It's the walls. And my darling girl, please don't discourage Tom." Aunt Alice beams. "He is so lovely and, well, quite the lover."

"What?" I slap my hand to my chest, my heart racing. What is she saying?

"I'm not sorry. You almost botched it last night, but I helped you out. Worth every second."

"Worth every..." Good. Maybe he'll ask me out again. I'd like that. I'll suggest a picnic on the beach— sunset with the water lapping on the shore. Yes, it would be a perfect setting.

The curtains fall in place.

A weight leaves the padding, the room disappears, and a heavy arm drapes over my stomach.

Awake…and frozen in shock for a moment as

awareness of crisp linens against my skin takes hold. I lift the comforter and gently slip out from under, grabbing my robe and leaving the room. Not believing who's in my bed, I look skyward, pacing the hallway, cursing out my aunt.

My hand slaps my chest as I realize the lack of birth control used from my end. *Aunt Alice, you better have made him wear a condom. If I get pregnant or catch anything from him I'll kill you all over again.* I grab the wall to steady myself. *What am I thinking? I can't kill a dead woman.*

Pregnant?

Bug-infested? Ahhh.

I spin on my heel, eying the bedroom door. A naked man in my bed. I've had sex, that was apparently lovely, but don't remember a thing. What else is she going to do to me?

This can't continue. I need to do something, learn something to shut her down.

The door opens, and I crack an elbow jumping backward. He wears a big goofy smile on his face. "Mind if I have a shower? I've got stuff to do today, and I can't be late."

I keep my eyes on his face, without looking I open the linen closet door. "Sure, help yourself to a towel." I pushed my back into the wall to make room for him to pass. My breath catches in my throat as he ducks down and kisses me.

He offers me an easy smile. "I'll do your back if you like."

"Ahh, thanks, but no. I'll start the coffee." I replay what just happened as I inch away. I pull a random towel from a shelf, and blot my neck.

"If you change your mind"—he leaves the door ajar—"my door is always open."

The water splashes as Tom sings about a ponytail hanging down, and I hurry toward the kitchen. Was this a one-night stand? I try to remember what happened while I put the coffee on. This not knowing is tough, and impatiently I will the coffee to drip faster. I need a cup. I need it now.

When it's ready, I rush outside. Not looking around the garden. I hide giving him a chance to make his escape if he wants it. Across the fence at Mrs. Perkins', dark windows sit cold in the morning light.

How silly am I? I have to stop running away. I'll go back and offer him some toast before he leaves. As I turn to head back in, I walk into Tom's chest. I bounce off sloshing coffee down my front. The satin robe sticks to my skin with a rush of too hot and an immediate cool down. I glance up, and his pupils swell.

I step back.

"Hey, steady there." Tom takes my hand and pulls me toward him.

"Did you get a cup?" I lift my coffee hoping it makes what I said clearer.

He shows me his other hand which holds my travel mug.

"Yep, mind if I borrow this. I'll give it back on Monday. No better make it Tuesday. I have a lunch on Monday with Jane."

"Tuesday?" *Jane? What the hell. Who's Jane?* It sounds like I know who she is. Playing along I say nothing.

"You still want to go out? Remember we were going fishing." He laughs. "Okay, I promise not to catch anything." He slides his hand up my arm and under my hair, pulling me in for a kiss.

I don't know him, not really, but can't stop myself and kiss him back.

In a voice husky and inviting, he whispers, "We're still going out, right?"

As tempted as I am to kiss him again, I step back. "Sure, sounds great."

"You look a little shell-shocked."

I smile. *You have no idea.*

"God, you're beautiful."

"I am?"

"Oh yeah." He strokes my cheek running his thumb along the edge of my bottom lip. "I'll see you soon." Another quick kiss and he's walking around the corner of the house.

Chapter 8

The moment Tom's sedan drives off, I race over to Mrs. Perkins' house. I don't knock, just storm in through her back door. She's sitting at her table all dressed to go out, a stack of toast, rosebud china plates and cups before her.

"He's gone, is he?" She sniffs as if something foul has been dragged into the room.

"Yes, he's gone." I collapse onto one of her kitchen chairs and carefully set my thermal mug on her spotless tabletop.

"I knew you had bad manners but this." Mrs. Perkins expels a hiss much like a pierced balloon. "Wait 'til your aunt hears about this."

"Don't blame me. It was Aunt Alice." Tipping my cup slightly, I watch the crescent of liquid gather on its lid and disappear again.

Mrs. Perkins' whole demeanor changes. "Alice? She took a young man to her bed?"

"Yes and left me with him in the morning not remembering a thing. Your antics were bad enough. Now, this. Tom and I have a date for Tuesday." I take a long drink of coffee and shake when I place the cup on the table. "I'm stunned."

"You're shouting, Emma." Her calm voice not betraying her pale deeply lined expression.

"Oh, I am. Sorry." I eye the plate of whole-wheat toast and take one. "And Aunt Alice dropped by this morning and told me we need to go to the Schmidt's anniversary party tomorrow afternoon. And we have to buy a gift."

Her delicate cup stops inches from her painted lips. For a moment, her lips disappear between her teeth. "You talked to Alice?"

"Yes, just before I woke up. Or maybe it happened while I woke up. Might have been a dream…oh, I'm not sure." If someone told me last week I would talk to my dead aunt, I'd've driven them to the loony bin myself. Now, I don't know. I'm actually going to go to a party because I dreamed I should. How can things change so much so fast?

"Does it matter? The point being we need to go to the party. What shall we bring?" She mulls it over while chewing the last of her crust.

"Just like that?" Something stinks. Nothing is ever

easy with Mrs. Perkins. "You believe me? What if I'm lying?"

Mrs. Perkins puts her cup down. "Don't be silly."

"Tell me why." Heck my own mother had me locked up.

"I've talked to Alice remember. If I can do it, so can you." Mrs. Perkins puts marmalade on a toast triangle.

"Don't do that…that…old lady logic thing. Just tell me plain and simple."

"The only person in this room who thinks you're crazy is you. There I said it. Alice explained the whole split personality thingy. A visitation gone wrong. No horrific trauma in your history. Everyone, including the doctors, assumed you'd blocked it out. Psychiatrists don't have all the answers, but for some reason no one questions them." Mrs. Perkins wipes up invisible crumbs. "I talked to Alice, and she is as real as you are."

"I did tarot cards for fun and wanted to believe in something after death because I didn't like the idea of nothing. But if someone came a long and overheard us talking like this." I shiver.

"Just because this is hard to believe doesn't mean it isn't true. Fact one, we want to save a man's life. Fact two, Alice is dead. Fact three…"

"You got nothing. We have nothing." I puff out some air and take long drink of my coffee. "It doesn't matter if we're crazy. I couldn't live with myself if something happened to Peter Schmidt. So I gotta go and at least check it out."

"Okay then. What do you want to take?"

As Millie Perkins natters on about gift ideas, I'm thinking of Tom and his voice, husky and warm, saying just one word—beautiful.

***

Even as I drive in to the police station parking lot, we still haven't decided on a gift for the Schmidts. I'm ready to take a goldfish in a cup, anything to shut her up.

"It will take five minutes. Maybe ten." I park in a slot close to the door. "Come on. I'll sign the papers, but I need you to do the asking. Throw Dr. Logan's name around or something."

"Emma, he won't do it if I ask him." She gathers her purse in her lap.

"Yeah, well you know him. I bet he turns me down flat."

"Benny can be a handful." She opens the door to my minivan and gets out. "No matter how we discuss this, it comes down to the same thing. We have to ask, together."

"It's more than that. If Aunt Alice has evidence on her, we need it."

"Well, when you put it that way." She pulls her hanky from her sleeve and dabs at her nose.

I open one of the thick glass doors leading to the lobby of the police station. She walks through first. The top half of the outside wall is glass to the ceiling. Below the windows sit two vinyl chairs with a table between them. A half-dead plant is busy wilting on its fake wood tabletop. Across from the door hangs a bulletin board with most-wanted posters and a community service announcement about fingerprinting children.

She stands at the glass window between the lobby and the office. It has a small tray under the thick glass. She dips her head and swerves her body back and forth. I smile realizing it is the dance of a woman trying to see through the reflection from behind her. As I move closer the sun's reflection blinds me unless I peer in from the correct angle.

It takes a moment before anyone notices we're there. When they do, it's a chestnut-haired woman in a blouse and slacks, not a cop in uniform. She smiles and signals she will be a moment. Her telephone headset sits prominently on her dark curls while she types madly on a keyboard. The hum of her voice barely reaches my ears.

Suddenly a man's face appears behind the glass. He laughs at us jumping as if choreographed. I slap a hand to my chest. Mrs. Perkins lets out a gasp and a surprisingly unladylike word.

"Benny, really." She recovers first and huffs at him. "We need to talk to you about Alice Bontaine. May we come in?"

"Oh, about what you called about?" His voice projects through the closed window.

"Yes." I don't raise my voice, and wonder if he must read my lips.

"I'll be with you in a second." Benny disappears.

"He's not living up to his name." Benny the Bully seems polite and helpful considering the solid glass barrier between the lobby and the office. It might be an old nickname. I smile to myself. How silly am I to believe local gossip.

"Give him some time before you jump to any conclusions." She pulls her hanky from her sleeve and dabs at her neck.

"Are you nervous?" Of all the things I would expect from her, nervousness is not one of them. I could understand her back stiffening with stubbornness, but this—little beads of perspiration gathering on her creased upper lip—surprises me.

"Yes, well you've not talked to him yet." She carefully dabs her lip and puts her hanky away. "I get so tongue tied around him. I'm afraid Alice did most of the talking when it came to Benny. She could talk him into almost anything."

"But not you?" Bad news, very bad news. "You don't expect me to charm him, do you?"

"Er…I don't think you could," Mrs. Perkins mutters.

"Pardon?"

"It's nothing personal. It wasn't charm. More like not taking any guff. I'm afraid no one knows how to stand up to Benny like Alice does."

I could stand up for myself if I wanted to. "Mrs.—"

The security door pulls open, and Benny waves us in. "Ladies, follow me please."

When I go through the door, I expect guns on display and cops sitting at desks talking on the phone solving crimes. I'm disappointed. To my right is a cloakroom, ahead four desks bunched together with mismatched desktop computers. The phones might have touch tone buttons but are an older model with square red and white buttons along their face. Toward the back, a cubical contains a microwave sitting on a little fridge and a table with four metal chairs.

The woman on the phone also has a fancy radio. Her desk is stationed between the coffee area and the front window. Besides us and Benny, she is the only one here. A gray door across the office appears to be metal and secure with a large keyhole. My mind says it has to lead to the cells. Our heading is toward the other door. To an empty conference room.

I'm not fooled. It's an informal, beige on beige, interrogation room. I'm sure a camera and microphone hide somewhere inside.

"Would you like coffee?" Benny offers.

"No thanks." I sit down in a chair at the conference table.

"Thanks, Benny, but we have a few errands to run today and popped in on the off chance you'd have time for us." Mrs. Perkins sits beside me. She gently pushes the table to spin the chair to face him.

"Okay." Benny sits down too and folds his arms resting them on the work surface between us. "What can I do for you?"

"Well, it's about Alice."

"Alice?" Benny leans back in his chair and smiles. "Mrs. Perkins you're not up to your old antics again, are you?"

"Benny." Her pink lips pull tight over her teeth. "Please, don't be difficult."

He swivels toward me with exaggerated patience.

"I need my aunt exhumed." Already, I can't meet his eyes.

"Do you?" He offers me a hand palm upward. "May I see some ID?"

"Um, sure." I open my purse and dig around. I pull out my phone, a brush, some used facial tissue, a couple mints, a notebook, and, finally, my wallet. Opening it, I show him my driver's license.

"Take it out, if you don't mind." His smile reminds me of a snake.

My cheeks burn as I pull the license from behind the plastic window. "Here you go." By the time I pull it free and hand it over my palms are damp and I'm shaking all over.

He takes it for a count of two and hands it back which ticks me off. "You said something about an exhumation. Since you're not related and have not proved a family connection, this conversation ends here."

"Benny, she lives in Alice's old house." She taps the tabletop to make her point. "She's the one who inherited the place."

"Mrs. Perkins, that is not proof of anything but generosity on Alice Bontaine's part." His smile widens, lifting his hands in a what-can-I-do manner, making me fume.

I bend so far forward over the table I'm hyper extended. "I'll get you proof if that's all that's stopping us." I bite the last word off with a snap of my teeth.

Benny stretches out on his chair bending his back awkwardly for a moment. There is a subtle crack and a sigh. "I'd like to help, but until I see proof—"

Snap. I shake my head slowly staring at him. "Okay, but let me make something perfectly clear." I stand up, glaring down my nose and stepping around the edge of the table. "If I need anything else and you've not told me about it,…and if I, for any reason, have to jump through more hoops because this thing you're doing happens to be a giant ego trip on your part…I won't be stopping with you. I'll go to your superior and their superiors until you're barely a memory, Constable."

His cheeks redden, but he doesn't move.

I gently turn his chair to face me straight on, lean

down so our faces are only inches apart, and push his chair away from the table. Now it's against the conference room wall. "We're talking about my great aunt here, and I'm not playing games. If there's a form, I want it now. If there is a procedure, I will hear it now. I will accept any and all help you offer today because I'm willing to go to your superior with that information too. You are a public servant. You are here to serve the law abiding citizens of this wonderful community."

He is stunned and stares with his mouth hanging open. He nods once and looks down at his lap. I let go of the armrests, stand up straight, and walk back to my chair. I figure the camera is in the smoke detector and nod at it.

"Give me a moment to find what you need, Ms. Johnston."

"Thank you, Constable."

Mrs. Perkins smiles behind her hand. After Benny leaves, she mutters, "Alice is that you?"

"No. For crying out loud, don't say a thing like that aloud. They could be recording us." I stare at the smoke detector inwardly cursing. "I'm glad Benny helped us, but I doubt my stunt will work again. Is there anything else we need before we go?"

"No, I'll take it to Dr. Logan once you sign it, and

he'll do the rest."

"Excellent."

***

Downtown Dunster is a town block between two crossroads leading back to the highway between Ravenglass Lake and Loxton. Although it offers minimal shopping, it has most everything a person needs. Pie 'n' All is on one side of town and the post office on the other. Its parking lot is always bustling with online deliveries.

As we check out different shop windows seeking the perfect gift, a far off voice calls my name. I peer up and down the street, examining each face, trying to sort out where the voice comes from.

Soon Glady rushes down Main Street, one hand on her wild blue hair the other on her chest. "Oh, Emma, I was wondering if you'd ever hear me."

"Hello Glady." Mrs. Perkins glances expectantly over Glady's shoulder and down the busy street. "Where's Jay?"

"Oh, that's why I wanted to talk to Emma. Tell me will she be okay?" Glady stares up at me with a half-smile on her lips.

I stare back. I immediately notice her missing BFF and realize we are talking about Jay. From the concern on

Glady's face, I know things must be serious, but I don't want her to worry. "Jay will be fine. No need to worry."

Mrs. Perkins blinks at me, sucking in her bottom lip.

"Exactly what I told her, but since we ran into each other I thought I'd ask what you think." Glady moves her purse to her other arm.

I smile, trying to load my expression with every bit of all-knowing-understanding I'm able to muster. "Feeling better?"

"Yes, thank you. We were having dinner and suddenly she grabs at her chest. And she's been in the hospital ever since." Glady pulls a hanky from her purse.

"Why didn't you call me?" Mrs. Perkins voice cuts in.

"Didn't you tell Millie about Jay?"

"Oh, ah, I thought it was nothing then, and I still do." Not daring to meet Mrs. Perkins' soul-burning gaze, I catch myself fanning my face and, slip my hand into a pocket.

Glady nods her head. "It's settled then."

"Not hardly. Next time something like this happens, you call me immediately." Mrs. Perkins turns the edges of her lips downward.

"Really, Millie. You have a psychic next door and will probably know before I will."

"You would think so, wouldn't you?" Mrs. Perkins tears her glare away from me, and I relax a bit.

"Well, you're busy. We'll talk later." With a quick wave of her hanky, Glady turns on her heel and goes back to her business.

"Bye, Glady." I offer a finger wave.

"Sometimes I think you're more trouble than you're worth." Mrs. Perkins huffs and puffs as we walk away.

"Hey, let's not take our eye off the ball. What Glady does or doesn't do is beyond my control." I glance at the display in the drugstore window. A sale on boxed chocolate.

Mrs. Perkins looks like she needs to go home.

"Give me a moment. I'll pop into the drugstore and pick up wrapping paper, a card, and box of chocolates then we can head home."

There is a bench at the corner with some freshly planted flowers. Mrs. Perkins examines a blossom and pinches off a deadhead, dropping it in the planter. Then she sits on the bench and looks down into her hands. "You said what you said about Jay to make Glady feel better, didn't you?"

"Yes." I check for eavesdroppers and add. "We both know I'm not a psychic."

She smiles. "Yes, but Alice is."

Chapter 9

I park my used minivan in the hospital parking lot across the street from the Schmidts' Tudor. Bunches of pastel balloons reach for the sky from the fence posts. A table with a white paper tablecloth centered near the back garden is loaded with salads, desserts, and a punch bowl. Streamers rattle in the breeze as I reach into the back collecting our gift, a wrapped box of chocolates on the backseat. Groups of guests sit and chat, some lucky enough to be in the shade of a small maple tree. A light baroque floats through the front windows.

Way too uppity for the likes of me.

I swallow and glance down at my one summer dress. A yellow job with a big round skirt that looks best over a crinoline. Because of the sun, Mrs. Perkins makes me wear one of her straw hats, decorated with a thick yellow ribbon, and, to prove I am a lady, little white gloves. I feel ridiculous until I walk through the gate. Every woman my age may be in a different color, but she's in a summer dress, hat, gloves, and delicate sandals.

I'm a mannequin in a fashion show. It's apparently

the standard uniform for my age and sex. Women of Mrs. Perkins' age carry large handbags and wear colorful skirted suits, like her mauve outfit; the men in ties, the older ones with sweater vests, and the younger in shirtsleeves.

Fortunately, the children, free of uniforms, wear festive shorts, overalls, sandals, t-shirts, and runners, in any and all combinations. I smile as a young girl runs by holding a paper windmill pinned to a stick. Another young lady runs with a green streamer flapping behind her. Both laugh and wave their arms.

Mrs. Perkins and I stop by the gift table to place ours with the rest. As I turn to take in the crowd, someone deposits a wine glass in my hand.

"Come on. We need to find Peter." Mrs. Perkins grabs me and pulls.

I follow her, struggling to remember what Peter Schmidt looks like but not seeing his face among the men in the yard.

Barbeque smoke catches my attention and leads me to a tall slender man wearing a red and white striped butcher's apron. Smoke wafts up from the gas grill as he waves a paddy flipper at it and takes a drink of a long necked beer. He spots us and puts the bottle down.

"Ladies, ready for some food?" He asks cheerfully.

"Oh, not just yet." Mrs. Perkins looks around again. "I wonder. Where can I find the happy couple?"

"Inside. Mom's fussing over what to put out next, and Peter is hiding in his den. Not much of a partier."

"I see. Well, this is Emma and I'm Millie."

He nods. "Charlie, Mrs. S.'s son."

"Mrs. S.?" Mrs. Perkins tilts her head.

His gaze parks on her for a moment then scans over the crowd. "What everyone calls her and I'm sure you're welcome to do the same." He winks and flips a burger. "Hey girls, ready for a hotdog?"

Behind me the same girls run by, but now both have fists full of streamers flapping behind them.

"Would she mind if I popped in to say hello?" I try a smile.

He smiles back. "Danny, come over here and eat something." A small boy of maybe five pokes a stick into the grass.

"No thanks, Uncle Charlie. Dad's made salad 'specially for me." He spies the girls and yells, "Hey, where'd you get those?" He jumps to his feet and chases after the two girls. They squeal and run off.

Across the lawn Tom jumps aside as the young trio run around the corner of the house. A young woman latches on to his arm and follows him to a group of people near the fence. A sharp stab of jealousy hits hard. I should have known he was too good to be true, and I quickly drag Mrs. Perkins in to the house.

"Ladies." Charlie calls after us in a strong Spanish accent, raising and dropping his eyebrows playfully. "I'll save something special for you."

As we enter the kitchen door, Mrs. Perkins projects in a singsong voice, "Anyone home?" She smiles widely and pulls me up beside her. "Hello, Grace. Need any help?"

A woman in a pale blue-skirted suit spins on her heel and smiles brightly at me when she meets my eyes.

"Thank you, but…yes, you might be able to help. Go down the hall to the end and pry my husband out of his cocoon." Mrs. Schmidt puts on her apron.

I can't help laughing. "Not much of a party person, huh?" I dump my wine and leave the glass in the sink.

"No, and we have too many guests that haven't seen him since the wedding." She opens the fridge and pulls two plastic bowls free. "It looks like everyone brought a salad. Are they trying to tell me something?"

Mrs. Schmidt places them on the counter to pop their lids.

"Oh, macaroni. I better put this out next." She

quickly pulls a serving spoon from a drawer and sticks it in the bowl. "Go on." She gives me a gentle push toward an arched doorway.

I stick my head around the corner and find a hallway leading to five closed doors. I nod at her before she steps outside.

"This is it, Mrs. Perkins." A man's life rests on our shoulders. Again I fill with a generous mix of doubt and hope this won't be a wild goose chase.

I try a door and find a linen closet.

Another pang of realization hits. Tom with another woman. Why would someone like him waste another moment on me? What's attracting him? My lips tighten when Alice's young face slips through my mind.

I try another door, and I find the bathroom.

"Mrs. Perkins, give me a second."

I leave her outside the bathroom door and examine myself in the mirror, not seeing beautiful. I'm blonde, sure, but not a tall slender blonde, not model tall and slender. My images blurs as tears gather in my eyes. Beautiful indeed. I bring a tissue up to catch the tears. What a fool I am. When will I learn men aren't for me? Love is but a pipe dream and stupid foolishness. I breathe in, stuttering, and another sob breaks loose. I cover my mouth so I don't make a sound. The last thing I need is Mrs. Perkins seeing me this way.

I let the tears come until the ache around my heart eases. Then I force them to stop. If I want to cry some more, I'll cry at home after this whole nightmare ends. I splash cold water on my cheeks, fix my make-up as best I'm able using my lipstick for blush.

When I finally step out of the bathroom, Mrs. Perkins is gone. I follow voices down the hall to find her with a friendly faced man in a wheelchair. Both gaze at a photo album.

"Oh, there you are. Emma, let me introduce you to Peter Schmidt. Peter, this is the girl I was telling you about."

"Close the door." His voice shakes, and he invites me to sit.

"Peter has been explaining the events leading to his annulment." Mrs. Perkins raises her brows, giving me the listen-to-this look.

"Yes, when Claire became ill she ended it. She said she didn't want to be a burden. I argued she shouldn't be alone? It still breaks my heart to think of what she faces. She wanted the annulment and because stress steals months of life, I did as she asked."

I'm not sure I buy it. "Kind of you."

His eyes tighten with unsettled sadness which seems real enough, to my surprise, and relief.

"It was the right thing to do." He sniffs, pulls a linen hanky from a pocket and wipes his cheeks. "I still loved her, but don't let Grace hear it. She'll blow her top. It's our first anniversary today. The party was all her idea. To me, it's just noise and chaos."

"It is quite a crowd out there." Mrs. Perkins shifts in her seat.

"Mostly family on her side." Mr. Schmidt flips a page and smiles. Another set of wedding photos much like the ones in the paper.

"Well, everyone's having a nice time." I lean back. The similarity of the two women, the one in the photo album and the one in the kitchen surprises me again. This man has a type—sturdy, strong, and handsome.

"They always do. It's all payday to payday, not a penny saved among them. It's a zest for life. Grace brings it out in all of them. They sure know how to have fun. And, Grace, she's a natural hostess."

"She likes to throw parties?" Mrs. Perkins takes an educated guess.

"Yes, she's never lived without a budget." His lined

face smiles, and I can tell he does a lot of it. "I've made wise investments. Luckily, they survived the country's economic troubles, and Claire gave me some funds with the understanding I would give the money to her heirs after she passed."

"Are you a lawyer?" I blurt it out and blush. "Sorry."

"A banker. Retired now. But I know enough about money to keep Claire's safe. She trusts me you see. Always has. We have some strategies in place for her and her daughter, Tammy."

"You're a good man." Maybe it's a generation thing because, good or not, people seem to trust him. Tom's image with the strange woman pops into my head again. Compared to Tom, Peter wins hands down.

"If I was fifty years younger, young lady, I would be chasing you around the desk."

I giggle, knowing I'd let him catch me if for no other reason than to piss off Tom.

"Easy to be a good man when you're stuck in a wheelchair and everyone offers to take care of you. I'm the lucky one here." He stares at the wedding photo, the same one in the paper. A faint smile stays on his lips.

"Yeah, you didn't need a wheelchair when you two

posed for this." Mrs. Perkins points at the man in the wedding photo.

"I had a small accident," Peter mutters under his breath.

"Accident?" This didn't sound good. What was he doing? Rollerblading? Skateboarding? Not likely.

"I tripped on the back stairs. Wrenched my knee. It's taking forever to heal." He spread his hands palms up. "What can you do?"

"Stop hiding and join the party." Mrs. Perkins stands, removing the album and setting it on the desk. Past her in a dark corner stands a large old-fashioned safe like in the old westerns.

Mr. Schmidt shakes his head. "I should have known. Grace sent you in here to drag me out of my hole."

"Charlie is at the barbeque cooking up a storm, and there is so much food you may wind up eating leftovers for months." I stand up and open the door noticing Mrs. Perkins has abandoned the warning-Peter-of-impending-doom plan. I go with the flow. "What is your favorite food?"

"Why it's…"

I stop listening as Tom enters the far end of the hall. Mrs. Perkins follows me out with Mr. Schmidt on her heels.

"I thought I saw you." Tom's voice stops me. His beautiful blonde friend stands beside him flashing her bright blue eyes at me. "Emma, I want you to meet my cousin, Jane. Jane, this is Emma."

"So you're Emma. Come with me, my new best friend, and I'll give you the latest on this guy here." Jane wiggles her penciled eyebrows and laughs.

Tom pales slightly and shakes his head. "Oh no, you don't. She'll leave me without a second thought. You keep your trap shut." He gently spins Jane away from me. Her wide blue hem flaring as she turns. With his hands on each of her shoulders, Tom pushes her down the hall. "I'll be back once I get rid of this one."

I stand there like an idiot. Every time I meet him, I jump from one side of the fence to another. I watch him walk away, lost in such a nice view Mrs. Perkins has to give me a little shove to start me walking again.

"Emma, really." She huffs. "We have bigger fish."

"Right, oh right." I focus back on the reason we're here.

"Ladies, I love the view but can't get through." Mr. Schmidt snickers at this joke.

"Okay, okay, I'm moving." I rush into the kitchen.

"Well, he's out. Now what?"

Mrs. Schmidt pulls more food from the fridge. "You did it!"

"Yep, but I think it's mostly because he's starving." Winking at Mr. Schmidt, I step aside to let him move closer to his wife. I glance down and see the same wrapping paper I used for our gift in the recycle. Someone besides me has good taste.

"You won't be for long. Come on, Peter. I'll recruit Charlie and Tom to help you down the stairs and while Emma here makes up a plate."

"What can I do?" Mrs. Perkins picks up a plate of squares.

Mrs. Schmidt nods. "Would you take those out and…." She smiles. "I'm sorry to put you to work. Are you sure you don't mind?"

"Mr. Schmidt, what do you like best? Burger, salad, or both?" I rest a hand on his shoulder.

"First off, call me Peter. A burger, please, and make sure it's well done and loaded."

I give his shoulder a quick squeeze. "I'll see you outside." I go to the table covered in not only salads, but fresh fruit, breads, and cheese. There were pies, squares, and the same brand of chocolates we brought. A little thrill goes through me knowing I finally did something right.

I grab a plate, flatware, and a napkin and put a spoonful of potato salad on Peter's plate. A loud laugh gets my attention and across the way sways a woman on spikey heels. "Who's the redhead in the gold dress?"

"Oh, she's Marcy." Mrs. Perkins places the squares with the desserts.

"Well, Marcy needs to eat something or at least put her wine down."

We watch her, trying not to stumble. Little tufts of dirt and grass cake around her stiletto heels.

"Take this." Mrs. Perkins hands me some flatware and goes after Marcy.

I watch for a moment making sure everything will be okay. Mrs. Perkins leads her to a chair and spends a few minutes talking to her. Knowing Mrs. Perkins will take care of the woman, I continue with my mission.

"Someone said the burgers are good today," I tease Charlie as I walk up.

"Yep, ma'am, the best." He gives me a salute.

"Well, your dad needs one with all the fixings. Paddy well done, please."

"Dad?" Charlie's face goes blank for a moment. "Oh, you mean Peter. He's my stepdad."

"Sorry, I didn't know." I could've sworn Charlie called Peter his father.

"It doesn't matter." He waves it away. "What I mean is, he treats me as if I am his son." Charlie takes a long drink of his beer. "Dead soldier. Do you mind? There's a few of special stock in the fridge crisper."

"Special stock?" I echo, not understanding what he means.

"Near Beer." He winks at me. "I'm cooking."

"Okay, I'll be back in a shake." I take his empty and hand over my plate.

A moment later, I'm looking inside the fridge. It's stuffed to breaking. I open the crisper and pull out a cold one, bringing it up to my forehead for a moment. It feels heavenly.

A blood curdling scream comes from outside. Still holding the beer, I rush through the backdoor.

Between the food tables and the fence, Grace stands over Danny. The little boy seems to have trouble breathing. As I come closer, I see his little lips swelling before my eyes. Without a moment's hesitation, Grace calmly picks the boy up and runs.

"It's okay Danny. It's okay." She holds him tight to her chest. "Get out of my way. I need to take him to emergency." To Danny she says calmly, "What did you eat honey? Do you remember?"

As I looked past the scene I wondered what she means. I turn on my heel, looking for Peter.

Chapter 10

Peter, grim as I've ever seen anyone, settles at the single table in Dunster General's family waiting room. With him sits Grace, Marcy, Charlie, and Mrs. Perkins. As footsteps quietly pad along the hallway outside, we turn as one looking through curtained window. Seeking answers, hoping, and worst of all waiting to find out how Danny is doing. A squeak of flesh against green Naugahyde cries out as someone shifts their position.

My making coffee or tea seems useless at a time like this, but I pick up the kettle at the serving station to fill it anyway.

The shockwave hits me again. Someone so young, so full of life and fun rests on a sharp edge between life and death. I swallow my feelings and push them deep down, for what I'm feeling pales compared to what the family suffers with right now. They sit gathered together discussing why they didn't test him before today. A hand clutches my forearm. Mrs. Perkins stands at my shoulder.

"Let's put the kettle on. If nothing else, we'll sober up Marcy," Mrs. Perkins whispers up at me. "Would you do that for us?"

I blink at her. "What?"

"Come on. We have to hit while the iron is hot."
She gives my arm a final squeeze.

Only a heartless person would stick their nose in
now. Mrs. Perkins settles herself beside Marcy, leans in,
whispers in Marcy's ear as the tipsy redhead sits
whimpering between Mrs. Perkins and Grace.

"Emma." Her gray head nods at me encouragingly.
There she sits. If she'd been a cat, her bottom would be
slowly swaying back and forth readying to pounce.

The lines on her face remind me of how young the
boy is and another shockwave hits. An image of Danny
chasing after the girls passes behind my closed eyes. I
shake my head. *Enough of this.* I fill the kettle, checking
the cups, and I wash them while waiting for the water to
boil. I imagine their faces as I listen to the voices from
round the table.

"Where's Bob?" A female voice, possibly Marcy's.

"He's in with the doctor." Definitely Peter's gruff
voice. It trembles as it did in the den.

"Not that Logan character." Charlie's playful voice
jumps to cold and sharp.

"I didn't see who treated Danny, dear." Grace takes

her daughter's hand and glances over at me mouthing *coffee*.

I nod my understanding, check the kettle, and organize the clean cups on a tray.

"Thank God you were there." Mrs. Perkins' voice beyond consoling. "How did you know what to do?"

"I…oh, yes. Peter has an allergy to peanuts. Bob and Peter sat down with me explaining what needs to be done if I see certain symptoms. He carries an auto-injector on him at all times." As Grace's expression softens, I find nothing but genuine love glistening in her eyes. She's thinking what I'm thinking.

It was an allergic reaction to something.

"Did anyone know Danny had allergies?" Marcy straightens in her chair and sobs. I realize she will need more than one cup of coffee.

"Who would? Can someone inherit allergies?" Charlie's back is to me, and I wish I could see his face. Mrs. Perkins gazes at him, and I wonder what she sees. Could it be anger or realization?

"And no one else has this allergy?" Mrs. Perkins' tenaciousness will not let it go.

"Unlikely." Grace glances back at me. I nod and pour hot water into the mugs. "They are mostly on my side of the family."

"Grace, that explains why you know everyone so well." Mrs. Perkins encourages her to continue with a wink and a smile. "Your extended family is a year old."

"Yes. Well, I'm learning melding two families has its challenges." Grace glances at Peter tension stiffening her shoulders. "There were some surprises."

Some nervous giggles erupt round the table. The tension in the air goes up a notch. Marcy's face pales, and I wonder if she'll be sick.

"You figured anaphylactic shock?" Mrs. Perkins nods as though in complete agreement.

"Yes, I..." Grace glances at her hands. "They didn't tell me I'd feel completely helpless after I found help."

"Mom, you were incredible." Charlie leans back in his chair. "But it has to be an accident." I wish I agreed with Charlie, but, until proven otherwise, Aunt Alice is right.

Marcy covers her face.

"Well, it's the second accident around Peter in two months." Mrs. Perkins motions me over.

"Oh, you mean the fall." Peter snorts. "That was nothing. Just me not being careful enough. Tripped over my own feet."

"What are you getting at, Mrs. P.?" Charlie leans forward again, and I wonder if his back is bothering him since he's not able to sit still.

"It seems too coincidental for my liking."

"Yes, Millie. I remember hearing stories about you and Alice. It may have slanted your point of view, and now you see things that aren't necessarily there." Peter throwing in his two cents worth changes Mrs. Perkins' thoughtful frown to one deeper and more intense. Her glare doesn't sway him and he turns his attention away under her withering gaze.

I bring over the mugs and set about giving each person a cup of something warm. They helped themselves to the teabags, instant coffee, sugar, and powdered cream. After I hand Marcy her coffee, I take the tray back to the station, refill the kettle, and plug it in.

With everyone warned of Peter's allergy, why would anyone bring food with peanuts in it?

As I turn back to the group, a man of about six feet tall with a barrel chest and baldhead strolls in. Everyone rushes to him except Peter—who turns his chair toward the newcomer. The man waits until everyone surrounds him, leans back on his cowboy boots, and raises his arms for silence.

"Danny, will be fine. They want to keep him for observation since this was his first reaction." Bob seeks out Grace. He takes her hand and kisses her knuckles. "Grace, how do I tell you—" His voice cracks, and he can't continue. The big man drops his chin, releasing a shaky breath.

"I'm glad he's okay." Grace smiles up into Bob's face. "Should we take shifts, so Danny won't be alone?"

Bob grins, and his frightening size and powerful demeanor evaporate. "Dad, she is beautiful, smart, and kind. You're one lucky man." Bob pulls over a metal chair and sits beside his father. "Where'd you get the drinks?"

"From me." I wave a cup at him. "What would you like?"

"Tea. Sweet tea would be best and more coffee for Marcy." Mrs. Perkins speaks up. I pour some hot water in a mug for him.

Bob leans back in his chair and stretches. "I appreciate your staying, but not much left to do except wait. It's unlikely anything else will happen tonight. His stay is just a precaution."

"I'm sure Danny would like his own pajamas and something from home, a coloring book or stuffy." How obvious can she be? Mrs. Perkins is not fooling me. As she speaks, her face changes from open concern to curiosity then lands on wise understanding. "We could take Grace and pick up some clothes or toys for Danny."

"Thank you." Bob smiles at me as I hand him his hot water. "And you are?" He stands and offers me a hand to shake.

"Emma."

"Nice to meet you…Emma, part of the 'we' I presume."

I nod and back away, taking Marcy more coffee. Even with all the upset over his son, Bob remains calm and collected. I glance over at Peter. He smiles when I meet his eyes. They share a slight resemblance around the mouth and nose.

"Okay, does Grace have keys to your place?" Mrs. Perkins stands up.

Bob quits dunking his teabag. "Um, no, and if you don't mind I'd rather go with you ladies."

"Of course." Grace gets up too. "I'll sit with Danny until you come back." She rests her hand on Peter's shoulder for a moment. "You don't mind, do you?"

***

Bob ushers us into the kitchen through the backdoor of his home. As he follows us in, he notices the state of the kitchen and shrugs. Dirty pots and pans sit in the double sink's greasy water, and the stove has something crusty smeared across its top.

He quickly encourages us to keep moving, pointing down the hall to Danny's room. This room is as tidy as the kitchen is messy and themed with blue wallpaper and printed teddy bears. It reminded me more of a nursery instead of a room for a five-year-old boy.

I walk to the nearest dresser and open the top drawer, finding socks and underwear. I pull two of each. The next drawer holds t-shirts, and I pull two of these also. I set them on the bed and look for pants knowing I'll find PJs eventually.

Mrs. Perkins comes in the room.

"Oh, what a cozy room for a young boy." Mrs. Perkins glances around. "Comic books, coloring book, or both? What do you say?"

Bob nods. As he walks to the desk, he pulls out a drawing tablet and some crayons. Then from under the pillow he retrieves a hard covered book.

"We'll read this together when he wakes up." He shows us the book's title, *The Hobbit.*

On the opposite side of the door, swinging from a doorknob, hangs Danny's knapsack. Bob dumps its contents out on the blue and brown striped comforter.

"He uses it for the daycare." The knapsack contents consists of a balled up change of clothes and some shiny snack-food wrappers. He hands the bag over.

"Thanks."

"He'll need his toothbrush." Bob leaves the room, but his voice carries from the bathroom. "Mrs. Perkins, anything else he'll need?"

"No, the hospital will supply the rest." She walks from the room leaving me to stuff the knapsack. I quickly grab a teddy bear from the bed and follow her out.

Bob pops out of the bathroom with a strange shaped green toothbrush and toothpaste. I can't help smiling and take them from him, tucking them into a side pocket.

"Will he like this little guy to join him?" I hold up the teddy bear.

Bob takes the bear and brings it to his nose. He inhales deeply, crushing the stuffy to his face. I stare at my feet, wishing for more people skills.

"He'll love it." Bob's expression changes. The lines in his face deepen and his lips disappear into a line. "Before we go back can we talk? The three of us."

"If you like." Mrs. Perkins peeks in, waiting to lead us back to the kitchen. We follow her to the table.

Bob's neck flares with color. "I was late to the party and—"

"This isn't your fault?" I hand him the knapsack and give the kettle a little shake. "Empty." I drop the pack on a kitchen chair and take the kettle to the sink. Instead of working around the dishes, I steady myself and plunge my hand into the greasy water pulling the stopper. After filling the kettle, I turn the spout to the empty sink and fill it with warm water.

Mrs. Perkins, who has been no help in this crisis, is demurely examining something on the kitchen table. Bob, looking glum, joins her, pushing the breakfast dishes aside. He sits, sighing, I grab a cloth, dunk it several times in the soapy water, and join them at the table. Mrs. Perkins moves out of my way while I wipe the tabletop.

I wish Bob would tell us what's going on. I'm dying to hear what's on his mind.

"What can I do for you?" Mrs. Perkins rests her hands in her lap. I know she doesn't mean the dishes. I rearrange the pots to soak, splashing around in the sink, and can't quite hear what he says. When the water stops and the dishes are loaded into the dishwasher, Bob's low, sad voice is finally audible.

"...She hasn't been seen since." Bob's hands clench

together, knuckles whitening.

"Well if she can walk away from you and your son, she isn't worth another thought." Mrs. Perkins meets my eyes.

"With only Grace and Dad for help it's been tough." The bald man expels a long breath. "I'm worried about Dad."

The kettle whistles and, while I collect what we need for tea, I find a large sealed container of macaroni salad sitting on the top shelf of the fridge.

"Well, I'm sure you can count on them." Bringing what we need to the table, I then sit across from Bob.

"Did the doctor say what happened?" I drop a teabag in each cup.

"Peanuts. They tested for everything, but it was peanuts he reacted to." Bob takes a drink then pulls the teabag free with his thick fingers and plops it on the table. "Not one person would bring any peanut products to the party because of Dad's severe allergy. It makes no sense."

"Could he have picked something up on the way there?" Mrs. Perkins ponders aloud.

"No, we had breakfast here, then I made the macaroni salad and off we went. We were in a rush because we were late."

"You made the salad yourself?" Mrs. Perkins beams at him.

"There's not really a choice. Danny's on a kick of eating nothing but macaroni salad for lunch. It's his thing right now. Not that I mind. It makes making lunches for him simple."

Mrs. Perkins looks at the fridge. "And when you shop, you check every label?"

"What are you getting at?"

"If it's the one thing Danny would eat, how did this happen?"

"This wasn't an accident?" Bob's cup shakes in his fist.

"No, but Danny wasn't the target, and until today peanuts were only dangerous to your father. And then there are the stairs. Put the two together, and someone might try to hurt Peter again." Mrs. Perkins leans forward, grasping Bob's sleeve and speaking about things that run blood cold.

"If you're right, they've already hurt him." Bob quiets for a minute and sips his tea before shaking his head as something occurs to him "No, wait. That can't be right. Charlie examined the back steps after Dad fell and didn't find anything wrong." His skin goes pale and his face pinches. "Dad's as agile as a cat. He's played golf twice a week for as long as I remember. The man is young at heart, and it's keeping him healthy."

"Now, he's in a wheelchair." Mrs. Perkins points out, like we don't remember.

"Wait, do we know it was peanuts?" I can't help but wonder why this didn't happen earlier.

"Yes, Dr. Logan did the test himself. It was peanuts all right." He takes another sip of tea.

I push away what might have happened if Grace hadn't been there. A shiver runs up from my toes to the top of my head, and the cup between my palms isn't warming me up.

Mrs. Perkins waits as if she knows what will happen next.

Bob nods to himself obviously struggling with an inner battle. "You know what I'm going to ask, don't you?"

Mrs. Perkins didn't move.

"Okay"—Bob clears his throat—"Mrs. Perkins will you look into this before someone kills my father?"

She glances at me and takes my hand tightly in hers.

"Yes, yes we will."

Chapter 11

I'm driving back to The Lake with Mrs. Perkins strapped in beside me. Darkish twilight barely lets the stars sparkle above the highway. Watchful for deer, I wait for my high beams to hit their eyes, the only warning I'll get before they jump on to the tarmac.

I'm jumpy but not because of the deer. I'm used to anticipating them, it's Aunt Alice. Whether she is a ghost or my imagination doesn't matter now because her warning about Peter rings true. I made a choice to believe in Alice, and now I might have to make one to believe in myself. It's freaking me out because I'm not sure it's possible.

I glance over at Mrs. Perkins hoping for reassurance and get exhaustion.

"No more hospital today?" It's a stupid question considering the fact I'm driving in the other direction, but I'm hoping it will prompt her to share her plan.

"No, we need to talk to Alice." Mrs. Perkins adjusts her seatbelt over her chest.

"Aunt Alice won't help us now." *Emma, just say it.* "Even if Aunt Alice wants to talk, would she tell us what we need to know?"

She clears her throat. "You need to have faith in yourself. Not all roads end at the psychiatric ward."

"Psychiatric ward?" I gasp. Aunt Alice held nothing back. "You won't say anything. If anyone finds out and I—" I bite the word off as clamp my teeth into my bottom lip.

"You're scared. Always so scared and it's ridiculous. No one will reject you because of Alice." Mrs. Perkins clears her throat again. "You are one of many odd people living in the tri-town area. No one judges them."

"Right." My throat tightens, and my eyes burn. I slow the minivan blinking away tears. "And these people have known and accepted one another all their lives. I'm new. No one knows me." A sob catches in my throat. I pull to the shoulder and put the vehicle in park, staring straight ahead. "Mrs. Perkins, I've never had friends. Since the day they diagnosed me, I've been alone. Sure, people were around me, like family or paid companions, but to them, I was a job not a person." Another sob follows my confession and then another. I drop my forehead on the steering wheel and let go.

A small hand lightly strokes my hair. "It will be okay. You'll be fine."

"I've never been fine." I scrub my face and dry my

hands on my crinkled skirt. "They'll come for me. They always have, and they always will."

"No, they won't. Not this time because you have me." Mrs. Perkins rubs a circle on my back between my shoulders. "And your aunt."

"Right." I check my mirrors for traffic and pull back onto the highway. "I'm not sure asking Aunt Alice for help is the thing to do."

"Don't be ridiculous." Mrs. Perkins barks a laugh.

I take my eyes from the road. Does she understand what I suspect? "I'm not convinced we'll be able to keep him safe. Have you considered the fall out if something happens to Peter while we're involved?"

"Emma!" Startled Mrs. Perkins points at a red flash of light, a reflection of an animal's eye.

"I see it." I pump the brakes and don't take my eyes from the deer until we pass. "It's one thing to suspect foul play, but now you're asking me to accept the responsibility for Peter's life and safety. What if I fail?"

"Don't forget both Alice and I've done this before."

"Yes, and one of you is dead." I regret the words as soon as I say them.

Mrs. Perkins brings a hand to her throat, lips pursed and her face pale as I've ever seen it. "Let's focus on the positive. First, the person in trouble is Peter. Second, Bob has asked us to help keep his father safe. Third, the culprit doesn't know we are on to them."

I shake my head very, very slowly. "Let's keep it that way."

"That's a good idea." Her voice is pleased, happy even.

Why the excitement?

"Tomorrow, during daylight hours we will examine the stairs where Peter fell and ask about the food." Apparently the plan is clear in her mind.

"Um—"

"You might have to ask Benny to help. He has the connections to have samples tested."

"Benny the bully." I hoped for more of a rest between bouts with him. "Let's try not to involve him unless we have to. If he gets wind of my past, he won't trust a thing I'll say."

"Emma, you need to have faith. We've all had challenges." She sniffs and looks out the side window. "I have faith people are kinder and wiser than you give them credit for. You'll learn that what we do is good for both of us."

"I understand some people accept I'm psychic and

that's fine. It's better than telling them the truth." *Okay, now it's all out.* I can be myself.

"You have your opinion." Mrs. Perkins tightens the seatbelt across her chest. "And Alice and I have ours."

I glance down at the speedometer, take my foot off the gas and let the van slow to the speed limit. "But you won't tell?"

"No." Her lips pull tight in a smile. "Not yet."

"I won't follow blindly just because you're older or have more experience. Expect questions."

"Emma, it's time to move on. Let it go. We need to be ready for tomorrow."

"Tomorrow." A niggle begins. I'm haunted by the fact Aunt Alice and Mrs. Perkins met behind my back at first. I suspect not all the talk was personal. Is she trying to change the subject? Is something else going on? Sure, Mrs. Perkins wants to talk with Aunt Alice. Wait a minute. "Do you want to talk to Aunt Alice about the case, or are you planning another gossip session?"

"Gossip? We never gossip. We do talk about things. For example, we both think Tom will be a nice addition to your life." Mrs. Perkins shifts in her seat. "And it's time you forgave this old woman for spending time with her best friend. Since it came out, I've told you everything."

I glance over at her, and she looks earnest enough for me to believe her.

"Okay, I'll consider it." It's up to me. Trust Mrs. Perkins and have a friend closer to me than my own family, or don't and be alone until I shrivel up and die inside. *Some choice.*

"Thank you, Emma." She grabs the door handle as I take a corner too fast.

"Mrs. Perkins, can we be sure Danny'll be safe until tomorrow?" I remove my foot from the accelerator and hit the low beams for an oncoming car.

"This occurred to me, too. Our villain made a mistake and almost killed Danny. If I'm correct, and I think I am, our culprit was shaken up by their foolishness. By now, they've calmed down and are able to hide their reaction to the whole thing. We need to discuss what we remember, talk to Alice, and then work on a strategy."

"I don't get it." I blow out a puff of air. "You act like everyone in town is your friend. What's with that?"

"It's a small town. We've seen each other's faces all our lives during school, in the grocery store, and at community celebrations." Mrs. Perkins shrugs. "How can't we feel acquainted?"

Until this moment, I didn't understand there was more to the small-town living than traffic-free streets and friendly hellos.

"That sounds crazy." Inwardly, I cringe at my choice of words.

"It's why new folk in a small town have trouble making friends at first. Once the first town member accepts the newcomer most of us follow suit."

I don't doubt her. In a strange way it makes sense. Which means they will be curious about my past and probably ask why I came to Ravenglass Lake. More sharing?

"Can we drop by on Danny tomorrow and make sure he's okay?"

"Yes, now you're thinking." She nods with approval.

As we turn onto Sandspit Crescent, I'm still not confident. "Even if we do find something on the stairs, who's to say they were tampered with?"

She sighs. "We must set priorities. Forget the unimportant details and recall whatever you remember about today."

"But I wasn't looking for trouble, and don't remember every detail."

"Assume nothing, Emma. Just tell me everything you remember, and we'll go from there." My shoulders tense, but I tell her everything I remember right down to the Near Beer.

As we park in front of my garage door, she unfastens her safety belt. "You better come in for a bit."

I follow her to her yellow door wishing for an excuse to go home. An envelope sticks out from the doorjamb, and she tucks it into her bra before we enter the house. Well, either it's none of my business or she's keeping secrets from me—again. I follow her into her dark house to find out what's going on.

"What's the envelope about?" I feel like another disaster is waiting to happen, and I'm poking at it with a stick. Kicking off my shoes, I free myself of the gloves, tuck them in the big straw hat, and leave them on the desk by the stairs.

"Let's settle in first. It looks like Dr. Logan's writing."

The exhumation forms I got from Benny? All I did was sign them, and Mrs. Perkins did the rest. I'm not sure I'm able to wait. I glance out at the street, close the door, and turn the deadbolt, locking it. In the house, we should be safe enough.

"Hand it over." I offer an open palm as I enter the kitchen.

She nods.

"Come. Sit." Grabbing a cloth, she wipes the table. "It might not have worked out like we planned, but all things considered we did okay today." She pulls the envelope free. "I'm sure our presence threw everything off."

Here she goes again. "What are you an egomaniac?"

"No." Mrs. Perkins puts her hands on her hips. "You were so nice when you first moved in."

I tear the envelope open and free two sheets of paper. The top one is covered in chicken scratch, and I can't read a word. As if by divine intervention, my phone rings. I jump out of my skin and dropping the pages on the table. Tom's number appears on my display as I walk out the backdoor. Thoughts of Jane and Tom standing by the fence, teasing each other in the hallway, and Jane knowing things about me when I know nothing about her, irk me.

"Hello." I slowly walk toward the Lily of the Valley garden in its wishing well design of river stone and two thick wooden beams holding up a cedar-shake roof.

"Hey, what happened? I expected you back after

Grace took Danny to the hospital." His voice fills with tension.

"Nothing. Mrs. Perkins and I picked up some things for Danny."

Tom lets out a long sigh. "I thought he was fine."

"No one had any idea he was allergic. The doctors tested him, and he reacts severely to peanuts like his granddad." I sit on the stonewall around the waxy spears.

"Well, that's just wrong. Everyone knows not to bring anything with peanuts in it to the Schmidts'." Tom's voice grows louder, from shock or anger I don't know.

If it's common knowledge, how did the peanuts get to the party? "And what does that tell you?" I glance up at the sky and enjoy the starlight.

"I don't understand." Far off voices chatter through the phone.

"I'm saying if it's common knowledge then it isn't much of a leap to say this wasn't an accident."

"Now hold up." He releases a long hiss over the line.

In my mind's eye Jane is right beside him smiling. Who's breathing am I hearing?

"You have any idea how it happened? You were outside with um…what was her name again?" I clench my teeth.

"Jane."

I don't want to be childish, but I can't help myself. "Right, you and Jane, your cousin, were outside when it happened. Do you remember seeing anything?"

"Just everyone having fun." Dead air. I wait, hoping for more. "Bob picked up two plates. He loaded up his and kept asking Danny what he wanted. But I'm guessing 'cause I couldn't hear. Danny kept shaking his head and Bob didn't make a big deal out of it. Finally, Danny nodded, and Bob piled it on."

"That's more or less what I know already." Even I could hear the disappointment.

"Sorry, not much help." A definite female voice in the background.

"Actually you were a lot of help." I decide to see the positive side. "But if you remember anything else, you'll tell me, right?"

"What are you jabbering on about? Mrs. Perkins didn't con you into anything did she?"

"I promised not to discuss it." I'd like to tell him everything.

"Why?" The phone rattles as he changes ears. "From the sounds of it you are helping her."

"Because…" My heart jumps to my throat, and I barely breathe. "If you find out on your own I'm not breaking my word."

"I've heard rumors about Millie Perkins." He doesn't hide his anger. "Stay out of it."

"Are you telling me what to do?" I bite my tongue hard before I say something I'll definitely regret later. "Just stop. Stop and think a moment. Something is wrong."

"Really." He grumbles something impossible to decipher. "And why is it your business?"

"Why isn't it yours?" I clear my throat. "Tom, just let it go, okay?"

"I've seen this before. Mrs. Perkins should stay out of things." When I close my eyes, I imagine steam coming out of Tom's ears. I bite my lip to stop the smile.

"Don't you get it? She thinks it's our fault." I look up high into the night sky and know Mrs. Perkins is right.

"That's effing nuts."

Perfect. "I'd better go." Standing, I head toward Mrs. Perkins' backdoor.

"Before you do, how about getting together later?" Female chatter comes over the phone while he waits. "Just a sec."

I don't know if he means me or the person with

him. "Hello?"

"Do you mind if Jane comes along?"

I swallow hard. "Sure, the more the merrier." What the hell is he up to? "I gotta go."

"I'll come by in an hour."

"Sure." I didn't say goodbye, just disconnected. *Bringing his cousin on a date? Wait a minute.* If Jane is there, maybe the conversation will flow better…and Aunt Alice will stay where she belongs. I cross my fingers as I enter the backdoor.

"Oh good. What would you like to eat last of the stew or a serving of chili?" Mrs. Perkins lifts two containers from the freezer.

"Stew if you don't mind."

"Not at all." She pops the lid off of the stew and opens a cupboard to reveal a microwave oven. I'm stunned. She hides her microwave in a cupboard. The gillibebop I presume. "Who was on the phone?"

"Tom. He wants to get together tonight." I sit at the table picking up the dropped pages.

"What happens will be on you this time." Mrs. Perkins freezes for a moment then shakes her head, eying the pages. "What are those anyway?"

Nice. Very polite.

"I can't read it." I drop the first sheet on the table surface and read the form. Someone else filled this in. "It's Aunt Alice's exhumation papers." I flip the pages to the end. "Looks like Dr. Logan has his approval."

"Good." Mrs. Perkins digs through the silverware drawer.

I fold them up again and replace them in the envelope. "You're acting like I was there with Tom the other night."

"Not exactly what I mean." She laughs. "It's the fact Tom doesn't know who he was with that bothers me."

"Cut me some slack." My face burns, and I wish I had remembered *that* before I made my date with Tom. "Nothing will happen tonight."

"Okay, okay." She sets the silverware on the table and removes the envelope.

"Besides he was at the party remember. I'll ask him about what he saw." And she'll never know I have talked to him already. A few choice questions for Jane is just what I'm interested in. But nicely, so Tom doesn't catch on.

"Good idea. You already sound like an investigator, a chip right off the old psychic block." She smiles at me and places a plate of stew on the table.

I blink at her. What's she up to now?

"You said we should talk to Aunt Alice." The microwave beeps, and she turns back to her chore to remove the steaming food.

"This is real life and not the time for carelessness."

"Pishposh." Mrs. Perkins snickers. "What would you like to drink?"

"Pop or water. Whichever." I'm getting nowhere. "Are you listening?"

"Try not to be difficult." Mrs. Perkins finally sits down. The table is set the food is ready, and I'm starved.

As we eat, it occurs to me Mrs. Perkins hasn't shared her observations. "What did you see? Anything interesting?"

"I had just stepped out and was cleaning up the main table when I saw Danny and Bob selecting food." Mrs. Perkins dabs her mouth. "Danny is a picky eater."

Her statement raises a flag. That's two people claiming Danny only had salad.

"Did you see anyone around the table messing with the food?"

"Well, of course." She smiles like I've said something funny.

"You did?"

"Yes, Grace and I were clearing paper plates and

tossing them into the garbage. We had replaced empty bowls, and Grace went back to get a cloth to wipe up a spill."

Not what I meant and Mrs. Perkins knew it. "Nothing else?"

She shakes her head slowly, thinking. "You know who would have seen something?"

"No, who?" My shoulders ache with tension.

"Charlie was right there all day." She samples her food and nods.

True, but was he watching? "You mean anyone with any sense wouldn't try it in the open. And if they did it in the kitchen…back to anyone could have done it."

"People were in and out all day." Mrs. Perkins agrees.

"That's just it. Everyone who attended the party will be suspect." I almost lick my plate clean, the stew was so good. Instead, I stand.

"Thanks for dinner, but Tom's coming over in a half hour and this time I'd like to clean up and be ready to go out." I look down at my wrinkled skirt and wonder if I have time to iron it.

"Emma, he calls and you drop everything and go out with him. It will give him the wrong idea about you.

Next time insist on a day's notice. You appear…incredibly…easy."

"Well, then I guess he's about to learn something new about me."

Mrs. Perkins' face goes a beautiful pink, and I can't help but smile.

Chapter 12

As my curling iron cools in the bathroom, the doorbell rings. I'm excited enough to dance to the door. To my surprise and disappointment, Jane, model blonde and beautiful, stands in front of him, a bottle of rum and a bag of nacho chips in hand.

Oh, no. Our wires must have been crossed. Jane's first impression of me will not be good. Not good at all. Sighing, I stand back to let them enter, and motion them into the living room which I haven't tidied for days.

The book, a best seller on mental health, remains abandoned on the throw rug and Aunt Alice's pansy tea service is spread out on the coffee table. There is dust mounting up on pretty much every surface.

"Come in." I take a quick glance around. My face heats up. "Excuse the disaster. I swore you said we were going out for a drink."

"My fault." Jane pushes the rum against Tom's chest, and walks right through to my kitchen. Clinking of glassware and the fridge door opening have me turning to join her. Before I take a step, she returns with a bowl full of big cheese flavored triangles and the three glasses full of ice. "No mix."

"You're fault. How?"

"I thought we should meet." She wags the glasses at Tom. "You better hit the store."

"No." The thought of being stuck alone with her almost snaps me in half. "I rarely keep pop in the house, but I'm sure I have juice somewhere."

Jane smiles, bright eyes crinkling, and sits on the couch.

"We're imposing already. I'll go to the store." Tom, as though realizing he's hugging the rum like a teddy bear, puts the bottle on the table.

"No need. Pineapple okay?" I back step toward the kitchen.

"You're sure?" Tom, fumbling his keys, steps forward. "Nice place."

If this is nice, I'd hate to see his place. I quickly load the tea tray on the coffee table, grabbing the cups, rattling china and leaving rings. What's worse?

"I inherited the place from my Great-Aunt Alice." My face grows warmer and warmer. Old news I'm sure I'm repeating from our first date, and force my lips together to make myself shut up.

Jane opens her purse in the middle of the couch and pulls out a lipstick, looking in a compact she reddens her lips. "Nice."

Does she mean my inheritance or my decorating skills? I scan the room. Jane is right. It is nice and more than I deserve, considering how close we were.

"I wish I'd spent more time with her." Something fuzzy has been growing in a teacup and I lift the tray, needing to move it into the kitchen.

She becomes still. Her eyes cut to mine.

"Jane, behave yourself." Tom, larger than life, settles in the chair by the windows as the curtains billow with a gust of evening air.

"Sorry." Her cheeks color slightly. "I didn't mean it like it sounded. I put my foot right in it." Jane offers me an embarrassed smile through the kitchen doorway from the couch.

She's feeling as awkward as I am. "It's okay." I slide the tray onto the marble work surface. After pushing my dirty dishes into a crooked pile, I fetch the juice. "Give me a second. I don't know about you, but I'd love some refreshments." There is only one problem. I shouldn't drink, not a beer at the pub or rum in my living room because of my meds.

I recall my conversation with Mrs. Perkins in the van on our way home from Dunster and mentally cross my fingers. Honesty it is. *Mrs. Perkins, I hope you're right.*

A lone carton of juice lies on its side in the cupboard. To steady my shaking hands, I gently grip the counter and take a breath, letting it out nice and slow. There is no option two. It's either maintain control or Aunt Alice steps in. At that moment, Alice isn't welcome. I want friends, real friends, more than I want to live free. Could I do it? Maybe I've done it already. Guests have come to my house to see me, to spend time with me.

Another breath. My muscles relax. Calmer, I reach for the carton, press it over my heart and join my visitors in the living room.

"It's my one and only. Someone will need to take a trip to the corner store when we run out." I carefully set the juice down in front of Jane, who has finished filling our glasses.

Eying the drinking glass, I tip it. More than an ounce and a half of white rum churns between the small round cubes. I remind myself I'm brave and good. Mrs. Perkins told me they would understand.

"Sorry, but I can't drink alcohol. I'm on medication right now. Any amount would have me sleeping in twenty minutes." I cringe, remembering the pub with Tom. I bring up my eyes, hoping for a positive response from Jane.

"Here I go again." Jane face goes deeper red. To the ceiling, she mouths, "Please let me do something right tonight."

"It's not you. Please, don't let this bother you." I glance at Tom, hoping he'll jump in.

A half grin changes his face to a mischievous boy's.

I give up. "Don't sit there watching all this. Say something."

"I'm speechless." Tom bursts out laughing and points at Jane.

Her pale skin flares almost purple, and the contrast is ugly. "It's the town. Have you noticed a bar at every corner in downtown Dunster?"

"Tom that's enough." My voice firm and demanding. I'm acting like Mrs. Perkins and blush. I try a different tack. "Why don't we forget the last few minutes ever happened? Please, you would be doing me an immense favor."

"I'm game." Jane passes the juice.

Tom takes the carton, pulls its tab, and adds mix to his glass. "So, you fine dine at Perkie Perkins'?" He takes a long sip and leans back.

"You were with her at the party too. She lives next door?" Jane accepts the juice and pours some in her glass. "I thought this neighborhood looked familiar. I live in Dunster. Doesn't Madame Bontaine, the world renowned psychic, live around here somewhere?"

I do my best to keep my face blank. How can I say anything? I'm hopping from one hole to another. "Mrs. Perkins and I eat together sometimes, and Madame Bontaine is, I mean, was my Great-Aunt Alice."

"You hang out with Millie Perkins? How old is she?" Jane pauses, then mutters, "Sorry for your loss."

"I bet she's a really good cook," Tom offers an attempt at support. "But you still need friends your own age."

"Yes, she is." I push my glass away. Is Tom trying to lead an intervention? "What bothers you so much? Her age, or what we are doing?"

"No, I mean yes." Tom shakes his head, his hair catching on his collar. "Oh, I mean no. You told me you spent time with Perkie and hinted you investigated Danny's allergic reaction like it is something sinister."

"Yes." A tremble goes through me. Mrs. Perkins was wrong. They did not understand in the least. In fact, they sit here trying to interfere with my life and say things behind her back. They're judging who I hang with and what I do with my time. Invisible steam chugs from my ears.

"Don't stop now."

Jane holds up her hand to clarify my sarcasm, but he happily continues, trying to fix it with a few more choice words.

"I mean you're young and beautiful, and you should be living life not seeking death." He is completely missing the point.

"It's not always about death. In fact, if you must know we were there to prevent someone from getting hurt."

"Great job looking after Danny." Tom waves away the only laughter in the room which comes from him.

That's it. I understand I don't know him and I doubt very much he knows me, but here he goes spewing on and on about my life. My life. "Jane, take him home."

"No, I mean…I said something wrong. Why aren't you laughing?" He sits, blinking. "You don't like hanging with Perkie and snooping in everyone's closet, do you?"

"I don't know what we're doing. All I can say is Millie Perkins is a close family friend, and it turns out my only friend." I hold up my hand to stop him, but again he doesn't shut up.

"Emma, come on. Do you really like hanging with that old lady?"

"Truth be told? Yes." I glare at him, bringing Mrs. Perkins' glare to its knees. "She's never said a foul word about anyone. Not like some people I know."

He stares at me. Still not understanding what I mean.

"This isn't a friendly drink. It's a pity drink." I stand and walk to the door. "Time for you to go."

"Come on." Jane gathers her purse and stands. "Tom, apologize."

"I'm sorry. There's no pity here." He spreads his arms.

"You get out." Jane pokes Tom in the shoulder. "I'm not leaving until I finish the drink I came for, but if we kick him out, I'll have to spend the night or you'll have to give me a ride home."

"Wait a minute. How come I'm not allowed to finish my drink?" Tom takes hold of Jane's finger and brings the poking to an end.

Jane and I burst out laughing. This man is incredible.

"Do you want to stay?"

"You know I do." He flutters his eyelashes like a teenage girl at me.

"Okay, but not another word about Mrs. Perkins. She was my aunt's best friend, and I like her. A harmless lonely woman and when I'm around her I feel…well, I feel good."

"Okay, okay." He raises his hands in surrender. "I'm sorry it won't happen again."

"And you like her." Jane lifts her glass in a toast. "To Mrs. Perkins."

"Thanks, Jane." I pour my rum into her glass leaving me with one ice cube. I fill my glass up with juice. "To Mrs. Perkins and Alice Bontaine."

Jane chokes on her drink. "I will go blind drinking this."

I smile. "Let me find some more ice."

When I come back, Tom picks up his glass. "To Perkie." He sips and sets his glass down on the ringed coffee table. "In my defense. I tried to do a good thing."

"Make it up to me? Tell me about the Schmidts." It's funny, I was sure standing up for myself and Mrs. Perkins would cause trouble, but instead I'm closer to Tom and Jane.

"Can you do me a favor?" Jane wiggles in her seat,

her bright blue eyes glistening.

I nod.

"Can you get me Mrs. Perkins' recipe for her Oatmeal Raisin Cookies?"

"I'm not sure." I imagine talking to her and it's not pretty. "I thinks she keeps them locked up."

"Oh, here she goes with the Bambi eyes." Tom laughs.

"Okay." Bambi eyes don't work on me, but she is damn good at them. "I'll try, but she may not want to part with her family recipe. And, Tom, Bambi has brown eyes."

Jane snorts. "I'll take that as a yes." She sips again, shivers from her toes, and pours in more juice. "The Schmidts and I go way back. When I was young and stupid, I borrowed money from him. I had a car accident and didn't want my dad to find out about it. To have the car fixed quickly, and under my father's radar, I went to Peter Schmidt. The only place to lend a kid like me money. I didn't have a job, just a small allowance."

I mutter under my breath. "You're saying loan shark. Here in Dunster. Peter Schmidt is one surprise after another."

Tom spits his drink into his lap. "What? Only a dimwit would be fool enough…You didn't tell Peter it was a secret?"

"Yeah, I did. It took a long time to pay it off." Jane sighs. "He tried to keep it going, saying I owed him more in interest. But I added it up, and I paid three times what I borrowed. Then he asked if he should sit down with Dad. Horrified, I told my dad everything. One phone call from him. No secret. No leverage. No more payments."

"All this time I thought you two were friends. You dropping by almost every week." Tom glares at me. "Let me guess, you and Perkie want to keep someone from hurting Peter Schmidt. Why?"

"Why? Because he's a human being." I steel my nerve. "Jane, have you seen Peter's safe or what he has in there?"

"I've seen the safe. Huge sucker, but not what's in it. I can guess. We all can." She rolls her eyes. "The man's a frigging millionaire."

"That's worth killing for?" Tom finishes his drink in one swallow. "I wonder how many owe money and don't want to pay it off? Or can't."

"Or have been blackmailed." She shakes her head.

"And if he dies, who'd get it?" I cringe sounding more nosy and cold hearted than I mean to.

"No doubt about it, Bob and Grace." She sounds

like an authority.

"Okay, there is a will." It's like eating one potato chip. I can't stop.

"Don't all rich people have them? His money would take care of the whole extended family and some." She leans back on the couch. "I paid him back probably four or five times what I borrowed."

"Have another drink, Jane." Tom smiles momentarily at her and winks. I don't get a wink. I get an explanation. "Asshole doesn't want to claim it on his tax return, so he's forced to keep it in his safe. It all makes sense to me." He goes into the kitchen and comes back with more ice. "How greedy do you have to be? With that much money, couldn't he give some to everyone?"

"Are you suggesting a family member?" I can't believe what I'm hearing. "They all seemed concerned about Danny. They rallied, clinging to each other for support."

"Close family sure, but it wasn't over Peter, it was over Danny. Ask yourself, would they have done the same for him?" Jane drops several ice cubes in her glass and stirs it with her forefinger.

She definitely has a sick mind...or a suspicious one.

"It could be anyone." Is this what the investigation

is all about? Wondering about blackmail? Knowing family members murder each other over money. Where are all the good folk of Dunster and Ravenglass Lake?

Tom stares at me, his face not as friendly as before. "True. The question is who?"

"I shouldn't be saying anything else." This is true. The list grew longer. It wouldn't take much to put a drop of oil in food that would only hurt Peter Schmidt? "I need your oath you'll not to say a word about this. It might tip the bad guy off and make him even more dangerous."

"Who would be more dangerous?" Tom wants to know.

I don't wait for his word. "Bob was the one that pulled us into the case."

"Wow." Jane sips. "Bob appeared shocked but not overly emotional. I mean his father dealt with this allergy his whole life. I'm sure there have been close calls before."

"You're thinking Bob is out." Tom takes a handful of chips. "And Danny is too young. Who else is there?" Using his free hand, he sticks out a finger for each name. "There's Grace, Charlie, and Marcy." He pops a broken chip in his mouth.

"Did you see Marcy at the party? Drunk enough Mrs. Perkins almost force fed her coffee to sober her up." I frown. "Even after two strong coffees at the hospital, she was still flying high."

"Neither Charlie nor Marcy should drink," Jane admits. "Their father passed away from a bad liver."

"He was the local drunk." Tom states it so matter-of-factly, I blink. "Charlie battled with it too, but he's sober now."

"It could be any of them." Jane puts her drink down, picks up some chips, and leans back, munching.

"I saw nothing suspicious. When the family ran off to take Danny to the hospital, Tom and I hung around to hold the fort and clean up a little. Once they came back Charlie helped Tom get Peter in the house. We left right after."

"And that was the whole story." I quickly glance down at my watch wondering if Mrs. Perkins would answer her phone. "It's been a long day. Anybody mind if I make it an early night?"

"I'm tired myself." Jane gathers her purse.

"Great. Let me make it up to you tomorrow or the next day." I smile, looking forward to being alone. "Jane, you pick what day would suit, and I'll take us out to dinner."

"You don't have to." But she smiles wide, teeth and

all, and I'm hoping it means she'd like to go out.

"I want to. What do you say?"

Tom nods and takes my hand.

"Sure, I need to check my schedule, but I'm pretty sure tomorrow will work."

"Great." I stand and slowly lead the pair to the door, then notice the bottle of rum. "Don't forget the bottle."

"Keep it. No doubt we'll be back." Tom looks hopeful. "Jane, would you start the car? I'll be right out."

"Sure." She nods. "Nice to meet you, Emma."

A quick finger wave and she's gone. Her heels click on the cement as she walks away. Tom reaches for my hand and swings it back and forth.

"The one reason I brought Jane with me was to chaperone." His smile turns to a gentle curve of his lips. "Lucky for me I did, or you'd've dumped my ass."

"Count your lucky stars." I lean against the wall.

"I am." He raises my fingertips to his lips. "Jane has a heart of gold."

"Like me?"

Looking down at me, his pupils swell and jaw softens. "Yes, yes you do." He leans down for a slow soft kiss. "I miss you already."

Chapter 13

When I step out into the backyard, the sunlight filters through the maple tree canopy, Mrs. Perkins sits on my patio reading a pocket book and sipping the last of her tea. Her garden gloves lay at her feet, and I notice my dandelions are gone.

"Well, hello." I'm bursting with news.

"Emma, you sleep like the dead. I tapped on your door fifteen minutes ago."

And she didn't come in? "I was in the shower." My lawn looks great. Should I ask how she does it or leave it to her from now on?

"And Tom? No car in the drive." Mrs. Perkins marks her place by dog-earing a page and tucks her book in her pocket.

"He didn't stay. He brought a chaperone trying to keep Alice at bay. I met Jane."

"Now, Jane is a lovely girl." She nods approvingly as she collects her cup and gloves.

"She is, isn't she?" I'm lucky they are related, or it would be her all the way. They act like best friends. "We got along pretty well too."

"Why don't you sit and tell me what happened last night." Mrs. Perkins sits ramrod straight in her lawn chair. Feet planted on the cement, gloves on her lap, she examines her empty cup.

I told her everything that happened.

"We agreed to keep this investigation secret." She hints harder, letting her empty cup hang from a fingertip and swing freely over her lap, proving there is not a drop left.

"You've got to be kidding me?" I blink. "We have more dirt than before. Our sweet old victim has turned out not so sweet. Anyone who owes him money moved to the top of the list. Never mind a family member might want to inherit early."

"The motive seems too simple, too direct. Our person is more sneaky." Mrs. Perkins hands me the cup. "Would it be too much trouble for you to fetch me a cup of coffee?"

"Of course not." As I walk away, my smile slips into place. I giggle while I pour and prepare her cup, enjoying how long it takes Mrs. Perkins to come out and actually ask for something when she really wants it. When I return, she's reading. "Do you agree someone tried to kill

Peter yesterday?"

"Yes and no." She sips, thoughtfully. "We agree someone went after Peter. Whether he admits it to us or not, he knows of the danger. Somehow, I doubt the goal was to kill him, or he would have been long dead."

I lean back in my lawn chair and rest my toes on a planter. "What's the plan? We go over to the Schmidts' and question them about Peter's dealings."

"Yes, let's start there." Mrs. Perkins frowns. "You three decided the motive is greed, did you?"

"Seemed most obvious to us." She's on my nerves again, and I stand up to pace the patio. "To ask Peter directly will be a waste of time. He's won't tell us the truth because he's avoided trouble until now."

"He will if he wants to live."

I don't agree. "He came across as if he's perfectly safe. Didn't bat an eye or say a word. I mean Danny eats one thing..."

"Let it go, Emma." She meets my eyes. "You're harping."

"Go home, get ready. I'd like to hear the other side."

"Okay, I'm going." She dumps her coffee on the lawn, picks up her things. "I'll meet you at your car in about fifteen minutes."

"Sounds good." I kick off my shoes and do my morning ritual, a short one, while thoughts of Dr. Logan wander through my mind.

***

"I can't believe it." Mrs. Perkins stands with her hands on her hips in the Schmidts' kitchen, an expression of utter disappointment and disgust on her face.

I want to reason with Mrs. Perkins. How do you expect the Schmidts to control the happenings here when they were at the hospital? I didn't bother. Mrs. Perkins firm jaw tells me she is in a stubborn state of mind. I stand back and wait for my cue.

"I couldn't leave the place the way it was and had to clean up." Grace worries her apron, examining it carefully.

"No, and you shouldn't have to." I turn to Mrs. Perkins. "You don't expect them to sit in an after-party mess until we come around. They had no idea what we were planning."

"Yes, well." She moves to the counter and wipes an invisible speck of dust away. "I suppose you have a point, but pishposh it all." Her eyes flare momentarily.

"Millie, I'm sorry, but Emma's right." Grace inches closer to her husband.

"Grace, please stop apologizing." Peter takes her hand. "I gather you think the allergy attack was not accidental. Millie, a murder, a crime, evil under foot is not truly everywhere you look—"

"Peter," I interrupt. "Mrs. Perkins and I need to speak to you privately."

"And why is that? You suspect me?" Grace's whisper bellows with insecurity. "Whatever you want to say to him, he'll tell me anyway."

"It's not about secrets." I lift a hand before Mrs. Perkins begins again. "We want to talk about loans with extremely high interest rates."

"Yes, well. Peter gave up his *home business*." Grace's voice changes to a confident one. She releases her apron and smooths it. "He wouldn't dare go against his word."

"Grace, some loans are still unpaid." Peter wheels between his wife and Mrs. Perkins. "I'm not a thug. They pay me as they can—"

"Peter." Grace's face pales, and she shakes her head.

"Don't worry. I lowered the interest rate to zero. It's outstanding principle. They should finish up this year." He smiles reassuringly at his wife. "Care to check my records?"

"Yes, thank you." Mrs. Perkins moves closer to the couple. "I promise to be the soul of discretion."

This is too much. I need space. "Do you mind if I satisfy my curiosity about the backstairs?"

"You're not on about the fall again are you, Grace?" Peter's lines deepen, as he adjusts to a more comfortable sitting position.

Grace ignores him. "Go ahead, Emma, but Charlie checked them already and they're fine."

Peter shoos me toward the door. "Off you go then. If you must."

I open it and peek out. "Charlie didn't check for tampering," I mutter as I step out on the wooden deck.

A table with a folded umbrella in its center sits in the opposing corner. Two chairs tucked in under it. To my left are the stairs. I jump on each step, and each one is as solid as the next. After I download a magnifying app, I carefully record my examination starting from the top step.

The usual scratches and scrapes from use until the second from the bottom. Here I find a small hole. I have seen the same hole when I fixed a picture frame. The eyelet pulled free, leaving the wire loose and the whole thing hanging too low.

Caught in the spur near its edge awaits a fiber. Mrs. Perkins insists I tuck tweezers and zip-lock baggies in my purse. Lucky for me I listened and take a picture with the tweezers beside the hole and then collect the substance.

A black silk thread.

It could have come from anywhere and meant anything, but it was also hard to see unless you looked for it. For Mrs. Perkins' sake, I collect it and note on the back of the bag where and when I found it.

I sit on the steps listening for voices but discover silence in the kitchen. Mrs. Perkins must have bullied them into seeing more than Peter's books.

Spouses were the best suspects according to television, and Grace would probably profit most. She seemed ticked about the loans though. It wouldn't hurt to check the kitchen.

"Grace, do you mind if I have a glass of water?" I come in fanning myself with the zip-lock baggie. Finding the room empty, I go to the hallway entrance and listen for their voices coming from Peter's study. On a roll, I turn on my heel, quickly searching the cupboards.

I find dishes, pots, and pans. No peanut oil or anything else obvious. I pick up a cake mix and am examining the ingredients when they come noisily back down the hall. In my rush to put the mix away the cupboard door slams closed.

"Grace, do you mind if I have some water?" My voice carries to them because when they come out of the hall, Grace walks past me and opens a cupboard to the right of the sink.

"Here." Grace pulls a roundish tumbler from a collection of glassware and heavy mugs. She examines it in the light. When she sees my expression, she smiles. "Old dishwasher. Sometimes leaves a film, but this one's okay." She quickly pours, hands me my drink and I force it down wishing for cola.

"Thanks. Very refreshing. Do you mind if I ask you some questions about where the money goes if anything happens to Peter." As I say the words my face burns. The words sounded better in my head.

"Really Emma, I wanted to ask that." Mrs. Perkins huffs and sits at the island between the kitchen cupboards and the dinette set. The high barstool raises her height slightly.

I put the glass in the sink. "Then please do."

"Grace, if Peter dies are you the beneficiary?" As I'm trying to take this in, I realize Mrs. Perkins is staring at Peter and waiting for the answer.

"I don't know." Grace picks up a cloth and wipes the shining breakfast bar and counter at Mrs. Perkin's elbow.

It makes little sense. How can she not know?

"Actually Grace and Bob are." Peter takes Grace's hand, and I notice how white Grace's knuckles have become. They are like children in trouble, clinging together and looking as guilty as any child caught with their hand in the cookie jar. Peter's grim face stares razorblades at Mrs. Perkins, and Grace won't meet anyone's eyes.

"If something happens, then what?" Mrs. Perkins' muscles tense, and I'm wondering if she is on to something.

"Well, if something happens to Grace, her children will receive her inheritance, but Bob and Danny inherit the house. And without Bob, it goes in trust for Danny."

"No one gets his money if he inherits?" Mrs. Perkins kicks at the hornet's nest.

Both Schmidts pale, but Peter looks up. "No, but he's a child. He wouldn't be behind this."

"No, but a greedy someone might try to get rid of him," Mrs. Perkins suggests.

Now I pale. "You're assuming a fact that was unknown until yesterday. Mrs. Perkins, no one knew Danny was allergic." This whole thing makes me sick.

How could anyone be that heartless? "To think someone would hurt a child is barbaric."

"I agree." Grace brings up a shaking hand and pulls it across her cheek.

"Millie, what are you getting at?" Peter stirs in his chair.

"No offense meant. I need facts to help me figure this out."

"No offense? Are you listening to yourself?" Peter locks the wheels on his chair and struggles to stand beside his wife. "This has been nothing but offensive."

"Peter really. I have to ask. Bob asked us to investigate." Mrs. Perkins stands. "Please quit it. We'll go."

"Yes, go." Peter settles in his wheelchair, frowning. "Millie, why is it always up to you to stir up trouble and search for murderers before anyone dies."

I tell Jane and Tom, and, now, Mrs. Perkins tells the Schmidts.

"Would you rather I wait?" Mrs. Perkins herds me out the back door and turns back to the couple barricading the door. "Danny home yet?"

Peter presses his lips together.

"Sometime this morning I've heard," Grace mumbles.

"Grace, I'm sorry. Mrs. Perkins and I will settle this as quickly as possible. Please, try not to worry." Again, my face burns. What a horrible business.

"Good, we'll drop by Bob's." Mrs. Perkins turns on her thick heel and marches down the stairs. "But let's stop at the hospital first."

The front yard is directly across from the small parking lot for the doctor's office. The whole hospital building looks like a fallen capital tee. Where the base should be is a small half circle of offices. I check both directions before we cross the road.

"Are we going to visit Jay?" I ask. She slows for the double doors, and I bump into her. "Sorry."

"No we are here to visit Claire. Apparently one loan involves her." She crosses the waiting area and follows a hall past the administration offices.

"Catch anything else." I look around to keep my bearings.

"No. He had his step-son, Charlie, on the books, but he was already written off. There were no other names."

"Why does the name Claire sound familiar?" Across from the elevator is the nurses' station and reception. Down one wing of the long hallway is the emergency entrance the other end is a lobby for visitors.

"Claire was Peter's first bride of the two Alice was talking about." Mrs. Perkins stops and pushes the up button for the elevator. She smooths her skirt and runs a palm along the back of her hair.

"Good. I guess you have questions for her too."

"I have a suspicion about the annulment."

"You think she left because she found out about his…home business."

"You and I both like being cared for when ill. Most people do. So, what's the real reason she rejected Peter?" Mrs. Perkins hints there must be more, and leaves it to me to work it out.

"I guess I like someone to check in on me, but when I need rest I like to be left alone."

The doors open, and we enter the elevator car. She pushes two.

"I wonder what kind of person Claire is." She squares her shoulders and waits for the doors to open again.

"Right." I follow Mrs. Perkins down the hall. "What did Dr. Logan say?"

"He'll be looking at Alice sometime this afternoon."

"Oh, that's fast."

"Not fast enough if you ask me." She sniffs. "I tried when Alice first passed, but I wasn't a relative and I didn't know you then."

"Right." I was still in the hospital. After reassuring my mother I'd be taking Aunt Alice's house and not staying with her, she fully supported my release.

As I walk down the hall, memories haunt me. My old hospital wasn't this hospital, but the energy and the color scheme were a match. I try to hide a shudder as I follow Mrs. Perkins past the second-floor nurses' station. "Isn't that Marcy?" I recognize a familiar mass of red hair.

"Yes, she's a registered nurse and worked here for years." Mrs. Perkins waves. "She looks green."

I didn't notice. An old memory of white starched uniforms and the tightly pinned hair slaps me back. Closing my eyes, I rub them. When I glance back at Marcy, she is in pastel scrubs, her hair tamed with a French braid. The queasy feeling of being trapped with no escape is still there, and I bite my lip to keep myself steady. I follow Mrs. Perkins down the hallway.

She leads the way into room 211. "Hello, anyone home?"

"Millie is it you?" Claire's voice is strong, and I can't help smile. It's a sure sign it's a minor illness.

"Hello." I force a pleasant tone.

"Oh, come in. Come in. You picked a good day."

Claire sits in a straight-backed chair sunlight warming her face. A halo hovers above and around her thin hair. It's an illusion, but my throat closes all the same.

"You up to a visit?" Mrs. Perkins looks around for a chair and pulls one over. The other bed is empty, and I shudder again.

"Yes, I'm even sitting up today. It's my daily exercise. Please come in." Claire smiles as she turns to greet us. I catch the healthy peach blush on her pale skin.

"You've color in your cheeks." I find another chair near the door, place it by the window, and sit.

"I'm on these experimental drugs, and they do wonders." Her eyes are bright but tired around the edges.

"I'm glad." Mrs. Perkins smiles widely. "You look wonderful."

"Yes, I started them about a month ago. I still have some bad days, but I feel lucky. More good than bad lately. And if the meds keep working, I'll see my grandchild before I pass."

I stop and stare. Claire's not as healthy as I thought. I hug myself then purposely relax my arms letting them fall away. "You're not getting better, but you—"

"Nothing can be done except make me comfortable." She meets my eyes, holding the connection for a moment. I see the woman in the wedding photo—strong, sturdy, and vital. The moment passes, leaving me with a wisp of a woman.

"Well, you may be thin, but your color is good and your eyes sparkle," Mrs. Perkins says cheerfully.

"I talked to Tammy. You remember my daughter. She always perks me up." Claire shivers and adjusts the blanket on her legs.

"Do you want to lie down?" Jumping up, I organize her bedding.

"If you don't mind giving me a hand. Suddenly, I'm chilly." She reaches out, and grabs hold like a talon.

It takes a moment to help her into bed and become comfortable. Once she settles, I take her chair in the sunshine, looking out the window I see my minivan parked in front of Peter and Grace's red mailbox.

"Tammy doesn't live far, does she?" Mrs. Perkins asks, politely.

"Far enough. They live in Vancouver. Difficult to travel when you're pregnant. She wants to see me and even talked about having me moved out there, but I won't go. The air is filthy and the city's too big. I'd hate it. After a long talk, we decided to make daily phone calls, and it's been good."

I don't think it's enough and promise myself I'll visit Claire. They sound close, and a thread of jealousy slides through me.

"I'm glad." Mrs. Perkins offers an understanding frown. "I see little of my children. They moved for work and then married. They send cards and gifts at Christmas and my birthday though."

I see our relationship with new clarity. We are surrogates for each other.

"Are you up for some questions about your marriage to Peter?" Mrs. Perkins pushes on. I steady myself for round two of this unpleasantness.

Claire smiles weakly. "I thought the gossip died down over that ugly scandal."

"There's been trouble. Why did you ask for the annulment?" Mrs. Perkins slides Claire's water jug toward me. "Emma, please get some water for Claire."

"When I realized I was sick, I also realized how rushed we were getting married. I refused to drag my love down with me. It wasn't right." Claire sighs. "How is he? Did he have an allergy attack yesterday?"

I bring over the water jug and pour water for Claire in a clean glass and put it within arm's reach. "Not Peter. It was Danny."

"He's so young." Claire leans back on her pillows and pulls up her blankets.

"Danny's fine." Mrs. Perkins stands and puts her chair back. "Were you okay with the loans?"

"Loans? Oh, I see." Claire blinks several times. "It's how he supported his family. Some people are foolish. Peter told me long before he proposed."

"And you know about the blackmail?" My hand slaps over my lips after I blurt out the question.

"Blackmail? Impossible. Wherever it came from disregard it. Peter is a good man." The color has left her skin, and I knew we stayed too long.

"Mrs. Perkins, it looks like Claire needs to rest." I stand and place my chair out of the way.

"You're right of course," Mrs. Perkins agrees. "Can we do anything before we go?"

"I'm afraid I'm beyond help." Claire's eyes flutter closed.

My heart cracks.

Chapter 14

"After what Danny has gone through you'd take a chance on ordering squares for him at Pie 'n' All. What about being peanut free?" We have been arguing all the way from the restaurant to Danny and Bob's house.

"You worry too much." Mrs. Perkins waves through the window as we drive into Bob's driveway. Danny waves back and runs into the house, leaving the ball he dropped abandoned in the middle of the patchy lawn.

"And you don't worry enough." I turn off the engine. "Put your happy face on. Here he comes. And leave those deadly weapons in the car."

She slams the van door. "All better?" Mrs. Perkins uses her singsong voice with Danny as she walks toward him.

He scrunches up his face. "Why does everyone keep asking me that?"

I smile at him and pick up his ball as I join them on the lawn. "Who wants to know?"

Danny puts out a finger for each on the list. "The ladies at the hospital, Dad, the doctor with the cold heart listener." Then he reaches out for the rubber ball, and I hand it over. "And you." He points at Mrs. Perkins.

"Quite a list of people." I agree. "Your Dad around?" I expect Bob to step out at any moment since Danny ran in to announce us.

"Yes, he's in the house." Danny takes my hand and pulls. "He's cleaning up."

Hard to believe. "Okay, let's say hello. I'm glad you feel better." I let him pull me slowly toward the door. "Boy, you're fixed right up. Let me feel your muscles." I pinch his scrawny arm.

"That's nothin'." He smiles, and I notice two missing teeth. "You should see my dad's muscles."

I'm almost to door when Mrs. Perkins saunters over from the center of the front lawn. "Danny, what did you eat at the party yesterday?"

"Um…" He drops my hand. "I only like my dad's mac salad."

"You sure?" She smiles.

Wide eyed, he nods at her. "It's the best."

"I bet." As Mrs. Perkins goes to the front door, she musses his hair. "Hope you don't mind, but I need some luck."

"I'm not lucky." Danny half runs, half hops after

her.

"You are one of the luckiest kids in the world."

"Mind if I help myself." I muss his hair up too.

Danny giggles. "No way to mess up my dad's hair."

I laugh aloud. Danny's acting like nothing happened to him yesterday.

"Knock, knock." Mrs. Perkins walks in without knocking.

I follow on her heels, looking over her shoulder. The place looks the same. The sun catches the dirt on the front window. Whatever Bob did I wouldn't call it cleaning.

"Hey, Bob. How are you today?" I return his nod.

"Good, now. Half-pint is home." To Danny he murmurs, "What did I tell you about balls in the house. Put it in the box, please."

Danny looks at his hand in surprise. "How'd that get there?"

I hide a smile behind my hand.

"Ladies, sit. I'll put the kettle on."

"Love a cup. We came from the hospital." Mrs. Perkins sits with her back to the wall.

"Looking for us?"

"No." I take a seat at the far end. "We visited

Claire."

Bob rinses out a cloth in the sink and wipes down the tabletop. "I'm not able to keep up with him. It's one sticky mess after another."

"With my children, they only ate at the table and washed up before and after." Mrs. Perkins pushes a dirty plate aside.

"I doubt it will help." I center the salt and pepper on the table. "All kids are messy, but some are major dirt magnets."

"Any news about Dad?" Bob sits at the table bringing his son onto his lap. He wipes Danny's hands. "Try to stay clean for five minutes."

Danny giggles. "May I play in the front yard?"

"Sure, son, but leave the door open."

"I will."

Bob adjusts his chair to watch the boy and then looks back at us. "Well, what's up?"

Mrs. Perkins frowns. "You didn't tell us what kind of business your father ran from his home."

"Don't tell me you didn't know." Bob scrubs his face with his palms. "Hell, I thought everyone knew, and why you suggested Dad being the target."

"Now, half the town is suspect," I mutter to myself.

"Great!" The whistle goes on the kettle, and Bob fills the teapot. "Have you learned anything else?"

"When you put it that way, no." Mrs. Perkins sniffs. "We came by to find out what Danny ate yesterday, and he says only your salad."

"Someone could have messed with it after it was on the table." I suggest.

"Makes sense. Dad loved it too. Mom used to make it before she died." Bob sets a cup in front of each of us and pours a round. "She left me her recipes. I was only three when she died."

"Did you know much about his business?" Now, I'm probing.

"I'm no banker. One of my friends needed a quick loan a ways back. He talked to Dad about it, and they worked something out." Bob pulled his lips into a straight line making them disappear for a moment. "After a few weeks, we stopped hanging out. He never said it right out, but I figured it was the money."

"I met someone last night who borrowed money. It took years to pay it back, but that wasn't the worst of it."

"Blackmail?" When he meets my eyes, the hope dwindles bit by bit until he looks away.

"Good guess." I nod, tipping my cup and peering in.

"You made your point." Bob passes the doorjamb and looks out. As he comes back, he snaps, "Are you out? Want to walk away because my dad's an asshole?"

Who wants out? "Don't put words in my mouth." I gasp. "It could be anyone. We came to you for a clue, a hint, anything."

He laughs, but it crackles like breaking ice. "You already understand more than I do."

Mrs. Perkins sips her tea. "Don't be offended, but I'm pretty sure Danny fibbed about what he ate. Would you ask him again and see if you're able to squeeze out the truth?"

Bob, dropping his chin to his chest, walks to the door again. "Buddy, come in for a sec."

"Ahh, Dad." Danny drops the ball in a wooden box by the door, his hands smeared with dirt. "What?"

"Danny, I'm going to ask you something important."

"Okay."

Bob clears his throat. "You need to be truthful."

"Oh, I will." Danny's eyes go wide, his face very serious.

"What did you eat at the party?" Bob, on his knees, meets Danny's eyes evenly.

"I…I ate salad." Danny looks away, examining his shoes. "I…Dad don't be mad, okay?"

Bob nods.

"I tasted a chocolate."

"From the box on the table?" I ask, pleased to know someone enjoyed the gift.

"Yes, it was good." Danny glances over to meet his dad's eyes. "I didn't snack…it was dessert."

"It's okay Danny. Now think. Did you have anything else?"

Danny squirms. "Dad, I tried to stop, but junk food makes me hungry."

"Keep going, son, you're doing fine." Bob's face softens.

"I took a cookie too."

"You telling me everything?"

Danny nods, exhaling a long breath.

Bob kisses his son's forehead. "You did good, buddy."

"Can I go now?"

Bob nods.

"What kind of cookie?" Mrs. Perkins wonders aloud.

"Chocolate chip or Ginger Snap." I answer for him.

"Still means nothing."

"What do you mean?" Bob doesn't get it.

"Because all it takes is a dab of peanut oil on anything to bring on a severe reaction." From her expression, Mrs. Perkins thinks she is stating the obvious.

"Well, crap." He slams his mug on the table and walks out.

We stare after him.

Did she have to be so blunt? Now, I'm the one with my chin on my chest. "Now what?"

"Give him a minute to cool down, and we'll brainstorm." She pushes her cup beside the dirty plate.

Bob's voice mutters something, and I smile.

"Is he processing aloud?" I lean back in my chair and look out the door. Danny's not visible. Nervous, I check on him. He throws the ball into the air, gets under it and almost catches it. Shaking my head, I come back and sit down.

Bob has his phone to his ear when he returns to the kitchen and sits at the table. "Okay…will do…bye." He sets it by his mug. "Sorry about the temper, but I won't have this happen again."

"Have any idea what to do next?" I slide my chair away from him, giving us some distance.

"I called Benny. He'll call around and get back to me."

"Are we out?" Mrs. Perkins throws Bob's words back at him.

"Benny will find out what's in the cookies. We all know who brought the chocolates."

Mrs. Perkins looks at me.

"What? The same brand on the dessert table." Before I finish speaking I understand what he's saying. "Not identical box. It was the same box?"

Bob nods.

"What are you saying?" Mrs. Perkins needs it spelled out.

"He's saying he knows we brought the box of chocolates." I rake my hair, dragging it away from my face. "And they contained peanuts."

The world slips away. Far off someone sounds like me. "Don't you dare blame us for this. Peter would have checked the ingredients, and no one knew Danny was allergic. Millie and I would never hurt anyone."

I lay on the white padding after Aunt Alice takes over. An image of Bob and Mrs. Perkins appears in a far window of the white room. Their faces flash between the flapping of thin fabric. Their voices muffled but clear.

"Yes, well someone did. Instead of giving them back to us and telling us to put them away, they put them on the table for everyone to enjoy." Mrs. Perkins defends me with an indignant hand on her hip and a bite in her voice.

"You're saying whoever targeted Dad attended the party." Bob shakes his head.

"I hate to do this, but tell us about Grace and your father." Mrs. Perkins taps her finger on the tabletop.

"When they met, she was in a bad way. Could barely put food on the table. Marcy and Charlie constantly invited her over for dinner and they both asked her to live with them, but she insisted on living on her own."

"You're saying Peter rescued her." Aunt Alice's disgust shows how sure she is that she has the culprit in her sights.

"Like the prince in Cinderella." Bob nods.

"That's ridiculous." Speaking under her breath, Aunt Alice pushes my cup away.

"What makes you think she's happy now?" Mrs. Perkins pushes a little harder.

He sighs. "You need to spend time with Grace. She celebrates every little thing. She did it poor. Imagine now. Not a greedy bone, and great with Danny." Bob smiles.

"You can't fake that."

"She really likes Danny." Mrs. Perkins nods her agreement.

"He's a kid. What's not to like?"

Good point.

We rise to leave. Well, my body and Mrs. Perkins stand up. Before we reach the door, there's a knock. Bob slips between us, not easy for a large man, to answer it. A broad smile crosses his face momentarily. "Benny, you find something?"

"I thought I'd drop by and see how the little punk's doing." Benny walks in passed us. He wears a thick vest with Velcro pockets and a gun bigger than a baby's leg strapped to his thigh. We step back. The man is taller than I remember, and his frown turns my blood cold. "What's with the women?"

"Who us?" Mrs. Perkins brings out her hanky.

He stares hard at us. His little wheels turning in his little closed mind.

"We attended the party," Aunt Alice confesses. "And wanted to check on Danny."

"True." Bob backs us up. "Want some tea?"

I step closer to the window as Alice asks, "Benny, have you found out something?"

Benny sways back and forth staring us down. "Ms. Johnston, you do understand the privacy act."

"Yes, I do." Mrs. Perkins answers for us.

"Well, then I guess you know my answer."

"Oh, you think she's prying. I always seem to be accused of that." Mrs. Perkins turns to Bob. "Thanks for the tea. I'm glad Danny is well." Mrs. Perkins looks up at Benny. "Constable."

She takes our hand and walks us out to the passenger side of the minivan. "Get in. I think I see a ghost."

Chapter 15

Alice gets me home, staying in the forefront, putting on a strong solemn face while I cry in the background. I can't bring myself to meet Benny's eyes after the first few moments of his snide smile. He is pleased it was us, pleased he can point a finger at us saying, "Mystery solved."

Bob knows it's accidental on our part, but the part we played set up all the dominos to fall on his son. If we hadn't stuck our noses in, we wouldn't have brought the chocolates, and Danny wouldn't have been harmed.

Logic even makes me see Peter would have never eaten those chocolates without checking the ingredients first. I shouldn't be ashamed or shocked…or afraid. Yet, sadness fills me to bursting.

Thank God for Alice. She took over, helped me home, and listened carefully not letting Mrs. Perkins know more than she needed to. She stood guard over me as many alters had before her.

I sob again, steadying my voice. "Aunt Alice, it's okay. I'll take it from here."

"If you're sure." She releases her hold and I slip into place, finding my tarot cards spread out between Mrs. Perkins and myself. Because I'm upset, nothing comes. I shift my attention to Mrs. Perkins, her green eyes full of disappointment.

"Thanks for getting me home." I take a deep breath to blurt out what's on my mind. When I try to talk, the only thing I let out is a warm breath of air. "I...didn't know."

Mrs. Perkins' face is grim. Her pale eyes without a spark sit flat in her face. "I'm as responsible as you are. If I didn't push to find out who was in trouble we wouldn't have been there."

"I don't want to lay blame." I swallow. Again the words don't come readily. They bottleneck in my throat almost choking me. "And I have no proof, but I firmly believe someone tried to kill Peter. I feel it. I know it."

"Emma, settle down."

"No, I won't. They used us, Mrs. Perkins. They used us to harm a child. To send a message to Peter. The message was...what?"

"A superb question." Mrs. Perkins picks up my tarot cards and shuffles them. She glances up at me. "This time, I'll ask the right question."

As I lay out the cards, the message refers to the

protection of a loved one, about memories pushing forward like echoes from the past, reminding us nothing is ever forgotten. Some things haunt us until we die.

I sigh. "If I'm reading them correctly, they say the killer protected a loved one from something most have long forgotten. They will do anything to reach their goal."

"You're saying?"

"The cards. The cards say." My voice, calm and strong.

"The cards say someone protected their loved one from Peter."

"They don't say it's a person so much as an action." I lay down another card. The queen of cups looks back at me. I drop my chin to my chest, exhaling softly, and with it releasing a frustrated raspberry. "Well, I've done it again. Peter is not a woman."

Mrs. Perkins pats my hand. "It's okay. You'll figure it out...eventually."

"Until then, what do we do?"

"Let's go up to the loft and light the incense to set the mood." Mrs. Perkins stops and stares at me. "We need Alice to read."

"No." I pick up the cards one at a time and offer each one a non-verbal thanks. "I'm not your local psychic line to Aunt Alice."

"She's the only one who can do this." Mrs. Perkins stands and walks away.

"Thanks." I snort, going after her. "Not debating it." *Sorry Alice, I hope you understand.* "If I'm not doing this, then I'm not doing this."

"Fine, but Alice Bontaine, my dearest and closest friend, always listened. She even sought me out when she needed to talk."

"Over and over again. I keep hearing the same talk. She was your best friend. She knew everything. Only she can help you. Thanks." I wave my hand around as we go up the stairs. "So tell me what am I good for? Since you understand everything else."

"Emma. Alice was the driving force behind our team." She tries to sidestep her part. "She was and is a trouble detector."

"No, you said she offered a direction." I put force into my tone. *If she wants this then she needs to be as active as I plan to be.*

"Ah, to be young and rude."

"You didn't answer my question." I sighed. "What am I good for?"

"You link us together." She waves her hanky at me

as she grabs the lofts railing. She looks down her nose at me. "Don't forget we need to call Dr. Logan."

She's right. I'm a link between two worlds. "Yes." I pull my phone from my pocket. I hold it out to her, but I'm facing her back as she glides up the stairs. When she's at the top, I tap her shoulder showing her my phone. "Would you call him? If it's bad news about Aunt Alice I'd rather you be the one to tell me."

That sounds selfish, but I don't care. My esteem has dropped through the floor. I guess I should feel lucky with what I have. I push my disappointment down deep.

She takes the phone. Her hand trembles as she punches in the numbers. I drop the deck on the table then select a short blue candle and two yellow tapers. I arrange candles on a large platter with melted wax all over it and place it to the side of the tabletop. The air fills with a wonderful scent of sweet and spicy. Breathing it in uplifts me.

Mrs. Perkins glances up during the call and turns her back. My gut clenches as I wait for the news Aunt Alice didn't die of natural causes. The murderer struck long ago. A tear sides down my cheek. A child and an old woman, two harmless people, and one bastard I would make pay.

That is something I can do.

"Well, you were right." Mrs. Perkins joins me at the table perching herself on the edge of the winged chair. "He was very thorough and found something inconsistent with natural causes."

"She didn't have a heart attack and fall from the loft?"

"Apparently someone struck her in the back of the head with a slightly imperfect sphere-like object. He's passing the details to the police."

I picture the crystal ball I gave Mrs. Perkins, remembering its perfect smooth surface filling my palm. It's strange shape. *Don't assume anything. You can't be sure.*

She sighs. "I asked him to send me a copy because everything went in one ear and out the other."

"Someone hit her from behind." My gut burns. I'm mad. "Snuck up behind her because she was such a threat and hit her on the back of the head."

"And tossed her down the loft stairs." Mrs. Perkins chin trembled. "I need to be alone. Please excuse me." She raises her hanky to her quivering lips and rushes away. A sob bursts free as my front door closes.

I close my eyes and breathe the wonderful scent in,

visualizing the white room with the bellowing white curtains and the bright light everywhere. I imagine the bed and lean back, no longer sensing the chair. The air moves in gusts making the curtains snap angrily. Sheets scented of fresh spring air and crisp to my fingertips. I pick up a pillow and inhale deeply.

"Aunt Alice." I whisper this because I don't want her to appear.

"Here." She stands behind me across the bed. A line deepens between her brows.

"You came." I turn, pulling one knee up on the mattress. "Would you tell me what you remember about the day you died?"

"I had an appointment with Dr. Logan, and he took me for coffee afterward. It was a nice day. After I returned home, I did my usual clean up and prepared a light dinner and watched my shows while I ate. A noise came from the loft. I remember going up the stairs. Then nothing."

"That's it." Disappointment is in my voice. "We heard from Dr. Logan. He did as you asked and checked your…um…checked you for evidence."

"Good. What did he find?" Her voice seems pleasant, but the line between her brows deepens.

I suck in my bottom lip and nip it until the burning

behind my lids stops. "Well, you were right."

"A clue."

"More like proof of foul play." I release a breath
and meet her eyes. "You were murdered, Aunt Alice. I
need you to go over everything you remember from that
day. It might be wise to start a few days earlier."

"Murdered?" Aunt Alice paces, and, as she walks
by a window, the curtain billows violently away from her.
An electrical charge tickles my skin, the hair on my arms
stands up, and ozone fills the air.

"Calm down." Not feeling too safe. "Should I go?
Mrs. Perkins needed time alone too."

"Millie." Aunt Alice faces me tears in her eyes.
"Poor Millie."

"Yes, it's bad. She's torn up. Both of us are." I can't
imagine my mentor, my rock, cracking even a little. "How
about you? Are you okay?"

I lean forward watching as the curtains rage,
growing in length and creating walls of flapping and
snapping fabric.

"I'm upset." Alice stands in the chaos, her shadow a
silhouette in white. "I've done nothing but help the citizens
of Dunster and Ravenglass. I don't understand."

"Well, put your brain to work." I shiver. "Could you

have said something that was taken the wrong way?"

"Or the right way."

"Okay, or the right way." I don't dare smile knowing it doesn't matter. What matters is she remembers what drives someone to murder. "He's dragged us both into this. I gather by your silence you remember nothing that will help us."

"I'm sorry." She comes closer letting violent wind become her backdrop. "I can't think."

"It's okay." I stand. "It might be best if I go. Contact me if you remember anything and try to be discreet, please."

She flashes a sad smile as the room disappears.

I wake up with a start. The sun no longer shines in the living room window, and the short thick candle gutted. I go to Mrs. Perkins. When she answers her door, her eyes are puffy, but otherwise she is calm. We go into her kitchen.

"I wanted to tell you I talked to Alice after you left." I sit at the kitchen table running my thumbnail along the edge. "She saw Dr. Logan the day she died."

"Makes sense. She was on quite a few pills. He liked to keep on top of things, make sure she took them properly and she wasn't having any issues."

"She said they went for coffee that day."

"Very likely. They were friends." Mrs. Perkins dabs her nose and sits down with me.

"I told her about being murdered." My throat releases its tension once the words are out.

"Shocked, I'm sure." Mrs. Perkins whispers.

"Shocked, upset, disappointed in Dunster and Ravenglass." It seems so much more real and we need a plan. A way of moving forward. "What's next? We need to protect Peter, and, our feelings aside, we can't fail."

"There's one place we can watch from that wouldn't be obvious to anyone." Mrs. Perkins taps her chin. "Claire's room is the perfect place to keep an eye on Peter."

Sure, it's perfect except for the sick woman in the room we would be disturbing. "I don't know. I do plan to visit, but we wouldn't stay long. It isn't right to keep tiring her out." I blink at the little woman across the table. "She'd never manage an all day visit. It would kill her."

"Being dramatic again? Claire is lonely. She needs us there."

I raise a hand. "I won't do it. You come up with another plan. One that keeps Peter out of trouble and hurts no one else. Then I'm in."

"Fine." She huffs. "You're always so difficult. What if I convince Dr. Logan to okay you helping Claire instead of her daughter?"

"I can't believe you." My whole body tenses at the suggestion. Knowing her, she already knows he'll go along with this. A slow hiss escapes my lips. "I keep an eye on Peter's place and act like Claire's personal nurse. Wrong again."

"Emma, really." Mrs. Perkins tsks. "You need to be more of a team player."

"Team player!" I can't believe my ears. "Listen, I have plans tonight, and this conversation is going nowhere. If you call Dr. Logan and he agrees, we'll talk about it tomorrow morning. If he doesn't, we'll decide on something else."

"Tomorrow then."

Chapter 16

I walk into Quackers, stand by the door looking for familiar faces. It's packed. A huge party of over twenty fills a section nearest the pub's west wall. At the head of the table sits a man, pushing up an oversized golden crown of cardboard and colorful candy out of his eyes. The rest of the group wears cone-shaped paper hats in assorted shiny pastels. Loud whistling and cheering crescendos when the king of the court stands lifting his cup in a toast.

I scan the rest of the loaded tables, not seeing anyone I know until my gaze reaches the fireplace. Tom and Jane sit at a table in the back. Tom has his chair turned, hands out, warming them on the gas fire.

It's summer, early evening, and still warm. Not getting it, I give Jane a wave when she sees me. Tom turns around giving me a nod. Every time I see his face the world disappears. A spark of warmth swells deep inside, and I'm happy—scared but happy.

"Hi there." I sit in the empty chair beside Tom. Our elbows touch as I take off my light jacket.

"So, what would you like to drink?" Tom stands

and waits for our order. "Emma?"

"Soda and lime. Thanks."

"What a gentleman." Jane reaches out to him. "You almost forgot me, didn't you? I'll have a half pint."

Shrugging, Tom leaves the table, and Jane winks at me. "You sure have impressed him."

"Have I?" I lean toward her. "Tell me while you can."

Jane laughs. "In the office today, every subject wormed its way around to you."

I don't remember where they work or they worked together. "You work together? Where?"

Jane waves a hand in front of her face. "I thought you knew."

"No." I'm wondering if I should know this. "It's not a secret, is it?"

"No, it's not a secret." Jane glances at the bar. "He sees a lot of confidential data, and I'd rather he explained it to you himself." Her whole demeanor changes.

"What you do or do both of you do the same thing?" Sticking my nose in is becoming a habit.

"Heck, no." Jane barks out a laugh. "My job. Boring mostly. I answer the non-emergency line at the cop shop."

I follow her line of sight, and Tom bends over a table for a quick word with a group of women.

"Boring? Somehow I doubt it." I picture the chestnut haired woman on the phone at the police station. "You mean you take calls and use the radio?"

"I'd leave, but government jobs pay pretty well." Jane raises her shoulders and lets them drop. "I'm sure you understand what I mean."

Why would I know? I have never had a job. Tom's at the police station but not a cop. Access to confidential files?

"How about some shopping tomorrow? Maybe take a look at the shoe situation?" Jane snaps her fingers near my face. "Hello. You home?"

I jump out of my skin. "What?"

"Shoes?" Tom chuckles. "I'm gone five minutes, and the shoe talk has begun."

"But I like shoes." I take the pint mug he hands over and set it down in front of me on a cardboard coaster. Three lime slices floating among the ice and soda. Minute bubbles cling to the thick red straw. "Thanks"

"Sorry, one size fits all around here." Tom settles himself down and reaches for the flames again.

"Do you know today's special?" Jane replaces the

plastic encased menu on the table.

"Friday's fish and chips day." Tom glances between me and Jane. "What?"

"It's June, and you have your hands in the fire." I'm having trouble accepting he's cold.

Jane chokes on her beer and sprays Tom in the face. "Sorry. Wrong way."

Tom brings up a napkin and dabs his face. "Who doesn't like a good fire?"

I shake my head. Who am I to judge? "Everyone up for fish and chips?"

"Sure," Jane agrees. "It's good here."

"Rather have a cheeseburger." Tom pulls away from the heat. "Tough long day. I sure needed a night out. Thanks for taking us."

"No problem." I go over to the bar. To my surprise, Charlie lifts his chin in my direction as he places two pints on a serving tray.

I squeeze my way to the bar. "What a nice surprise."

In his horrible Spanish accent, he butchers, "Looking good."

I laugh.

"Well, now I suppose you want a burger?"

"Yes, one cheeseburger and two fish and chips." I thumb over my shoulder. "We're at the table by the fireplace."

Charlie raises his chin again. "With Tom and Jane, huh?"

"Yep."

"Okay, we're kind of hopping tonight thanks to Murph's birthday." Charlie smiles. "You dating Tom? Inquiring minds…"

I shake my head. "We're friends."

"Good luck getting past Jane."

"I don't understand." I glance over my shoulder. The two of them have their heads together. "Oh, you will."

"May I ask you about the barbeque?"

He thinks for a minute and looks around. "Give me a minute to put your order in." Charlie steps away, jots a note on a slip of paper, and clips it to a metal circle. With a spin it disappears through an opening. He stops for a fellow waving a twenty in the air, pours two drafts, takes the money, and returns the bills dropping the silver in a cup under the bar. "You have my full attention."

Time to give my sleuthing skills another go. "Did you see anyone at the table messing with the food?"

"Well, sure. Mrs. P. and Mrs. S. constantly replaced

bowls from inside." Charlie motions to a waitress he'll be a second. "Anything else?"

"You're pretty busy here, but if you remember anything, would you give me a call?" I lean back, pulling a pen from my purse, and jot down my number on coaster. "I'd appreciate it."

"*Sí si, señorita.*" He takes my number. "Your order will be up in about fifteen to twenty minutes. Wanna run a tab?"

"Yes, thanks. Dinner is on me tonight."

"Don't let them drink too much. It's a long drive back to Dunster."

"Thanks, I'll keep it in mind." I give him a finger wave.

When I sit down again, Tom glares. "Is it true?"

"What?" I take a sip of my soda with lime and find it quenching.

"You and Mrs. Perkins brought the chocolates made with peanuts." Tom shifts his chair to face me and takes my hand. "Jane told me Benny came in the station beaking off about it."

"We didn't know. Even at the hospital I didn't think of it." I grip his fingers tightly. The responsibility of it all weighs me down as I wait for him to make a snide comment about what kind of idiot I am. "When I found out, when we found out…I feel awful."

"No doubt." Jane leans forward. "It's Benny. He came back from seeing you at Bob's and laughed about how it freaked you out. He doesn't like you much."

"Yeah, I don't like him much either." I frown, remembering.

"What's to like?" Jane takes a sip of her drink. "I'll be back." Jane takes her purse from the back of the chair, slings it over her shoulder, and walks toward the washroom sign.

"You okay?" Tom gives my hand a squeeze.

"Me?" I lean back, stretching my arm so I don't let go. "I'm fine because I'll never do it again. I've learned from my mistake."

"You'll need a plan to out run Benny." His face is perfectly straight and relaxed.

"That's not—" I try to pull away, but he holds on tight.

Then the side of lips turn up and he chuckles.

"Funny." I meet his dark eyes. "What do you do?"

"Me, nothing. I have thirty pounds on him." He smiles, bringing my knuckles to his lips. "But your aunt knew how."

A waitress comes with our food. "Hey Tom."

"Hey, Sylvia. Busy night?" Tom leans out of her way as she places the plates.

"Yep, busy." She smiles at me. "Ketchup?"

"You gotta know by now." Tom teases. "I'd drink it straight if I could."

"Right-tee-oh, then." She drops a ketchup container on the table and leaves without looking back.

"Ahhh, perfect timing." Jane settles herself in her chair and picks up a fork.

Tom grabs the squeeze bottle, pours some ketchup, and passes it on to me.

"Thanks." I pour some, too and place the bottle by Jane's plate before digging in.

"I've been wondering." Jane samples a French fry and moans.

"Oh, no here it comes." Tom points his fork at his cousin.

"Why Grace doesn't mark the food with peanuts in it." Jane dips a fry, swirling it.

The fish is delish. "What are you talking about?" I cut another piece free.

"My brother has an allergy to shellfish. We marked dangerous food with a red-X and he'd never touch it." Jane takes a bite of fish. "So good."

"That's it? They seem to be on major alert. Peter carries a needle in a case with him and everything." Although I'm talking to her, I glance at Tom.

He's not talking. Half his burger is gone.

"It depends on sensitivity. Some break out in hives or their eyes go puffy. Extreme cases go into shock and die." She shrugs. "You pick up a few things when it's in the family."

"So, what you're saying is Peter's allergy must be extreme." Even with the fire going I shiver. Anyone, family or friend, with access and armed with peanut oil would kill him.

"After everyone left, Jane, and I tidied up." Tom rubs his chin with a paper napkin. "Not much to do. The streamers and paper tablecloth gathered up and trashed, the barbeque put away, and the garbage bagged. The table stood against the fence had some covered dishes on it which we brought in, but I didn't see chocolates anywhere."

"Weird. I wonder how Benny got his hands on the box." Could someone have made a point of giving it to him?

Jane lifts her finger to say wait while she chews.

"He didn't find your chocolates. He asked about the brand and did an Internet search. It took two seconds."

"Well, Bob called to tell him Danny confessed to eating a cookie and chocolate." I put down my fork. Not so hungry any more.

"A sticker on the base of the box warned some of them may contain nuts." Jane continues. "It has to be marked or people would drop like flies."

No judgment or condemnation, just stated facts. The more time I spend with Tom and Jane the more I'm enjoying acceptance. I don't even have to try. I'm discovering a place inside myself I didn't know existed. Now that I do, I'll never give it up.

Friends. They were my friends. Mine. And I would do anything for them.

A few minutes after Sylvia, the waitress, takes the bill, she returns and leans in close to me. "Excuse me, Emma. Would you come with me for a moment?"

I follow her to the bar where Charlie waits with my plastic in his hand. "Hey, I hate to say it, but they rejected your credit card. Thought you'd rather deal with it away from the new love of your life." He uses a gentle tone. "What would you like to do?"

My cheeks grow warm, and I'm glad Charlie

assumed correctly. "Do you have a debit machine?"

"Sure, follow me." He takes me down to a fancy cash register and taps the keypad and points. "Swipe you card, with the black bar toward me."

It takes a while then rejects me too. I open my wallet and pull my last two bills out. "Try the machine again but for half the amount."

"I've some money. How about a loan?" Charlie offers.

I think of Peter. An innocent offer or not? Then another thought hits me. What if Charlie counts on inheriting Peter's business? Maybe he didn't want to wait anymore. "Oh, please don't ask."

I take a napkin from the stack by the debit machine and dry my palms and give him the last of my cash. Charlie patiently repeats the procedure, and I mentally cross my fingers trying the machine again. It works.

As I walk back to the table, Tom and Jane each drop a ten on the table, and I wonder if my face will ever go back to its natural color.

"For the tip." Jane points at Tom and herself. "It's the law. One pays. One tips."

"Thanks," I choke out. Two days ago, I had several hundred dollars in the bank and one credit card that worked. I'm not sure what happened, but it smells like Aunt Alice all over it.

Tom drapes my jacket over my shoulders as we exit Quackers. I stop in my tracks and take in the waves coming in on the beach. With the lights from the street, I make out the sand and the water's edge. I let the rhythmic sound wash over me and calm me down. Little by little my face stops burning, and I'm able to face my friends again.

Jane stands beside me during my silence. "It's beautiful, like living in a postcard."

"Yes, exactly." I sigh.

She squeezes my elbow. "I think I'll walk ahead to my car. It's such a nice night. Call me when you're up to checking out those shoes."

"I will." I grin shyly at her as she walks up the street.

She raises a hand. "Night, kids."

I pull my palms along my pant legs ridding myself of the last of their dampness. I'm nervous and have trouble meeting Tom's eyes. No chaperone this time.

"Something wrong?" Tom stands behind me. He rests his hands on my shoulders and his chin on my hair.

I try to answer, but no sound comes out. I swallow and try again. "May I be totally honest with you?"

"Sure, I mean. Yes, I'd like that." His hands become heavier.

I take a deep breath and as I exhale. "I'm always so nervous around you. It's driving me crazy."

His fingers tighten for a heartbeat. "Me too. Probably because we jumped into the sack so fast."

My cheeks start up again, and my throat tightens a little. "Probably." I know it's true.

He lets his hand drop to my waist and pulls me to his side. We start to walk back to my place. "Okay, I suggest this. We focus on friendship for a while." He lifts my chin with a fingertip and takes in my reaction. "I mean it was great, really, really great, but it's too much pressure. Let's give it some time, see how it plays out."

I agree. "No pressure."

"No pressure." He dips down and kisses me on the forehead.

"I like you." Somewhere in the back of my mind, a curtain shifts in the breeze. Aunt Alice reaches out and pulls me beyond the glass. From behind the gauze, I see my hand reach up and stroke his cheek. Aunt Alice grabs his hair tightly in a fist then pulls his face down to ours.

The kiss soft at first, slowly becoming more urgent until I'm afire. "No pressure, and incredibly hard to resist."

He takes his hand in mine, brings it to his lips.

My hand tightens on his as I fight for control. *Aunt Alice, Not now. Get back where you belong.*

Not happening.

Alice, stop it.

As we battle, I'm falling to the ground and can't stop my head from cracking on the cement when I land. Tom, not expecting me to collapse in his grasp, does nothing but follow me down. I grab Aunt Alice by the hair and force her back beyond the glass. I shut and lock the window. The drapes flutter down in the dead calm.

"Tom," I whisper. My hoarse voice cracking. "Help me up."

"What happened?" His eyes wide, voice panicky.

"I'll tell you, but please don't make me tell you right now." I reach out for his hand. "Please take me home then call Mrs. Perkins."

He takes my hand, gets me standing, and lifts me into the air. "She knows what to do?"

I cling to him, disliking being off my feet. "Yes."

Before I say another thing, I'm floating in the air as he runs full tilt.

Chapter 17

The light coming in the bedroom curtains burns through my lids. With a goose egg on the back of my pounding head, I creep out of bed and into the shower. When I step into the kitchen, the coffee's made and Tom munches on toast.

"Where's Mrs. Perkins?" I join him at the table.

"I promised to stay, so she went home."

"Thanks for looking after me."

He has my travel mug which he returned two nights before, in front of him. "You okay or should I give Perkie a call?"

"Please don't call her that." I drop my face into my hands.

"You're touchy this morning."

"Sorry. I need some caplets, and I'll be fine." Awkward but fine. "No need to call. She'll come over anyway."

"I'm glad you're okay." He reaches for my hand. "Mrs. Perkins said you fainted and it was nothing, but I'm not sure it's true."

"You're a smart man, and I do have to tell you some things, but not now." I clear my throat. "May I have some time? With you, I mean."

"You sick?"

"No." I shake my head painfully. "More of a condition I live with."

"I like to think of myself as patient, but this…don't leave me hanging too long. I'm also the curious type." He kisses my knuckles. "Don't be afraid to tell me anything."

"Don't laugh or take this the wrong way, but it's me not you." I stare into his eyes willing him to understand and back off.

"Okay." He squeezes my shoulder. "Think of me as a safe place."

I don't say anything, afraid to glance up.

He whispers, "I'd do anything for you."

A grin slides across my lips. My chest tingling with warmth. "Good to know."

He leans back in his chair, sipping his coffee. "I'm at your mercy."

"And I'm at yours." I clear my throat. "Let me put out a fresh towel." I stand with a triangle of toast pinched in my fingers. "The water should still be hot if you want to shower."

He stuffs the last of his toast in his mouth and chews. "Quick one. I'm meeting a client in fifteen and need to get going." He pulls me into a gentle hug and whispers in my ear. "You should rest. Fresh towels in the linen closet by the bathroom door?"

"Yes. Help yourself."

He leaves me at the table pressing on the bump at the back of my skull.

"May I come in?" Mrs. Perkins sticks her head round the door.

I jump, holding my chest. "Sure."

"How'd you sleep?" She joins me at the table and pushes Tom's plate away. "This business takes its toll."

"Don't worry. I'm good." I listen hard for a moment and water is still running. "You went home and left Tom here. I don't want him to see me like this. He asked me about…you know and I didn't…couldn't say anything. I said I'd tell him later. Now, I need to come up with a believable lie."

"If he's the one, you need to tell him the truth."

I take a calming breath. "Truth? We've talked about this. He'll think I'm friggin' nuts. I hate all this pressure."

"Oh, Tom." Mrs. Perkins stands and shakes Tom's hand. "Nice to see you again."

"Mrs. Perkins, look at you. Are you always this pretty in the morning?"

"Me?" She bats her eyes at him.

He kisses my cheek. "I'll call you."

"Okay."

He grabs the travel mug and leaves through the back door.

"I mean it. I'm freaking out here." I fan myself.

"He slept in the spare room." Mrs. Perkins looks around the kitchen seeing the coffee she gets up and helps herself. "It turns out Alice has excellent taste in young men. Pleasant to be around, and he genuinely likes you." She sounds surprised.

"So he says." I twist my hair several times and toss it out of my way. "You understand, Alice and I fought for control over who would use my body."

"And you won." Mrs. Perkins selects a piece of toast.

"It hurt and embarrassed me, but yes I won." I stare into my cup. "She scares me. If I had been driving she would have killed us."

"I wouldn't worry about it." Mrs. Perkins finishes her toast. "Come on. Alice would never hurt you. Think of her as your mentor."

I sigh. "You're my mentor. To be honest, Alice is a threat, popping in whenever the mood hits her. And then there's stopping a murderer."

"Relax, you are coming along. Alice doesn't interfere that much. We should talk to her about it, and I'm sure she'll be reasonable."

"She wants Tom." I wave my hand to show what I mean. "You know…after him. Tom and I agreed to slow the intimate part of our relationship down, and Aunt Alice tries to take over and bed the guy…again."

"And you crack your head fighting her off." Mrs. Perkins wide eyes make me wonder if she believes me. "And you won."

"I'm not the one jumping into bed with men."

She stiffens her back. Mrs. Perkins stares at me.

"You should do it alone today." I leave the table and go back to bed, pulling the covers over my head.

Her little shoes tap on the floor as she follows me. "Emma really." Mrs. Perkins drags the duvet off of me.

I put a pillow over my head. "You don't take my problems seriously."

"Listen to yourself. We have a murder to investigate." She sits beside me.

I peek out. "If this was happening to you, what

would you do?"

"I would make myself stronger by doing what you did and be ready to do it again," she says.

"Right. Sounds easy," I mumble from under the pillow.

"Hard or not, you'll succeed." Mrs. Perkins tugs at the pillowcase.

I sit up. "You're right."

"Crawl out of bed and put on a nice dress." She walks from the room.

"What's the point?" I call after her.

"You always go on and on about the Internet. Why don't you look for your answers there?" I barely hear her.

"What? Search how to prevent possession?" I shout at her. "Or how about how to avoid your alter ego?"

"I don't know, but taking it laying down won't fix it." She sticks her head through the gap in the door. "I can't do this for you."

"Okay, okay I'm up. But I'm not dressing up for the Internet."

"No, but you do if you want to live your life on your terms."

"Okay, will you excuse me while I change?"

"Of course." Mrs. Perkins closes the door with a

snap.

I find clean jeans and a t-shirt. After pulling my hair into a ponytail, I examine my face in the mirror and dab on some moisturizer. As glamorous as it gets today.

She sits outside with a mug of coffee beside her. "You've learned how to make coffee. Not bitter like usual."

I smile. "Tom made it."

"He cooks. A definite mark on the plus side."

Who knew making coffee and cooking were the same thing? *Sure, why not.* I put my coffee cup down beside hers and remember my broken laptop.

To drop it down a notch, I close my eyes, emotionally reaching out for the calming of the yard, sky. I take baby steps and let the grass tickle my toes and breathe the coffee scent floating in the cool morning air. I open my eyes and walk the yard.

The crunching of footsteps grow louder and louder. I glance over my shoulder. Benny's angry, red face comes around the corner of my house. *Oh, good. More trouble.* I slowly walk back to the patio.

"I see you found us." I'm pleased with the strength in my voice.

He stands over us like superman with his cape caught in the breeze. "You kidding me?"

"Yes, actually. Would you like a coffee?" I offer the hospitality he offered me at the station and mean it about as much as he did.

"Both of you need to come down to the station."

"Why?" Mrs. Perkins blinks up at him.

"What do you mean, why?" Benny bounces back.

Mrs. Perkins and I glance at each other. I know I don't want to go, but I have no idea what she's thinking.

"What are we talking about here?" I state, more loudly than I mean to.

"I…" He drags his palms down his face. "Yes, coffee would be good."

As I walk into the kitchen, he sits in one of my two lawn chairs. I make fresh, put a tray together, and am out the door in record time.

"Did I miss anything?" I put the tray down on a side table and pour Benny a cup.

"No, he wouldn't tell me a thing." Mrs. Perkins looks ticked off.

"Would you like a refill?" I ready to pour her a cup.

Mrs. Perkins waves me away. "No, thank you. I'm fine."

I sit on the patio and lean against the planter I usually rest my feet on. "Okay, Benny, talk to us."

"Dr. Logan called me early this morning telling me your Aunt Alice passed away due to foul play. What do you know about it?"

"As much as you do." He waits for me to tell him more.

I shrug. "Weren't you there when I asked for the forms? I filled out as much as possible and gave them to Dr. Logan."

"Where were you when your Aunt died?" Benny pulls out a little notebook.

I blink at him and laugh aloud. "Not in town, but I'm not sure where exactly. I heard about Aunt Alice's death when they called me about her will. A huge surprise since I'd met her once."

"You're lying about something."

As he studies my face, my cheeks burn. I don't dare break eye contact, not wanting to be shifty. "I'm telling you everything."

"Mrs. Perkins, what about you?"

"At home. We argued over something ridiculous, and we separated to cool off. Well, okay, I needed to cool off." She gave a shaky exhale. "I still regret it to this day."

"So, why did you want her body exhumed and autopsied?"

"Why, Benny, you sound just like a real cop." Mrs. Perkins' cheeks pink.

His face reddens. "Please, tell me what motivated you. I need to move things along."

No way to tell him about Aunt Alice unless I wanted to be locked up, opening my mouth I hoped for the best. "Intuition."

"You're kidding me." Benny sips his coffee and makes a face. He shovels in some sugar. "Overwhelmed with a feeling."

I bite my lip. "Mrs. Perkins and I talked about her death. She looked after herself, and I saw no reason for her death. It made no sense. I wanted her exhumed and examined to be sure."

"Amazing." Benny leans back in the chair looking up at the sky. Sunshine lights his face. "You remind me of her more every day."

"I'm sorry." And I was. He looks mildly annoyed with me.

"I'll need a formal statement." He finished his coffee. "Come by in the next few days."

"I guess her being murdered so long ago makes this a low priority." I stretch my legs out. My green nail polish needs a touch up.

"Mrs. Perkins, I expect you to respect our agreement and keep out of police business especially in this case." He stands looking down at her. "I'll check into this without your help."

"I understand, dear." She smiles sweetly at him. His expression changes to one I recognize. He knows being called 'dear' means trouble, and he shakes a forefinger at her. "We have an agreement, and, according to Bob, you're up to your old tricks."

"It's completely different." She sniffs and then wipes her nose.

"When it comes to police business, I expect you to inform me and step aside." He paces the patio stepping over me.

My eyes almost pop out of my head as I turn to Mrs. Perkins. "Anything we should tell him?"

She sets her cup down. "I follow the law precisely."

He stops in front of her, hands on his hips. "But you agreed."

"No, Alice agreed. I argued." Mrs. Perkins' green eyes flash.

Oh, boy. "Mrs. Perkins—"

"Did you check the step where Peter fell? Did you follow up with all the food when I called you? I would stay out of it, but with an incompetent idiot on the job, I don't dare."

I jump to my feet. "O-mi-god! Mrs. Perkins shut up."

Benny glances at me. "Stay out of this little girl."

She stands, staring up at him. "How dare you?"

I back away from the pair of them. "I have to go shopping and buy a new laptop. And you…you will pay me back…Oh crap."

They both turn toward me momentarily forgetting their argument.

"What?"

"I have to call the bank." Or, I check online. "Mrs. Perkins, I'm borrowing your laptop. Your door open?"

"Yes, help yourself." She turns back to Benny.

Not looking back I run up to Mrs. Perkins' den. I collect the laptop and power cord, bringing them back to my kitchen table. After fiddling with the power cord and wall socket which only let me put the plug in one way, I open the lid and push the power button. Up pops the start-up message a laptop asks before it boots up for the first time, confirming Mrs. Perkins hadn't touched her computer since she put it on her desk.

I answer the questions as I think she would. Once

up and running, I install virus protection etc., and go to my bank account.

I refresh the page twice hoping the number will change. I have five dollars and twelve cents. Apparently two days ago I cancelled my charge card and emptied my account. A cash withdrawal from the ATM.

Cursing under my breath, I run the updates that need to be installed and try to remember the name of the free application I use for word processing. I'm busy writing up a flimsy excuse for a résumé when Mrs. Perkins comes in the door with the coffee tray.

"Well, he's gone for now, but I guess we should make time for a formal statement before the man has a heart attack." She sets the tray down on the countertop.

"I have no money," I mutter to myself like a mantra.

"What do you mean you have no money?" Mrs. Perkins looks over my shoulder reading my résumé.

"Someone cleaned out my account using the ATM day before yesterday."

"Alice and I took a trip to the bank." Mrs. Perkins cheeks redden. "I didn't think about it."

"She cleaned me out." Great, perfect. "She didn't tell you where she put the money, did she?"

"No, have you checked your purse?"

"Ah, yeah." Barely listening, all I see is white page on the screen with my name, address, and cell number printed at the top. "How do I create a résumé when I have no experience—no skills?"

"Don't worry. I'll make some calls." She reads over my shoulder. "What are you good at? I'll need something to say."

"Pick the qualities you like best."

Mrs. Perkins taps her chin, frowning.

"Oh, come on. I'm becoming quite the people person." No other abilities come to mind. "You'll still call, right?"

"Emma, being a people person means having a good attitude." Mrs. Perkins lets out a long sigh. "I think I can come up with a few names that might take you on."

Friggin' hopeless. "I don't have a sound mind, I don't have a computer, I don't have any money, and I have a bad attitude. So, I have a few issues."

"A few?"

"A few." I won't admit to more. "You might have to call in some favors, but I promise I won't embarrass you."

Mrs. Perkins rests her palms on the table. "Okay, put a résumé together, and I'll make the calls." Standing over me she adds, "And for heaven sakes, give me a list of things you do well."

"What can I do?" I sincerely want to know.

"Now, don't be difficult."

"Me." I stand and pace in a circle. "I'm being difficult."

"Oh sit down, quit over reacting. I have some nice paper you may use—"

"While you call around begging everyone you're acquainted with to hire me, I'll be making the best résumé you've ever read."

"Don't you feel better all ready?" Mrs. Perkins glances back at me.

Chapter 18

I've never been employed, so to need a job this urgently makes me tremble and my confidence hunker down low. As I pull open the door handle of Pie 'n' All, its brass bell tinkles my arrival. Glancing up, I give it a silent thank you, for cheering me on.

My life's accomplishments listed on a single page of expensive writing paper, double-spaced with a large font, securely pinched between my fingertips. Nervously, I stroke the linen texture knowing the paper deserves much better than displaying my very sad résumé.

Mrs. Perkins rushed me out the door saying Maggie needs me right away, but, looking around the café, I don't understand why. The quiet place remains as I remember it except for a decorated chair in the corner.

A special chair, for a queen or a wood nymph, sits in a corner of the restaurant facing the center of the room. Its carved wooden legs ended with claws for feet. Along its puffy arms and swollen backrest clings ivy and a silken daisy chain.

One of the round tables, naked of the usual things,

is covered with a dark cloth and a pale doily lays flat and plain.

Two women chat among a collection of shopping bags. Colorful bags with the store names obscured broadcast they have been down the street—Copper Kettle, Artie's Hardware, and Brittany's—the local ladies clothing store. They sit at a table near the cash register with a tea setting and a tier plate of cakes and squares between them.

The menu will be easy to remember, and I comfort myself with a mantra of waitressing is mostly attitude. Pamper your customers, give them good service, and be as efficient as possible.

As I pass, the ladies nod and smile. A rush of relief fills me up. My confidence sticks its nose out. I have no reason to worry. If I make a mistake, I'll apologize and make amends. It'll be fine.

Knowing Maggie must be around somewhere, I lean over the counter, craning my neck. Not able to spot her through a wide door leading to the back, I ring the bell by the register. A moment of waiting is all it takes before her round face pops around the doorjamb, she smiles brightly, and mouths 'come on back.'

I glance down at my black slacks and white t-shirt giving myself a last chance to come up with something else. With no other choice, I lift the counter and follow Maggie through the door.

"Welcome Emma, sit a minute." Maggie silvery voice fills with encouragement. Her notebook's open wide in front of her. "I must jot a few things down before I forget them."

I sit and have more time to fret as Maggie scratches at the paper with a fine-tipped pen, pausing now and then before adding another item to the list. The industrial kitchen has large silver doors leading to fridges or freezers, metal tables with loafs of bread wrapped tight in plastic, and a floor even Mrs. Perkins couldn't get any cleaner.

I've never been in a place like this. It's not like a hospital at all. My shoulders relax, and I open my fists under the table and shake out my hands. The fear, the nervousness, seems to leak away, replaced by excitement.

She finally looks up.

"Ready for the tearoom?" Maggie leans back and stretches for the ceiling. "I expect a long day. Hot, cold, hot, cold, like most long days I suspect."

"I'm sure I'll keep busy." I like my sure voice.

"Love the attitude." Yet Maggie gives me a hard look. "You surprise me. Such a conservative dresser at your age." She gets up and circles me. "Well, I guess they'll do."

"I'm sorry." My nervousness scratches at me again. "I wore what I thought other servers wear."

"Server?" She laughs behind her hand. "No, hon. I hired you to do readings in the tearoom. I thought it would bring in some business. You have two customers already."

No wonder the women seemed warm and friendly. I have their futures in my hands. My hands.

"Oh, I didn't bring my cards." It's a whisper. My sureness took my volume with it when it left me stranded. The only job Mrs. Perkins can find for me is soothsaying. Impossible to turn it down, and impossible to do.

"Cards?" She drops her strong manicured hand on my shoulder. "We're a tearoom. You'll be reading leaves."

"Leaves." My hands clamp on my knees. No way. I steady myself and don't allow my instinct to take over. I mouthed the word and then repeat, "Tealeaves." It still sounds strange. "I've never read tealeaves."

But I read Maggie's eyes as they narrow.

"I'll do it." My nervous whisper disappears. "I'm just not sure how well."

"Don't be so serious. Have some fun." Maggie barks out a laugh. "It's okay. We understand you're not your Aunt Alice."

"Right." I ease my hands and smooth my slacks.

"Too right. I'm no Aunt Alice."

***

The first two readings suck. Definitely the worst, but the two shoppers tell me when two people come to a reading together it messes with the each other's energy.

Why argue?

The clues come at me from all angles. Sometimes chewed nails, dark smudges under their eyes. Other times as simple as a knee not staying still or a trembling chin. I learn faster than I expect and when I'm stuck I hear tapping—like a fingernail on glass.

I close my eyes and find Alice, proud and pleased, behind the glass mouthing some hint or other as to why my client sits across from me. By noon, I am in my groove and anticipate my next encounter.

"Princess of all tea leaf readers." It's a masculine, musical baritone I know well. Tom sits before I'm able to send him away. "I booked an appointment with Maggie this morning."

My eyelids snap open when I realize what he's done. "I didn't know about the readings." I'm torn between making a fool of myself and having enough experience to possibly squeak by; sighing, I decide to roll with it.

Tom sips his tea. "This stuff is hot. It's gonna take a

minute."

"Take your time. Maggie has been spreading out my appointments. She gives me more than enough time." I glance up at his face, getting lost in his warm dark eyes. "I'm a fake. Don't you dare take this seriously."

"Oh but I do." He smiles behind his cup.

"Fine, but consider yourself warned." I relax and let the smile come. "Do you have the day off?"

"Oh, I take lunch when I like. I'm my own boss."

"Funny you don't come across like a business man." I lean back in my fancy chair, my finger playing with the ivy.

"My psychic dollars at work." When he sees my expression, he laughs aloud. "You don't have a friggin clue, do you?"

"I'm not a gossip." I cross my arms over my chest. Then remember why he's here. "Best for you to walk away."

"Nope." Tom takes his empty cup places the saucer over it and turns the two of them upside down. "Show me what you got, sunshine."

I accept his challenge. "Okay, let's see what we see."

Small twigs, and leaves cling to the cup. My first

impression reflects in my face, and he lets out another laugh. "Should I cancel my afternoon and go to emergency?"

I quickly rearrange my expression. Then an idea pops into my head. "Funny. I see a young woman." I take a pause for dramatic effect and turn the cup slightly. "Ah, yes, beautiful, charming, and more than you can handle. Run, run I say, before she traps you in her web never to be free again."

I turn the cup again, glancing at the saucer. "Sorry, I see nothing else."

His face in a state of shock—lips a tight line and a crease cuts between his brows.

"Stop it." I shake my head and drop it into my hands. "Stop it. I'm joking around."

"It's as if you read my mind." He takes the cup from me and tries to see what I see which is rich because I saw nothing. At the angle he holds the cup, an outline of a circle and to the right a steeple appear. I gasp and push the saucer at him. Not funny anymore.

Yet, a whisper tickles my mind saying the jokes on me. I have strong suspicion the once serious Aunt Alice transforms into a playful minx at times.

After several more hours of reading, I'm exhausted

and am comfortable saying whatever pops into my mind. Maggie knows I'm a fraud, and, if she's good with it, so am I.

My boss interrupts me with a cup of tea and two oatmeal cookies. "Here you go." She tsks and sits. "Too long of a day? Maybe we need to have shorter hours for you. How about working between about one o'clock and four-thirty tomorrow afternoon?"

"I…if you want." Embarrassed, I gaze down at the table playing with the edge of the doily. "I don't mind being tired though. Didn't Mrs. Perkins explain I need to make a living doing this?" I won't meet her eyes until I blink away my tears. "Would you rather I wait tables?"

"No need." She rests her fists on her hips. "Haven't you checked your jar?"

"I haven't earned enough for a jar, but someone did give me two dollars." My fingers go to my pocket to verify the toonie is still there.

Maggie points at a smoky-glass jar behind her counter. "It's right there."

"You don't mean the jar full of paper."

"It's money you fool." She barks it out, and I see the dollar signs in her eyes.

But I'm a fake, a fraud. "Eventually, they'll figure

out I'm full of crap."

"Like two peas in a pod." Maggie pushes the tea toward me. "Your Aunt Alice used to say something similar all the time."

"You knew her." I slap my forehead. "Of course, you did."

"Yeah, I did." Maggie scans the nearest table to us. "She used to do this for me over the winter months when it slowed down."

I sip my tea. "She would?"

"Alice understood business and stepped up to help out when she was able." Maggie sits down, playing with the doily.

Aunt Alice, not me. "No one ever said." I remember the picture of her funeral. "They'll figure me out fast enough. I wish I had her skill." Good or not, I will do this until I'm fired. "I'll come whenever you like, and between one and four-thirty will be more than fine."

"Don't worry I'll take care of you." Maggie pats my hand and stands.

"I hate to ask, but when do I collect my money." I point at the jar beside the register.

Maggie makes a face. "Now. It's yours."

"Mine?" With Aunt Alice locked up, the money

should be safe. "Great, thank you."

I'm still counting my money when Mrs. Perkins enters shaking her head in disbelief she walks over to my table and sits down. "I thought you would work the tables."

"Me too." I take in what she's wearing—long johns, army boots, my hat from the party, a frilly dress with a large flower print on it. "Miscommunication."

She sniffs as she straightens my stack of fives. "Looks like you're in the money now."

"Until they find out I'm a fraud." I drop the little stack of twenties on the table and sip my tea. "May I ask you something?"

She smiles at me, taking off her hat and fluffing her gray curls. "Sure, ask away."

"What are you wearing?" I gaze at it like a train wreck. "And why?"

She looks down, straightening her bodice. "I'm going for bag lady."

I think about the assorted clothes and wigs in her den and understand her scary appearance. "Disguise? Did anyone spot you?"

She smiles. "No, I went as myself in the morning and hid behind a newspaper in the clinic waiting room at the hospital, and I wore this in the afternoon while I gathered bottles and cans." She looks over her shoulder. "Maggie, cup a tea when you have a moment."

I cringe at the thought of her hanging around watching the Schmidts all day. She'd stand out for miles. In my gut, I know she drew attention, but if they recognized her or not was another matter. "Did someone call the police?"

"How did you know?" With an honest expression of surprise, her eyebrows rise to her tousled curls and make me laugh.

"A feeling." I pull out fifty dollars and put the rest in an envelope. "Would you take this, and no matter what don't give it to Alice? I need it for food 'til my next deposit."

She nods and puts her hand out. "You didn't answer my question."

"Not joking." I put the fifty dollars in ten, fives, toonies and loonies into my purse. "You're supposed to blend in when surveilling, not stand out. I would have known you didn't belong there too."

Mrs. Perkins' expression transforms to thoughtful while slipping my money into her big leather purse. Maggie brings a fresh pot and winks at me as she walks away.

"Well, give me a moment to refuel and we'll go."

"Go? Go where?" My gut says surveillance.

"We've been asked to help." Mrs. Perkins pours her tea, adds sugar and stirs. "You are a woman of your word, right?"

"Yes." I sigh. "The only thing to stop me would be death."

"Even that doesn't seem to stop your family." Mrs. Perkins chuckles. "Visiting hours start in about an hour."

"To see Claire then?" I munch on a cookie, pushing the other across the table.

"Yes, Dr. Logan gave us the okay." She sipped her tea. "Actually he okayed you to help out on the floor."

"The whole floor?" I don't think so. "For nothing. Like volunteer?"

"For the goodness of your heart." She carefully sets her cup down and breaks the cookie in half. "You're not bored, are you?"

"No, that's a fact."

"Well, don't worry about anything else."

My turn to huff. "You're okay with tiring out Claire all the while we spy on people. People who barely deserve protecting."

"We need to keep an eye on them." Her voice as determined as ever. "Give me a moment and I'll be ready for another session."

I hide my face in my hands. I'm not the crazy one. "When they called the cops on you, did they take you away?"

"Me? No of course not." Mrs. Perkins sips her tea staring at me expectantly.

"…I better go alone. You go home and rest." I want to stop talking, and not do this. Except not doing it is much, much worse. I won't let anything happen to Grace.

As Maggie comes around from the back she carries a plastic bag full of pastry boxes. "Mostly sandwiches. I thought you needed a snack."

I shake my head slightly. "Thank you, I'll see you tomorrow then?"

"Yes, see you then." Maggie smiles at Mrs. Perkins and wipes off the table beside us.

I take the last of the broken cookie.

"Thanks for suggesting we give Emma a chance here, Millie. It's been booming all day." Maggie organizes the sugar and cream at our table and moves on.

"Emma, you weren't kidding. They like you here." Mrs. Perkins eyebrows rise for a moment. "It is you, isn't it?"

Chapter 19

It feels great to move even within a Dunster General hallway with my e-reader under one arm and my dinner hanging from my wrist swinging in a plastic bag. My heels announce each step on the polished tile. I'm staring straight ahead avoiding the sickness, the weakness, and the hopelessness of such a place.

Marcy, red head down over paperwork, sits at the nurses' station. Hearing me, she glances up and gives me a feeble wave. Her eyes bulge then she sees the boxes from Pie 'n' All and hurries over.

"It's Emma, right?" Nurse Marcy's sober voice is all business.

"Yes, and you're Marcy." I sniff the air to catch the scent of booze. No drunk will care for my friend. She deserves better.

Her smile never spreads further than a curving of her lips. "Claire can't have anything from Pie 'n' All."

I glance down at my package. The plain white plastic bag could be from anywhere. How did she know where it came from? "It's not for Claire." I sigh, sharing my annoyance. "It's rude, but I haven't eaten yet and promised Dr. Logan to make time to come up."

"There's a note about you helping on the floor." Marcy leans back on her heels. "Didn't realize you'd start tonight."

"I'm helping Claire. Not the floor." My eyes bore into Marcy's for a moment. "She can have tea, right?"

"Not the kind from the teahouse." She looks up and down the hall. "I'll make some weak enough for her."

"Thanks." I walk away but turn back to her. I need to know she's more than what I saw the day of the party. "Your drinking at the Schmidts', is that something you do often?"

Marcy halts, turning with a smile that should have killed. She looks me up and down again. Afraid of us being overheard, she lowers her voice. "Don't assume too much. I have eyes too. Interesting reading only a click away."

I saunter back to her. "Anything happens to my friend and drinking on the job won't be your only problem." I match her hostility. "Don't eff with me lady. Do your job and do it sober."

"Why you—"

"Say it!" I expel a breath with a hiss. "Go ahead. You forget I'm psychic."

Marcy goes pale, freckles glowing, and she steps back like distance matters. "Stay away from me."

"No problem." I turn on my heel. Her stare burns my neck. I make myself stroll down the hall checking room numbers until I find Claire's open door. Before entering, I turn. Marcy hasn't moved. The shock on her face tells me my message was received.

She'll stay sober. I smile, a big and sassy one, showing my teeth and my sincere hatred of drunken nurses. Without giving Marcy another thought, I step into Claire's room. The second bed stripped clean and mixed feelings bubble up through my surface of calm. Was Claire so ill Dr. Logan wants to keep her alone, or is she so delicate and private he respects her deepest desire?

"Hello, Claire." I stop in my tracks and turn to leave. Claire is on her back. Her cheeks sunken in, and dark smudges hang in bags under her eyes.

"Emma," she whispers.

Not sure what to do, I take another step closer. Damn Marcy. She should have told me Claire's condition. "You up for a visit, or should I go?"

"Please come in." Her voice is quiet. I read her lips to understand what she says.

Stepping in, I pull a chair near the bed and put my

e-reader on the table. "I hurried over without eating. Would it be okay if I snack on a sandwich or two from Maggie's place?" I'm desperate to do anything that will hide how I feel.

Claire lets her head relax upon her pillow, and bit by bit it tilts to the side to see me better. Slowly her eyes close.

"She's had a battle today." Marcy's soft shoes let her creep up behind me with a small teapot and cup which she sets on the table by my e-reader. "She's been dropping off all day and will come round in five or ten minutes."

"A warning would have been nice."

"Being such a good friend and all." Marcy looks down her nose at me and clears her throat. "They changed her meds today. The side effects should only be temporary."

"Right."

Marcy leaves, and I'm not about to call her back for a better explanation. Watching Claire's chest smoothly move up and down, I eat the entire contents of a box, slip the box in to the trash by the door and hide the bag under my chair. My heart aches as I roam the room, placing each heel softly to minimize their clicking.

At the window, I find Peter's house down the block.

It's a quiet night with no traffic. Above the silhouette of mountains hang stars I've come to love. I settle myself by Claire's bed and pick up my e-reader. My voice is a loud whisper with changes of tempo and emotion as I read aloud.

"Still here?" Claire's voice croaks at me.

"Good morning sleepy head." I test the tea and put it into a paper cup with a straw. "Take a sip and try that again."

"Not…funny." Her lips curve up at one corner.

"Sorry, it's been a rough day today." I put the lukewarm tea down.

Clair's eyes flutter. "Can't keep my eyes open."

"How about I read—"

Her eyes grow wide. "You brought your cards."

If only I was thinking. "No, I mean from an e-reader."

"I dreamt such a strange dream." She waves a limp wrist and blinks her eyes open.

I stand, go to the window. Peter in his wheelchair. Odd lighting from the television flashing throughout the room. "If you need to sleep, please do."

After a struggle, Claire lets her eyes close.

"Stay awake or rest. I'm here for you." My gaze

stays on Peter. Grace comes in their living room and closes the curtains. Light and shadow pass over the fabric.

Slowly Claire's breathing becomes deeper. I go to the bed and straighten the covers, check her water supply and refill her jug and glass.

"Emma?"

I jump and grab my chest but keep my voice singsong. "I'm here."

"Thanks for coming," she whispers.

Before I answer, she's dozing again. I pace to the window. Across the street the living room curtain is dark, and the shadows gone.

Feeling lonely, I call Mrs. Perkins.

"Hello." Mrs. Perkins' voice is thick.

"Hi, it's Emma."

"At the hospital?" She shifts the phone with a rattle.

"Yes and I shouldn't be here. Claire's meds have taken their toll today. Peter has called it a night, and the house is dark."

"Excellent." She moves the phone again. "You still need to keep an eye on the house."

"Don't be ridiculous." Quietly, I cut off each word with a clenching of my teeth. "They're in bed. How long do you want me to stay?"

"Emma." The voice comes from the bed.

"It's okay Claire."

"Okay." Claire sighs and closes her eyes.

"She's asleep again already." Mrs. Perkins sounds surprised.

"Yes, I feel helpless. She's not up for visitors today."

"Don't want to stay, then don't." Mrs. Perkins' voice turns hard and brittle. "Sit in your van across the street."

"Great idea, you going to bail me out so I make it to work tomorrow?" I try to sound like her…and fail. "It's not happening."

She huffs. "Fine, stay until the end of visiting hours."

"Right, and, while I'm staring at a dark house, what's going to happen?" I roll my eyes and pretend to shoot myself with my finger.

"Anything unusual."

Oh, yeah. Narrow it down a little. "I have no idea what that means."

She ignores my complaint. "Come over before you go home."

"Fine." I hang up, fuming, not believing how

stubborn Mrs. Perkins can be. Maybe hinting is not how I get out of spending the whole night looking at a sleeping house.

"Everything all right?" Marcy stands at the door.

I slam my palm to my heart.

She chuckles. "Sorry. I tend to be quieter at night." But her face says she's glad she scared me.

"Back again." I pace the room.

"Voices came down the hall, and I thought Claire felt better." Marcy comes in and takes Claire's wrist. Glancing at her watch, she takes Claire's pulse.

"Just me talking to myself." I lie, not wanting to share anything.

When I turn from the window, Marcy looks down at her mother's house. I'm unnerved and wonder why. A woman should be able to check in on her family anytime she wants.

"All right then." I stand over Claire wanting to slap Marcy's hand away. "Chores done?"

Nurse Marcy doesn't ruffle. She takes the rest of her readings and silently leaves. Glad she's gone. I sit beside Claire, open my reader and read, keeping my voice steady and my sideway glance on Peter's house.

Down the hall sharp voices snap my head up. I rub

my neck and glance around the room. Through the door and down the hall heels connecting with tile quickly get louder. I only catch the last of her pant leg as I peek at the door. Voices then silence. It's the silence that bothers me. Is she cursing because it is too late, or is the nurse herself after a fight?

I strain to listen. A moment passes, quiet footfalls return down the hall. This time Marcy, her face flush and eyes flashing and angrier than she was with me, storms down the hall.

Curiosity has me.

I rise from the chair and glance round the corner, finding an empty, quiet hallway. No disturbance. I decide to investigate, leave Claire's room and seek the thorn in Marcy's side. Slipping into the shadowy hallway, I follow Marcy's path peeking into doorways, but the dim rooms are too dark for anyone to be awake. I glance at the time— 9:30. It's not visiting hours anymore.

As I enter the last room on the left, a reading light goes out.

"I promise to rest now. Please don't be angry." Jay's voice sounds upset and not like herself at all. I cringe at what Marcy must have done to the spunky woman I remember with the cane and chicken neck.

The voice comes from behind a curtain. I slowly pull it aside and peek in on the frail woman. Her cane hanging on the edge of her bed, linked on the side bar.

"Don't mind me. I thought I heard something." I store my hands behind my back.

"It was probably the nurse giving me heck for reading when I should sleep." Jay takes a long look at me. "Hey, Glady told me I'd be out right away."

"What? Did she talk to your doctor?"

"No, she talked to you."

"Oh." I examine the floor for flaws as I recall what I said to Glady. "Sorry. She was pretty upset, and I thought it would rid her of all the worry." I pull up a chair. "On the mend?"

"And you didn't tell Millie." Jay tsks to herself. "Who will cover the tourney next week?"

"I'll ask Mrs. Perkins to do it."

"And maybe visit?" Jay organizes her covers.

"Sure, I'll let her know."

"You won't forget this time?" Jay looks tiny in her bed.

I dig in my pocket for my phone. "Call her now."

"Now?" After a moment of staring, she takes the phone between two fingers and gives it a long evaluating stare. "Is this one of those fancy phones?"

I take it from her and dial Mrs. Perkins' number. "Here just put it to your ear, and she'll answer in a second."

A sparkle of delight fills her eyes as she listens. "It's ringing." She chuckles to herself and glances at the door. "Close the door or the wicked nurse of the north will be in here in a flash."

"She can listen from the nurses' station?"

Jay waves a hand at me. "Millie is that you...Yes, yes, she's here...Watching the door while I talk to you...Okay, I'll tell her." Her chicken neck quivers as she speaks. "Millie wants to know when you're leaving."

"Right after you're done with the phone."

She nods and covers her mouth, continues to talk but keeps her voice quiet. I pace to the window and adjust the curtains.

With a glance around the room, I see nothing special that would draw Marcy to it. It's just a private room—quiet and out of the way. I smile at Jay who is nervously watching me while she speaks to Mrs. Perkins. I walk to the door, and the hall remains empty.

"Okay Millie, I will." She smiles widely. "Goodbye."

"All done? Tourney covered?" I reach for my

phone.

"Yes, thank you. I need one of these. Where do you shop for a phone like this?"

"When you're released, I'll take you shopping for just the right one." It sounds like I'm bribing her to get better. She's not acting right. Jay should be waving her cane at me and calling me chickadee.

"Deal."

"You and Marcy don't get along?" I slip my phone into my pocket.

"She'll be back any moment. And she'll sit here for hours just staring and pacing and muttering."

"Staring at you?" I shiver at the thought, barely handling a few moments with her.

"No, out the window." Jay lifts a frail hand.

I pull the curtain aside, and there's Peter's house. If the curtains were open, I would see most of his front room. It must make her feel safer checking in on her parents anytime she wants. It would be easier than calling and much less intrusive.

"Not much to see."

"You don't get it?" She glances at the doorway.

"What?"

"Her mother lives across the street."

I nod my understanding.

"The way she talks. It's like Grace isn't safe over there." Jay jumps with surprise and blushes.

"Here you are." Marcy stands at the open doorway, gaze on me, and her arms crossed. "Visiting hours have ended for tonight."

"Thanks." I turn back to Jay. "I hope I didn't scare you."

Chapter 20

Marcy walks down the hall with me trailing after her, but my pace is slower and more deliberate. My aim is to annoy her, test her boundaries, and see what happens. I've never hated somebody, so truly and completely before—reason or not.

Something stinks. It hangs invisibly in the halls like wet vines, dragging along my flesh. Is it her or me? She appears innocent enough—lavender scrubs, a red cord clashing from round her neck, and an ID badge with utter power over the patients.

Rubbery shoes squeak quietly, arms loose at her side, she seems too relaxed for what's going on with her family. Wouldn't a caring daughter be more stressed and worried over her mother? She comes across as if it's business as usual.

Then spies out Jay's window. Why? I think she knows something.

In each room, everything is quiet and gentle. The rustle of sheets. A snuffle. A soft ring of a phone down the hall. When I return to Claire's room, all is still. I wait for her chest to rise and fall. The pause between breaths seems too long…way too long. I bite my lip and quietly gather my things.

"Take care. Be strong." My whisper thunders, leaving behind a larger and painful silence.

Outside the white room, Alice peeks in from behind the curtains. The window tightly secured. She is pressing her palms to the glass trying to see. I'm afraid and don't know why.

I walk to my van, thinking things over. Peter comes across like a fatherly soul until you learn his business practices. Heck, he turns his back on one woman and marries another. He's a loan shark, mild for the city types but unsavory for the locals.

His sleeping house is the most intimidating on the dark street. My shoulders relax once in my van to drive away.

Peter knew Jane's secret…and I'm sure he knows many others, adding to the list of possible suspects. Even Tom, gets riled up talking about him.

And Claire, not once while we talked about Peter did she mention he'd hurt her.

Hell, I'd be hurt even if he agreed to let me go and married within a year. Moved on and forgotten her. How dare he?

Is Grace a new victim…or a villain stealing another's man. If we think money, then Grace would be the obvious person to kill Peter. Yet I believe they truly love each other. I'm turning into Mrs. Perkins, seeing murderers everywhere.

***

I park in my driveway with a heartfelt sigh, turn off my van, undo my seatbelt, and rub my eyes. It had been a long day, and I'm looking forward to a hot bath and a sleep-in tomorrow.

Rest, maybe after a….

Mrs. Perkins waves from her front step.

Great!

Here I go, waving back lamely and gathering my things. *I'll pop in for a minute, report, and leave as quick as I can.*

With mixed feelings I drag my feet to Mrs. Perkins' front door, walking under the dim streetlight. A burning sensation runs up my shoulder blades and into my neck. The glare of eyes bores deep. I spin, taking in the street, houses of varying colors, and neat square stamps of lawn all in the shadows. Decorative plants and tree branches sway in the wind. Still turning, something snaps behind me, making me jump ready to run.

Barely visible, at the edge of a streetlamp, a cat twitching its tail readying to pounce on an invisible victim.

"Come on, come on." Mrs. Perkins flaps a hand at me to pick up the pace.

"What's the rush?" I watch the cat slink into the shadows. "Miss me or something?"

"No." She snickers. "I have something for you."

Food? I'm hoping for a huge steak sandwich or more stew. It needs to be substantial to hold me over until I grocery shop. The image of my empty cupboards, my fridge with two yogurt cups, a few slices of bread, and half a jar of fuzzy spaghetti sauce appear behind my closed lids. I shudder and pass her as I go in the doorway.

"Where have you been? I've been waiting."

"Doing what you asked me to, geesh. You want me on a schedule. Send me a copy." I look around the living room. "What's the rush?"

"Visiting hours were over a while ago." She takes my hand and drags me further into the house.

"And you talked to Jay." I remind her. "What's the big deal? Lost track of time."

"No one kicked you out?"

"No, but—" I stop at the dining room table. Staring

at a thin rectangular box with the word notebook written on its side in bold font. "What's that?"

"It's for you." Mrs. Perkins bounces on her toes, clapping her hands together. "I used a little of your money and the broken computer in trade."

My heart catches in my throat. I can't believe this. "Holy crap." I rush over, pushing Mrs. Perkins aside, and open the box to reveal the dark form of a new laptop wrapped in white bubbly sheets. "How much money?"

Mrs. Perkins purses her lips. "Not much for an old rebuilt model, and he did all the file transfers himself." She clasps her hands together. "If you don't like it, Tom said I can bring it back."

"I mean it. Give me a dollar value." Not able to stop myself. I close the lid.

"Half of what you made today."

"You're kidding me!" I tear my eyes away from my new toy. Tom?

"He said its full of wireless things and tarabitiesy and a wide screen to see better with."

"Thank you." I pull the laptop free, unwrapping it, taking a moment to run a hand along its sleek black case, and open it up. My fingertips slide along its full sized keyboard, just like my old one. A touch pad without missing paint and all the letters still clear on the keyboard buttons, and, the best part, little decals shine brightly. In a corner of the box, tucked away, is a little plastic bag holding a battery and electrical cords.

"Yes Mrs. Perkins. It's more than okay, and you said Tom built it." I let my smile loose. "This is the best thing ever."

"Yes, he's the local IT man." She smiles up at me pleased with my reaction.

"IT, that's his job?" With effort, I put my new laptop down gently and take her in a huge hug. "Thank you."

"Yes, he services everyone around the Dunster area."

"We'll keep this one away from Aunt Alice."

"Outstanding idea." She smiles up at me patting my hand. "Now, we can talk about what we need to do tomorrow." She leads the way into the kitchen. "Oh for heaven sakes, the kitchen is no place for a computer."

I walk it back to the dining room and force myself to leave it behind. Wait a minute. I have to work tomorrow. "When tomorrow?"

"I'll get a snack for you, dear. I'm sure you're hungry after working all day and then sitting with Claire."

She stops in her tracks. "Claire's not so well today?"

Sitting at the table, I stare into my hands. My thumbs won't stay still, and my throat closes. "No…not well at all."

"Sorry to hear it." She drops a hand on my shoulder for a moment. "No doubt Claire appreciated you dropping by and spending time with her."

"I yelled at Marcy." I drag hand over my cheek.

Mrs. Perkins nodded. "I'm sure she deserved it." With a quick squeeze, she releases me, and digs through her freezer drawer. "What would you like?"

I reach up and stretch and think back. Did she call me dear? "What have you done?"

"Grace called of all things. A complete surprise. Right out of the blue."

"Yes." Tension edges my shoulders skyward.

"And for some reason she felt watched all day."

"Imagine." I shake my head. "Did she see you getting arrested?"

"The constable didn't take me in." She stares me down. "He just asked me about my clothes. He called them a getup."

"Understandable." I purse my lips to stop smiling. "Then what?"

"Then she hired us as bodyguards." She states this proudly. I want to spit, but the shock sinks in and my mouth dries up. Take a bullet for Peter? Not going to happen.

Not a chance. Nuh-huh. "Bodyguards. Have you ever seen a bodyguard? They don't look like us."

Mrs. Perkins chuckles. "Nothing to it and just in the mornings before work." She roots around in the freezer again. Coming up with a silver pack, she reads the label.

"Omigod, tell me you're not covering for me while I'm at Pie 'n' All."

"Well yes." She shakes her head. "Who else?"

I imagine her in a Charlie's Angel's outfit with a gun in her hand and shudder. "This is just getting better and better."

"Listen to me."

I blink, straight faced. "Okay, but it would be easier with my mouth full. Feed me and I'll shut up."

Mrs. Perkins, satisfied with the package, removes the tin foil, and pops it into the microwave.

She explains why we will be bodyguards and I drool over the contents in the microwave, not hearing a thing she says. Until a warm piece of garlic bread and a large bowl of chili are placed in front of me. Silently, I use a napkin to wipe my mouth before I dig in.

"I felt guilty at first when Grace called. I spied on all their comings and goings but didn't dare admit it. One thing led to another." Mrs. Perkins drops a hand on her hip. "It just kinda happened."

I nod and fill my mouth with garlic bread. My eyes roll back into my head, and I groan happily.

Mrs. Perkins smiles. "It is good, isn't it? One of my better batches. I don't know why it happens. You add the same ingredients and do the same things."

I slam my hand on the table, widening my eyes.

"Right." She smiles shyly. "She had wanted help but didn't know where to turn. Anyway, I let her talk me into it. It seems like a better solution than sitting in the waiting room or roaming the streets with a shopping cart."

I put my palm out, hold my breath until the image of her pushing a shopping cart passes, and safely swallow. "Hey I'm visiting Claire anyway. She needs people around her. Wait a minute. Are we getting paid by Bob and Grace?"

"Paid? No, we're not getting paid." Mrs. Perkins stops talking and stares over my right shoulder.

I turn to see who's at the door. With the lights out on the porch, our faces reflect back at us.

I turn back to an empty bowl.

"What's the matter? Someone outside?"

"No, no it's nothing, just thinking."

"Think out loud, or I'm going home." I pull my hands over my face and rake my fingers through my hair. "What time do I have to show up?"

"Oh, they eat breakfast at six."

"Six! A! M!"

"Calm down."

"Shit." I stand.

"Come over at five-thirty and we'll have eggs."

"I'm getting up early and not getting paid?" I need my head examined.

"We do this for the love of our community, for decency, for the betterment of mankind."

"Okay, that explains why you do it." I sigh. "But I'm not like you."

Chapter 21

To keep my promise and help Mrs. Perkins, I arise at five, shower, and go with her to the Schmidts'. The morning seems overly long, and, when Peter announces he wants to visit Claire, I'm more than surprised and happy to join him.

"Peter, you want to spend more time at the hospital?" Grace's stressed out voice annoys me.

I understand Peter wanting to leave the house. I'm dying here, too. Peter and Claire are still friends. Visiting her will be enlightening.

"Come on Peter. We'll go together." I put on my summer jacket, sling my purse over my shoulder and walk to the door, looking at his ride. "I'm not strong enough to move you and the chair."

"It's okay." Peter pulls two canes from the side of his wheelchair, puts the brakes on, and stands. He seems wobbly, and I put out a hand. "I'm able to walk about ten feet at a time."

"He's getting better every day." Grace adds her comment from across the room at the breakfast table.

Mrs. Perkins sits with Grace at the table nibbling on toast. "Put some color in your cheeks." Mrs. Perkins gets up and retrieves the coffeepot. "But don't be long."

"Hurry before they change their minds." Peter smiles widely. "Freedom from under the magnifying glass."

I'm not too sure I agree. My job is clear in my mind. I turn away and open the door. "Stay put until I have the chair down the stairs."

"Will do." Peter leans on a stool near the countertop.

I collapse his ride and roll it outside, letting it down one step at a time. Once I reposition it, I aim the open seat at the stairs. "Come along slow poke. I'm ready."

Peter carefully steps through the door and cautiously takes one step at a time until he's in front of the chair. He sits, landing rather hard, and I suck my lips between my teeth in sympathy. "You all right?"

"Yes, but give me a minute to catch my breath." Glistening with moisture, he dabs at his high forehead with his sleeve and stows his canes away.

I come around. Peter's face flushes, and he manages each breath through clenched teeth. His eyes aglow with pain. "Should I go back and find some pain killers?"

"No pain, no gain." Peter dabs his upper lip and lets out a controlled breath. "I'll be fine. We better move before Grace sees me like this. She'll drag me back in."

I center the chair on the sidewalk and push it around the house. "Okay, but I'm taking it easy. I'm sure Grace expects you back in one piece." After a couple sudden bumps, I'm not so superior. He seems less like a menace and more like a harmless old man.

"You and Millie went to visit Claire yesterday?"

We come around the corner of the house.

"Yes, and we clicked." We wheel to the gate, pause while I open it and push Peter through. "She's quite brave facing what she's facing alone."

"Oh, don't be silly. You and Millie are two peas in a pod." He glances over his shoulder at me.

"I meant Claire, but yes, I admit Mrs. Perkins seems more like family than my own ever has." I push the chair down the sidewalk with the hospital looming over us from across the street. Little faces appear and disappear while they peek out the high hospital window. A chill from within runs through me as a warm summer breeze tugs at my loose hair.

"Funny, it's similar with Claire. When she asked for the annulment, I took it as a personal rejection. Devastated, but she needed to focus on herself and not money or a new husband. She still loves me and I her." He looks back at the house. "Don't tell Grace it would break her heart. They are both wonderful women."

"I agree." My hackles rise, complaining about love trouble at his age. I clench my teeth and push on. "I won't say a word."

We roll the chair past the house. He checks for traffic. "You don't have to walk all the way to the corner. Cross here. It's not like you'll be arrested by Benny the bully."

I chuckle, eying the gravel beside the cement, I'm not sure I want to. "What do you suggest? We cut through the gravel and across the road?"

"Use the driveway into the parking lot. We'll save wear and tear on your back."

It sounds like a good plan, but once off the broken cement onto the gravel, I'm forced to dig in my heels and lean forward. The chair fights me the whole way, and, when my hand slips, I almost fall on my face. He gets his hands down on the wheel and helps push. Six feet and we break free onto the tarmac. With a final gasp, we glide.

"I don't know about you, but I'll be glad to have you walking again." I mean it on so many levels, but mostly because then he won't be vulnerable and we can give up guard duty. Oh, how I hope we'll give up guard duty.

He laughs. "Yes, it would nice to go dancing with Grace. I've missed it."

I never considered Grace. How long has it been since the injury? She's been a good sport looking after him, the house and worrying about everything, too. Every time he shows his affection for Grace, I like him a little more.

We face more gravel on the other side of the road, but it only takes rhythm to rock us free and onto the driveway, easily rolling across the lot and through the double doors. The air conditioning blasts frigid air with a lovely scent of antiseptic. I angle us to the elevators and away from the stink, but Peter takes control.

"We need to make a stop first." He wheels himself to reception. A wide sign hangs over a half-circle of three wickets. Only one is wheelchair level. "You have an envelope for me?"

The young brunette opens a shallow drawer, looking through some papers. She pulls an envelope free. "Mr. Schmidt?"

"Yes." He offers an open palm and is rewarded. Peter opens the envelope, pulls the page out, and flattens it on his lap. I read over his shoulder—a bill for Claire. Without a second glance, he pulls out his checkbook and writes a check for the full amount, forty thousand dollars. What am I seeing?

Then he calmly places the bill with the check and hands them back. "Thanks, Deedee."

Deedee stamps the bill paid, and he slips it into his pocket.

Forty thousand dollars to a woman, a friend—unbelievable. Mrs. Perkins told me about a loan for Claire, but witnessing this makes me wonder if Peter prefers the poor house. Lucky for him Grace knows how to live on nothing.

Through the glass, Deedee gives us a small smile and a nod.

"Okay, let's go to the gift shop and take our girl some flowers." He almost runs over my toes when he pivots and rolls away. The little gift shop reminds me more of a magazine stand at an airport with books, flowers, candy, magazines, newspapers, and a variety of soft drinks in a glass cooler. Peter selects a festive bouquet of daises and asters which brings Easter bonnets to my mind. He hands them over, pays for them, and moves off toward the elevator.

"Feeling more like a pack horse than an escort?" Peter snickers. "Come on."

"Did you just call me a horse?" I gently cuff the top of his head. "You like to play with fire, don't you?"

We take the elevator to the second floor and find Claire sitting in a chair looking out the window. "I spotted you crossing the road. Peter, don't work her so hard."

"I volunteered." I sit, fanning myself with the flowers.

"Emma, you came back." She seems like her old self.

Relief washes over me. "I said I would."

"A woman of your word." Peter cheers. "Wonderful."

"Come say hello." Claire holds her hands out to Peter. She smiles wide and looks like she has nothing wrong except exhaustion. I push my worries away for now. No point in thinking about something beyond my control. I'm here to make her feel better.

Peter rolls closer to her and takes her hands. "How are you today?"

"Better, much better than yesterday. Lucky for me, I slept through most of it." She glances up at me.

I stop fanning myself with the flowers. "I'll put

these in water, shall I?" I tip the bouquet toward Claire.

"Beautiful."

"Peter has great taste." I glance around and don't see a spare water jug. "Excuse me for a moment. I need to find something to put these in."

The two of them have their heads together, speaking quietly. It reminds me of when I'm talking with Tom—the attentiveness of it, the look of pure affection on Peter's face. A gentle union between two souls.

I leave them to talk and walk to the nurses' station. "Hi. Marcy working today?"

A young wiry girl looks up from her computer. "Not 'til tonight."

"Oh, I guess I'll see her then. May I bother you for a jug or something to put these flowers in?" I raise the flowers over the high counter.

"Peter visiting again?" She sighs and rises from her office chair.

I don't want to say anything wrong. "No, I bought these."

"Sure you did." She winks and waves me to join her. "Follow me."

We go into a day room with one wall full of large windows. Sloppy blinds hang half pulled up, closed completely, or letting sunshine filter through the angled slats. A few patients sit watching television, dealing cards, or playing board games.

The day room didn't have a sterile hospital atmosphere to it. I spot an antiviral hand dispenser, tuck the flowers under an arm, and drop a blob of the solution onto my hands. The nurse nods at me approvingly. In an old cabinet, bursting with puzzles, games, and books, sit a collection of vases. She pulls one down and hands it over.

"Nicer than a jug, don't you agree."

Our hands touch, and my skin itches where it met hers. I step back.

"Yes, thanks."

But she's beyond hearing me, approaching a patient, and soon leans over to speak with him. She puts a boney hand on his sleeve and whispers reassurances in his ear. She nods, stands, and helps him to his feet, then walks beside him, pacing herself to him and listening to his mutters. His jowls shake when he speaks, and his gnarled hand clasps his cane, planting it carefully with each step.

The room suddenly becomes unfriendly, and I'm reminded at once about my stay. A shiver goes up my spine, and I rush from the room almost knocking a woman over trying to escape.

Jay's talons clamp tightly onto my arm. "It's chickadee."

"Hello, Jay." I take her elbow to steady her, moving the vase to the other hand.

"Help me into a chair before you skedaddle." She plants her cane and shuffles over to a sofa with two yellow cushions tucked in one corner. Its headrest meets the sill of a window, leaving a patch of light warming the seat. Jay drops into the center of it. "Ah, long walk down the hall when you've been lying around for a few days."

"Any more visits from Marcy last night?" I take a seat beside her. When she lets my arm go, I put the flowers in the vase and place them at my feet.

"After you left." She adjusts a cushion. "I didn't sleep well, and she popped in every hour on the hour." She pushes one cushion toward me, and the other she adjusts at her lower back.

"I hated leaving, but visiting hours had ended."

"She's wicked." Jay leans back to enjoy the sun on her face.

"What nurse isn't?" I lean back too, although I don't want a wicked nurse to sneak up beside me.

"I know why I don't like her, but what's your beef with her?" Jay opens her eyes and lifts a hand blocking the sunshine to see me better.

"Let's just say I know too many of them who didn't respect me." I huff. "Would gladly live without seeing another pajama clad witch for the rest of my days."

"I hear you sister." Jay squints at me. "Do something about the blinds, chickadee."

"Sure." I bring down the column of slats, and adjust them to block direct light from hitting her in the eyes. "I should check in on Claire."

"I saw she had a gentleman caller." Jay tips her head to the side and considers me with a knowing look. "Funny how Grace and Claire seem so much alike? Or did."

"Trying to tell me something?" I sit again, picking up the full vase.

"Might be?" She winks at me. "It might not be a coincidence Peter met Grace escorting Claire to an appointment."

"Who's the matchmaker?" I lean forward, vase clamped between my palms.

"Wouldn't know." She sniffs. "I'm not a gossip."

All the way back to Claire's room, I try to imagine a matchmaker at the hospital. What a novel idea.

I walk up to Claire's room, but arguing voices stop

me. I pause by the open door, torn between not wanting to eavesdrop and interrupting them.

"No, I won't do this anymore," Claire's weak voice cries.

"I want to help. Stop worrying about later." Peter's urgent voice demands. "Leave later to me."

"But some days, I barely cope."

I bite my lip knowing what she means.

"Think of the payoff meeting your grandchild, holding him after he's born." He takes a deep breath. "It will all be worth it, won't it?"

Claire sobs, and I bite my lip harder to keep from crying too. The wiry nurse comes up behind me and chins toward the open door, raising her eyebrows.

"Don't want to interrupt." My cheeks burn.

She nods her understanding. "Boy, do I know the feeling." Her voice carries purposely to Claire's ears, and I walk into the room as if pushed, glancing behind me at the nurse's blank expression. Both Claire and Peter stare at me.

"Listening outside the room, Emma? Have you no manners?" Peter rolls away from Claire and closer toward the door. His nostrils flaring.

"Sorry." I rub my face with a palm, wishing I could cool my cheeks. "I know better, but the angry voices made me shy about coming in." From the frown on his face, he doesn't believe me.

"Oh. How loud?" Claire adjusts her bedding with fumbling fingers.

"Into the hall." I take a step closer to her. "Not words exactly, more like tones."

"How embarrassing." Claire wipes her damp cheeks. "I'm frustrated with my condition, and yesterday—"

"I understand. Rough day yesterday." I take her hand, dip down and meet her eyes. "I've felt helpless too. For some, it's impossible to imagine."

"Don't encourage her. Emma, let's go. I'm sure Grace must be missing me by now."

"Sure." I hold up the vase, dry but full of flowers. "Just give me a moment to fill this up, and we'll be off."

Peter glances back at Claire. "I'll wait in the hall."

"Peter," Claire calls out. "Don't be angry."

"Angry? Angry is the least of my problems," Peter mutters over his shoulder. "I need a quiet place to mull things over. Give me time."

I fill the vase in the bathroom and put the flowers down on her side table. "Anything else before I go?"

"Take care of him." She speaks from behind her

hand, her eyes hidden, and her cheeks glistening.

"I will." It's a promise between me and Claire. Peter confuses the heck out of me. He's doing his best to help her, and I'm okay with him again.

"No, I mean it. Read this." She opens a drawer, pulls a crumpled paper free, and hands it to me. The torn half page is the standard threat you would see on any cop show. In magazine letters the note spells out. "Stop it or I'll kill him."

My breath catches in my throat. "Do they mean Peter?"

She nods, eyes wide.

"Stop what?" But I know. Forty thousand dollar invoice.

Before Claire answers, Peter calls out. "Hey, what's taking so long?"

Claire pushes me away. "We'll talk later."

I need to show it to Mrs. Perkins. "Sure. Okay." Pulling a baggie from a side pocket in my purse, I open it and Claire slips the paper inside. Then the bag goes in my back pocket. I walk away wondering if I'll see her again. On television, right about now someone dies.

***

We come out into a bright sunshiny day. I stop a

moment and put on my sunglasses, the glare of the
windows intense. A bold golden globe reflects back at us
without mercy.

"How are you doing down there?"

"Blinded." He pulls his palm over his brow and
glances around. "Those windows really catch the light."

"Why'd I ask?"

We cross the drive. Not hearing any cars, I keep my
head down as we move across the parking lot to the
sidewalk. I'm relieved and turn away from the intense light
avoiding most of the reflection. A breeze catches my hair
and whips and tugs playfully dragging a curtain of long
blonde hair across my nose. I push it away, controlling the
chair with one hand and losing the battle badly. Suddenly,
Peter takes control and pushes the chair toward the road.

"Let's cut over here."

My instincts say no, but I'm distracted by the note
and follow along with one hand on the chair. I let it lead me
across the pavement. Did I look both ways? No, did I listen
for an engine? Yes, but it seems far off.

Until it is too late.

A woman screams. What she says, I don't know.
The wind stops just for a moment, and I turn my face to
free it of my hair laying like a blanket over my eyes.

Grace's car revs at the end of the road speeding toward us.

I can't believe my eyes.

I grab both handles of the chair and tug it backward. Peter tries to go forward. Mrs. Perkins screams, and now I know what I need to do. I kick off my shoes, digging in my bare toes into the lumpy road surface and push with all I'm worth. The chair resists at first and for a moment, I realize Peter will not die alone today.

Leaning forward with all my might I push, Peter's hands, strong, yet awkward, don't move as fast as the large wheel and slow me down, but I keep pushing. Feet away from more gravel. I don't dare look, but I hear it coming. It's louder. The tires screech as it shifts down. The rubber squeaks, and I scream for my life.

I give up on the chair, come around Peter and grab both his hands, clamping on tight and pulling him on top of me. We fall between two parked cars. I land hard on my back with a full-grown man on top of me. My bruised ribs ache. I don't care. I'm too busy trying to breathe and hungrily suck in air.

A crash happens at my feet when the car collides with the chair. As the car scrapes along the parked cars and over the chair, it breaks into bits without mercy. I swallow, turn, and vomit into my hair.

"It's okay Emma. It's okay." Peter mumbles at me, trying to crawl out. The two of us are stuck because he can only move his legs partially. "Thank you. Thank you so much."

Mrs. Perkins runs toward us with a phone to her ear. "Yes, it was Grace Schmidt. She drove the car."

Now, I can't believe my ears.

Chapter 22

It seems like forever laying near the curb with Peter beside me. A few moments have passed. I blink away tears and try to squeeze out from beneath the bumper of a large green car.

Eventually, I'm forced to commando crawl out from beneath and pull myself up to sit on the sidewalk. My hands shake as I rake the hair out of my eyes. Peter inches free after me. Much slower, unable to use both his legs.

"Watch the vomit." I rake my hair again, realizing I should have taken my own advice and wipe my fingers on my jeans. My back burns from contact with sharp edges of the cars as we slipped between them.

Mrs. Perkins sensible shoes slap the cement as she nears me. "Emma! Emma, are you all right?" Her hands butterfly over my back. "Oh, you're cut and bleeding."

Peter drags himself beside me and examines my torn and bloody shirt. "Really, Millie. That is what you want to ask the girl?"

"Shut up, Peter, and let her answer me." She's in a panic.

She turns my shoulders to examine me. I grab on to her like a life preserver. She lets me pull her down from a crouch, and I relax my grip before her bones snap.

She gently rubs my back. Her face beaming. "Emma, you saved his life."

I swallow hard and clear my throat. "Well, not surprising. I saved mine too." Embarrassed, I let her go and pull my disgusting hair away from my face.

Then a woman's voice shouts, asking what happened. Stunned, I gape in disbelief at the woman who tried to kill us. I get my feet under me and stand shakily.

Bring it on, Bitch.

Grace, in her prim slacks and sweater, runs across the street, heading straight at Peter. I adjust my stance, spreading my rubber legs for better balance. "Back off." I raise a fist. One more inch, and I'll hit her. Hit her hard. But will I stop?

Mrs. Perkins rests her hand on my forearm. "Let's see what she says."

I slowly drop my hand to my side and shake my fists away. "Sure, but keep her away from him."

"Emma, Millie, I don't understand." Grace Schmidt steps around me to see her husband and doesn't move any closer. "Peter, how did this happen?"

I step between them and put an arm out to keep her at a distance. "No closer. Don't you dare move." A siren sounds and relief and regret wash over me. "The police won't be long."

"Emma, I don't understand. What's happened to Peter?" Grace comes as close as she dares and kneels at my feet. Her right hand reaching out to him. "Not another accident."

I push her trembling hand away from him. "What do you mean accident? You tried to kill us."

Grace smiles as if I'm funny and realizes I'm serious. "No." Her chin quivers. "Don't be ridiculous. I'd never hurt a soul."

I fist her blouse and pull her up. "Look at me." I step aside bringing her with me. "Look at him." My voice cracks, and I have to swallow to continue. "How did you not see his battered chair in the street? You walked right past it."

Mrs. Perkins pulls my fingers apart to release Grace. "Leave her be."

"You ran it over." I sob. "You tried to kill me."

"Peter, I would never hurt you. I hired these two to keep you safe."

He blinks at her from the ground. "You did what?"

"If you spend your money caring for your ex-wife, I'll spend some caring for you." Grace centers her blouse buttons and tucks the tails into her slacks.

"Emma, please let her pass." Peter pushes me aside. "She's my wife." He opens his arms to Grace. "Forgive her. She doesn't know you like I do."

I don't believe my ears. "Know her?"

A patrol car comes around the corner and double parks beside the scraped cars and broken wheelchair. Benny gets out and adjusts his gun. "What happened here?"

"I called it in." Mrs. Perkins runs to him pinching his sleeve. "Didn't they tell you what had happened?"

"Give me a minute to get some help from across the street." Turning away, Benny speaks into his radio. He takes a moment to inspect the parked cars and the broken wheelchair. "Mrs. Perkins, why don't you go first? What happened here?" He pulls out his notebook.

"Grace, she tried to run over Emma and Peter." Mrs. Perkins grips his arm with a clenching fist. "That mess might have been them."

"Sure she did." Benny eyes Peter and Grace clinging to each other. "Apparently, Peter agrees with your assessment. Let's get him up."

"For crap sakes." I slap his hand away. "He putters

around in a wheelchair for a reason. Hold on a moment and I'll fetch another chair from the hospital." I storm away with vomit in my hair, and a foul expression smeared across my face.

In a hurry, I help myself to one by the waiting room double doors and follow the sidewalk back, shoving my way through the group gathering across the street. As chills runs up me like tire treads, I stop for a minute doubled over, worried I might vomit again. I hold the handle of the chair for balance and breathe through my nose.

Yes I almost died, but it's over now. Why am I acting like it will happen again at any moment?

Every time my eyelids close, Alice frantically taps on the glass. She shouts something I don't quite understand. In my mind I call out, *later. We'll talk later.* She nods and mouths *don't forget.*

Once I settle down, I push the chair to where Peter sits on the ground with one leg sticking straight out and the other bent. I engage the brakes on the chair, and Benny carefully helps Peter climb in.

"Comfortable?" The constable's police-academy compassion could be bottled and sold as poison.

"Not really, but it will do for the next hour or so."

Benny nods and glances over at me. "I've listened

to Mrs. Perkins side of things. It's your turn."

Grace sits in the back of the police cruiser. *Good. Okay.* My shoulders relax, and the dried blood on my back and arms tugs at my shirt.

I tell him everything I remember. It doesn't take long. Benny nods and takes notes but doesn't interrupt.

"Thanks. I need you to come down to the station and sign your statement. That's two now."

I nod, staring down at myself.

Peter speaks up. "Give me an hour, and I'll be down too."

Benny pushes back his hat. "And why is that?"

"To sign your documents and meet Grace's lawyer." Peter wheels toward the house.

Benny follows. "Even after what Mrs. Perkins and Emma said, you still claim it wasn't her."

"I know my wife, and Grace wouldn't—couldn't hurt anyone." Peter studies each of our faces, pausing on each of us until we meet his eyes. "Not ever."

Benny gives Peter a grim smile.

"Come on, Peter. I radioed over. Dr. Logan is probably waiting for you right now." Benny tucks away his notepad and turns Peter away from the Schmidts' front gate.

"Oh, that's a great idea. He is the best GP in town." Mrs. Perkins glances up at me. "Maybe you should wash up." She pats my arm then follows Peter and Benny down the street. Grace watches them too. Her concern obvious on her face, she presses a cheek to the glass as her gaze follows them.

The wind changes, and I gag. "Washing up sounds good."

Peter looks out into the street and points. "My keys. Emma, pick them up, will you?"

"Great." I go out into the street, checking for traffic several times before stepping out. Another car comes up, and my heart stops momentarily. A distinctive gray sedan with a thick plastic barrier between the front and back and barred back windows parks in a spot by the Schmidts.

"Hey, how's it going?" Tom walks toward me.

I stop dead in the street. What I smell like brings a quiver to my bottom lip as I try to smile. "Hi, Tom. Is that a police car?" I keep some distance between us, scooping up my shoes, and resist testing the winds direction.

"My work vehicle. I bought it at auction. What happened here? You okay?"

I see the keys on the road, pick them up. "We'll talk later, I need to go." I run to Peter's front door and quickly try every key on the ring. It's one failure after another.

Tom's heavy steps crunch the gravel as he moves around the cars. I'm closing the door when Tom's voice reaches me. "I'll call you."

***

After I wash my hair at Peter's and borrow an outfit from Grace's closet, I leave my clothes balled up, ready for washing, and sealed in a grocery bag by the back door. I walk over to Dr. Logan's waiting room. Mrs. Perkins sits with Jay and Glady and frowns when I join them.

"Have they released you?" I crouch in front of Jay.

"Yes as long as I come back for my tests next week." She gently but firmly pushes me away with her cane. "Millie says she knows where to go for a phone."

"Good." I find a chair and sit across from them. "Any news yet?"

"No, Peter wouldn't go in until he called a lawyer." Mrs. Perkins looks at her shoes. "It delayed the exam. I'm sure it won't be long."

"Emma, were you hurt?" Glady wants to know.

My muscles ache and my skin screams in places. "I have a few cuts on my back and goose egg on my noggin, but I feel pretty good." Even as I say it, I feel a new twinge and pull my borrowed sleeve up to find my elbow a deep purple. Adrenaline is still wearing off.

"Peter said you saved his life." Glady's false teeth snap.

"Very brave." Jay has a spark of disbelief in her eyes.

"Yes, brave and foolish." Mrs. Perkins, once again, butts in. "Why didn't you stop when I shouted?"

I pull down the sleeve. "I didn't hear you. Why else wouldn't I've listened?"

"Oh, Millie, I see what you mean." Glady pats Mrs. Perkins' arm.

"Young lady, I think being a hero has gone to your head. Remember to use manners." Jay gives me a motherly frown. "It makes dealing with you much easier."

"Easier." I wonder what Mrs. Perkins told them.

Mrs. Perkins offers me a stiff smile.

She's trying to take the remainder of the glory for herself, is she? "Sorry. Almost dying does that to a person."

"Understandable," Jay mumbles, putting her cane between us.

"Of course," Glady adds, but her expression says otherwise.

"Time for our stories." Glady helps Jay to her feet. The ladies leave us, not glancing back.

"They didn't think I should be alone, and they stayed with me while I waited for you and Peter," Mrs. Perkins explains.

"Is that the only reason they dropped by?"

"No, they wanted to know what happened, but I promised Benny I wouldn't say anything."

"Well, we all know you can keep a secret," I mutter, more to myself than to anyone.

"Oh Emma." Mrs. Perkins laughs aloud.

I smile. "How long now?"

"Peter went in ten minutes ago. It will be what it will be." She straightens her skirt, leans back in a slump, and closes her eyes. I'm worried about her too.

Dr. Logan wheels Peter toward us frowning. Once he gets close enough, he nods at me and speaks directly to Mrs. Perkins. "Take him home and put him in bed. Once settled in give him these. No romping around or visiting the police station today. I've already called Benny and told him to expect Peter tomorrow."

Mrs. Perkins nods her understanding. "Okay, he must be able to move to some degree. We need to get him up the stairs."

"According to Peter, Emma is more than capable of dealing with the stairs." Dr. Logan then aims a comment my way. "You should be proud of yourself young lady. I heard you took the brunt of the fall. How are you doing?"

"Good. I'm good." I rise from my chair slowly, stiff from sitting so long.

"Call me if you need me." Dr. Logan hands me a card. "I mean it."

I take his card. "Thanks for everything, especially Aunt Alice."

Dr. Logan nods, lips in a tight line. "Okay, off with you. I have work to do." He gives my shoulder a squeeze that makes me wince. Most likely a bruise there too.

I take control of the chair and push Peter forward. "For the record, we're using the crosswalk. No arguments."

"Learned something, did you?" Mrs. Perkins' hard eyes take me by surprise. She's angry with me.

"Let me guess, that was what you shouted at me." I can't hide my shame.

"Yes." She stands taller. "Sometimes, you are incredibly careless."

"Millie, cut the girl some slack. I told her to cross where she did." Peter mutters. "I'd be dead right now if she wasn't on the ball."

"There wouldn't have been any danger if she had stayed on the sidewalks."

"Or cover if Grace's car did what it did at the corner." Peter takes Mrs. Perkins' hand. "Millie, she saved my life, and that's all there is to it."

***

We leave Peter all tucked in and Mrs. Perkins drives me to my car, so I'm able to catch up with Benny. As I go downtown to the police station to make a statement, she returns to the Schmidts to sit with him. The statements I intend on making excuse me from the discomfort at the house. I need downtime without thank yous or accusations.

The attack makes little sense. Sure, sometimes I want to kill Peter. Maybe Grace has passing bouts too, but her look of surprise moments after Mrs. Perkins saw Grace's car go by spoke to me.

How does anyone regroup and casually wander with an air of innocence into the aftermath of chaos? What does she have, nerves of steel?

I sigh deeply as I park my minivan, slamming the door. Someone, my guess Mrs. Perkins, had written 'wash me' on my side window.

I push my hands deep into Grace's polyester pockets and head for the lobby. *This should be fun.*

Benny glances up at the window as a bell goes off

inside. Jane's pretty face turns toward me, too. He signals to wait, and I sit beside the wilting plant, searching for my phone. Tears threaten to come, and I bite down on my lip fighting them. I left my phone in the grocery bag beside Grace's back door.

This is so stupid because I'm fine. I don't understand it. Bruises and phones are nothing to cry over.

"Thanks for making the time." Benny sarcasm shoots through the glass.

I stand, ready to follow him. "No problem." I want to sound strong and sure of myself, but my voice cracks and my bottom lip wobbles.

Benny leaves the window and opens the security door. "Come through. Would you like some water?"

"Thanks." Pulling my lips into a hard line, I walk through the door. I wave at Jane as she picks up a phone call and types into her computer.

"You know the way." He signals me to continue through to the conference room. "I'll be right behind you."

I walk ahead of him, his light tread absent behind me, and half turn. "You're not going to leave me in here." I scan the empty beige on beige room nervously, not trusting Benny.

Benny's smile, not his best feature, turns cold.

"You're not fooling anyone, lady." He presses his open palm on my lower back. The pressure connects with my cuts and bruises, leaving me no choice but to out run his invasive touch.

As I turn to leave the conference room, he closes the door in my face with a snap. I push closer to the mesh window and see him walking away. I try the handle, and it won't move. Jane's brilliant blue eyes meet mine. She continues with her call. Benny sits at his desk, winks at me, and picks up the phone.

I sit down, fuming. What's he up to now?

Tap, tap, tap. No one at the door. The bare walls might as well have bars. Under fluorescent lamp, shimmering and buzzing, I close my eyes.

"I called Tom." Jane's familiar whisper comes from a speaker near the light fixture. "He'll be here as soon as he's able. I hope Benny listens to him. Do you want coffee or water or anything?"

"Sure, thanks."

Nothing.

"Jane?"

I stand, pace, while Jane speaks with Benny. He's at the coffee station. Our eyes meet, and he smiles again. I don't like it. His whole demeanor screams anger. He takes one of the two coffees in Jane's hands, his smile widens, and he drops it in the garbage.

Jane pales.

"Thanks anyway." I sit at the base of the door and drop my head on my knees. This is too much. I hold my knees to my chest and let go.

Eventually, I settle down and wipe my face. The tapping begins again, and I glance up at the mesh window above my head. No one is there. It takes a moment to realize it's me. I'm tapping my leg.

Okay Alice. I have some time. Let's talk.

Chapter 23

The industrial carpet, taupe with green-gray flecks, invites me to rest. I move to a corner, sit, stretch out my legs, and use the conference room wall as a backrest. I breathe in deeply, close my eyes and let the surrounding room disappear. Recorded or not, I enter the white room. I'm expected to be odd since I'm the new local psychic.

The curtains of light mesh, hang limp and the windows around the room hold an empty darkness. I push one curtain aside then the next, wishing for light. The bedding crumpled on the floor. I make the bed and sit on the duvet cover to wait.

"Getting bored?" The voice booms from above.

I almost jump out of my skin. "Where have you been?"

"You figure it out." The curtains gust and a flash of lightning flares, outlining Aunt Alice's silhouette. "I've been watching you. Waiting for you to realize how much you need me."

"I've been busy." I fold my arms over my chest.

"You're sure on top of things. Someone tries to kill

you, and you land up locked in here." She snickers to herself. "Way to go."

"You going to help?" I snub out my anger before it gets in my way, and go to the window, holding the curtain aside. Alice's angry eyes narrow.

Her lips tight. "Did you get a good look at the driver?"

"No." Even as I say it I imagine myself back on the road, tugging on the stuck wheelchair. "I was friggin busy trying to get the heck out of the way."

"But she was there?" Aunt Alice prompts.

"Sure, I mean yes. Grace came out the hospital, acting like she didn't have a care in the world." The fabric snaps out of my hand and covers the glass. "Never mind, attempting murder." I pull the flimsy fabric aside, fighting to hold it still.

"You're sure it's Grace?" Alice paces into the smoky darkness outside, becoming more ghost-like the further she goes.

"Mrs. Perkins yelled and ran along the sidewalk. She recognized the car."

Alice says nothing.

I don't need to see it. I feel it. "It was Grace. It was Grace's car...you think someone else drove her car?"

"So, you're not a fool after all." Aunt Alice taps the side of her head, encouraging me. "Assuming nothing, choose between a gut feeling or seeing it with your own eyes."

"Okay, let's say you're right and the driver is someone else. Who?" Frustrated with the flapping of wild fabric I tear the curtains down with a sharp tug and throw the rod aside. "Who do you choose? Tell me since you know so much."

Aunt Alice steps closer, smooths her hair, and smiles at me. "May I come in?"

"Nah-huh." I'm in control of whether she comes in here or not. "If you want to help it must be from there."

"That's it then." She slaps a palm on her hip. "You don't need me anymore. Well, I don't believe you." Her eyes narrow. "Have you asked yourself why?"

Why would someone try to kill Peter? I try it aloud. "Charlie may want to inherit Peter's home business. I'm not sure Marcy has a motive, but Bob might need money, raising a child alone is expensive. Grace may want Peter to stop spending all their money on his ex-wife and his son."

"Is that all true?" Aunt Alice jeers. "Still true?"

I shake my head. No, Peter holds one active loan. "Not much money left in the business the way he's spending it on Claire, which knocks everyone off the suspect list."

"Again I ask is this true? What about Bob?"

"No. Grace has a clear and understandable motive. She won't inherit if Peter doesn't stop spending all their money. But then, that's true of Bob too. Changes Bob to a maybe." I'm confused. "Grace and Peter loving each other changes Grace to an unlikely."

"Anyone else?" Aunt Alice steps closer. Mist swirls around her legs.

"Motive? I haven't talked with Marcy much, but she's not going to inherit a thing if Peter dies, and she's definitely frightened of something."

"Don't expect Benny to help you work this out." She smiles at me. "But if you talk it over with Millie you'll figure it out together."

The room dims, and the curtains fall still. "Are you there?"

"You need to go." The voice echoes from everywhere.

"What?"

"He's coming," Aunt Alice calls from nowhere and everywhere.

I open my eyes as Tom walks through the opening

door. "Benny, she came in to sign two statements. They're on your desk all typed up and ready to go. What are you up to?"

"How do you know I didn't just this second finish typing them up?"

"Jane called me."

"She hasn't been here that long." Benny follows Tom to the table and drops clipboard on the work surface. He turns toward me. "Coffee?"

"No, I've had about as much hospitality as I can stand. Thanks." I get to my feet.

Tom sits down. "Love a cup." He takes my hand to stop me from storming out.

Benny walks past me as if nothing is wrong, and comes back a moment later with three cups all with cream in them and two printed pages. He pulls sugar packets and stir sticks out of his pocket and tosses them into the middle of the table. "Help yourself."

We did. I catch the pages pushed my way and read. The statements read exactly what I stated, and I sign them. Not wanting to spend another moment near Benny I stand, ready to go.

"Grace staying overnight until Peter can bail her out?" I ask as we walk through the office.

"That would have made me happy, but I don't have a witness confirming the driver. Whoever did it used her car though. We found it trashed and wiped clean." Benny speaks directly to Tom ignoring me completely.

"She's no longer a suspect." I scan the room. Jane, her gaze on us, places a fingertip over the headset microphone, muttering to herself. I give her a finger wave and mouth, thanks.

"Benny, someone tried to kill them." Tom crosses his arms, stopping at the exit.

"True and I've impounded the car, but we've found no proof Grace did anything wrong."

I push between them, hoping to be included.

"Someone needs to keep tabs on them." Tom chins the general direction of the Schmidts.

"I'll have a car drive by every hour." Benny raises a hand to stop Tom's rebuttal. "You see her pretty face. Blinded, you want Emma to be innocent, but I have to keep an open mind. She may be partnered up with the driver. Who brought the chocolates to the garden party?"

"Benny, what is wrong with you?" I shout, not believing my ears. "Only you could find a way to blame me for something like this. Someone tried to kill both of us."

"Yes and you had something to do with it." Benny

looks down at me, glaring.

"You took my statement."

"Yes, I did." He walks to the door of the lobby. "Now, leave."

"Benny?" Tom barks.

"I said I'll have a car go by the Schmidts'." He waves me toward the door. "I said nothing about her."

No proof, no arrest. I need a distraction, a break, and decide to visit Claire. I leave Tom and Benny arguing.

After a quick drive back to the hospital, I enter Claire's room. I find it empty and the bed stripped. Unsure what happened, I mull over what to do. I find Marcy at the nurses' station, and her eyes widen when she sees me.

Once I'm at counter, I ask as calmly as possible, "Hey Marcy, was Claire moved?"

"Sorry, but she passed away before I came on shift today." She swallows. "I had nothing to do with it. I wasn't even here." Marcy steps back from the counter.

I grip my elbows, my hands shaking.

"Emma?" She quickly moves out of the station, takes my arm, and slides me into an office chair. "Sit. Just breathe. It came on suddenly."

Marcy blurs behind my tears. "But she seemed stronger, as if she was getting better."

The blurry shape pulls away. "I know. I'm sorry."

"I can't believe it."

"Let me get you some water."

I wipe my face, processing the cold hard news. Marcy takes my hand and tries to put a paper cup in it.

"Thanks." My voice strained, and my hands clammy. I keep seeing Claire's image in my mind's eye—healthy and pain free. I choke on a sob.

"Here take this." Marcy firmly closes my hand around the paper cup and gently lifts my arm.

"Thank you." I complete the motion, lifting the cup to my lips and take a small sip. "I'm sorry for being such a bitch. Something about hospitals brings out the worst in me. It's the building, people, smell. It's not rational."

"I understand." She rests her hand on my shoulder. "I'm sorry for your loss."

I sip, longer, deeper. "It's too soon. She's supposed to hold her grandchild."

"I remember." Marcy nods. "Will you be okay?"

"I guess." I stand up and hand over the empty cup. "Thanks for the water."

With little thought, I walk down the hallway to Jay's room. I keep wondering if talking to her would help. When I enter, I find the bed messed. I gasp, grabbing the doorjamb. It takes a moment to remember she was released. I relax, walk to the window, and gaze down on the Schmidts' front room window.

Mrs. Perkins sits in the living room. My stomach gives me a quick pinch when I realize I'm supposed to work in ten minutes. No phone. Backtracking to the nurses' station.

When Marcy sees my face her hand goes for an office chair. "Now what?"

"Nothing. I was wondering if I can use the phone."

"Sure." Marcy lifts the phone from the lower counter and places it in front of me. "I thought you just met Claire?"

"I did. Some people just click." I let out a stuttering breath. "I don't know the number for Pie 'n' All."

"We call there all the time." She pulls a menu from a drawer.

The number is spelled out in finger sandwiches and tea bags. After two rings, Maggie answers.

"Hey, I'm sorry, but I won't be in today."

I imagine her looking for the list of scheduled appointments. "Sounds serious."

"It is." I take a deep breath. "Claire died."

"Oh, no." Maggie sucks in some air. "Don't worry

about a thing everyone will understand. We'll reschedule when you're ready."

"Thanks, Maggie. You're the best."

I hang up the phone and rush down the hall to the elevator. My hands recheck my pockets for my phone, and I make a mental note to find it.

Moments later, I run across the street and burst into Peter's house. Between calling Maggie and getting to Peter's something snaps in me. The shock slips away, and when I walk through the doorway my emotions overwhelm me. I find Mrs. Perkins, and kneel at her feet, choking on the words I need to say.

There is no other way but to say them—plainly and without flowers.

"Claire died today," I blurt.

Mrs. Perkins takes me into a hug and lets me hold on to her until I can think again.

"What's happened?" Grace comes from the hallway.

"Marcy told me." I pull away. "Claire looked like she felt better." I hiccup. "But she died. She died."

"I'll call Marcy." Grace turns on her heel. "She at work now?"

"Yes." I sit back. "At the nurses' station on the

second floor."

"I should call Dr. Logan." Mrs. Perkins pulls me close to her and whispers in my ear. "All too soon after Peter's attack. Much too convenient."

"Mrs. Perkins, none of this makes any sense. Benny accused me of being part of all this." It takes all I have to meet Grace's eyes. "He thinks we did it together."

"You need tea." Mrs. Perkins pats my hand. "We all do. What a shock." She adjusts her hem as she stands.

"I'm not sure how much more Peter will cope with." Grace stands in the kitchen doorway.

"I'm sure she tried to fight it, but sickness doesn't always give us a choice." Mrs. Perkins meets my eyes.

I know she's lying. She thinks Claire was poisoned.

I nod. "She did seem much better."

"True. Another mystery?" Mrs. Perkins seems to be testing all of us.

"Millie, please." Grace covers the mouthpiece of the wall phone and sits on the stool under it. "Not now."

Backing into the kitchen, I take Mrs. Perkins with me. "Maybe." I let that settle for a moment. "Maybe not. Are we seeing murder everywhere we look?"

"Yes, well. I've been right so far, haven't I?" She doesn't wait for an argument, but plunges ahead. "Give me your phone Emma. I need to talk to the doctor."

"He wouldn't have had time to do anything yet." My hands automatically go to my pockets.

Grace gets to her feet, dragging a long cord with her as she steps into the hall for privacy.

I frown at the bag by the door, and crouch beside, fighting with the knot.

"I need to know he'll be investigating this." Mrs. Perkins snaps her fingers at me. "Properly and not assuming anything like they did with Alice."

"First, Aunt Alice. Second, Peter." I hold up a finger for each. "Now, Claire." I carefully pick through my dirty clothes, pullout my phone and see the note. I stare at it. "Claire gave this to me when Peter and I visited her this morning." I hold up the page.

"And you didn't mention this to Benny when you were at the station?" Mrs. Perkins looks impressed as she takes it to read. "Well done."

"Not on purpose. I forgot all about it."

"We have to call Benny later."

"Later sounds good to me." Benny will take the note and think I withheld evidence. "As soon as he sees it, he'll arrest me. If we go to him, we better take answers with us."

"He can have it tested." Mrs. Perkins thinks aloud. "Check for more evidence. It's talking about Peter and Claire."

"Do you see any names?" I hadn't meant to snap. "He'll think what he wants. That stupid note will prompt him to arrest me and whoever he decides is my partner."

"Emma, you need to calm yourself." Mrs. Perkins puts out her hand. "I need your phone."

I hold the phone out of her reach. "Okay, but you're calling the doctor?"

"First Dr. Logan, then Tom."

"Tom doesn't need to be involved in this." Even though I complain I still hand over my phone. Deep inside, a vague image forms but too far away to be clear.

I walk over to the couch, and look Grace in the eye. "Tell me everything that has been going on between Peter and Claire, every detail. No matter how small. You know something, and I need to know it too."

Graces stares at me wide eyed and doesn't speak immediately. When she does it's in nervous spurts. "We don't talk about Claire very much, but her illness brought us together. I volunteered at the hospital after Marcy suggested it and did the book and magazine cart for the patients that had trouble getting around. I'd visit with some of the lonely patients. The first time I saw Peter, he sat with Claire in the clinic waiting area. As she worsened and began overnight stays in the hospital, I saw them more often. We talked about Tammy. One day, Peter dropped by the nurses' station while I waited for Marcy. She had to finish up paperwork and suggested that we go for a coffee and she'd catch up with us.

"I started off consoling him, and before I knew it, we were dating. He never stopped visiting Claire. I knew he needed to stand by her. When she needed money to try some experimental drugs, I agreed."

"So, that's why he picked up the bill when we visited Claire?"

"Yes, and they argued." Grace covers her face with her hands.

"He told you?" I wanted to hear her side more than I wanted to breathe.

"Peter told me she wanted to stop treatment. He feared she gave up." She sighed. "She reacted badly to the drugs this round."

Mrs. Perkins comes around the corner. "Well, I spoke with Dr. Logan. He says they've done all kinds of tests because the program she's on. Nothing shown up, but it is still early."

I need Grace to stay focused on our discussion. "Peter was a great comfort for Claire."

"You understand." Grace nods. "Peter loves like no one I've ever met."

I didn't understand. *Either he is a fool or I'm missing something.*

Chapter 24

Face blotched and red, Tom stands over Mrs. Perkins as if that will intimidate her. Bent at the waist, hands on hips, he yells. "You need to stop this."

I pull Mrs. Perkins away from him. "Go to your corners…Now!"

Tom slowly turns away and stares at the wallpaper in the Schmidts' living room. Mrs. Perkins paces back and forth, puffing and huffing like a wolf in a bedtime story.

"Let's keep this civil." I place myself between them. "Okay, Tom all the shouting in the world will not stop her from doing what she does and Peter rests down the hall. So, do me a favor and quiet down."

"You have got to be kidding me," Tom mutters under his breath. "Fine, I'm sorry."

"Somebody killed Aunt Alice…and Claire." A wave of sadness hits and I raise a hand to my eyes.

Tom's face changes from confused, to sad, to grim. "Okay let's say you had all the proof right in front of you." His gaze falls on the note secured in a zip-lock bag. "Who did it?"

"I'm not sure." I stomp my foot on the carpet and the thud I expected disappoints. "Tom, they tried to kill me and Peter today."

"We'll figure this out. We suspected something wrong long before Benny picked up the scent." Mrs. Perkins glares passed me at Tom. "Tom read the note again."

"It—" I close my mouth with a snap, pick up the bag, and wave it around. "It's not enough."

Tom takes Mrs. Perkins by the shoulders and calmly meets her eyes. "She'll be hurt, possibly killed. She's acting more like you every day."

"I knew it." Mrs. Perkins stops and drops her hands on her hips. "Even if we had the ability to solve this thing...doesn't matter, does it? Because all you're focusing on is Emma."

"I need her alive." Tom pulls his phone out. "It's a police matter. I'm calling Benny."

"Do what you gotta do." Mrs. Perkins takes the note I try to hand over to Tom. "But as soon as Benny becomes involved, all hell will break loose."

I sit down on the couch moving the curtain aside. I glare up at the hospital windows, and I see a flash of red hair and a pale face disappear. Creepy.

Mrs. Perkins sits beside me. "I need to think."

"Finally." Tom walks into the kitchen. The tone of his voice changes as he speaks into phone.

"Outstanding." I lean back and rub my forehead. "Let's maneuver Tom out of here and send Benny with him."

"Yes, take them out somewhere," Mrs. Perkins suggests. "I'll take it from here."

"No way. Not with Benny." I glance at the kitchen as Tom walks by the doorway. "Besides, Tom'd never fall for it."

"We need a plan." Mrs. Perkins taps her foot in mid-air.

"Tom leaves with Benny." I palm my face and take a deep breath. "If we give them the note, that will distract them."

"Our one solid clue?" Mrs. Perkins suddenly becomes serene. "I quit. Wash my hands of the whole thing. I'm going home."

"Walk away?" I'm not believing this for a moment. "That's great. Well, I'm not. Even if I have to call Aunt Alice. She'll be disappointed in you. She told me to depend on you, and together we would figure this out." I sigh. "Okay, tirade over. If you have to go, fine. You'll come back, right? When you do, please bring me a change of clothes? I can't wear Grace's clothes forever."

"Of course, dear." Mrs. Perkins looks around gathering her things.

"You are coming back tonight, right?" I hope the draw will be too strong to resist.

"I'm spending the night at home." She pats my hand, her lips tighten as she lies. "If I change my mind, I'll call."

I smile to myself. *She's up to something.* "Tomorrow then."

"What's going on?" Tom stands at the door.

"I'm going home."

"Finally, someone talking sense. Let me walk you to your car."

"I'll do it." I've had enough. "I don't want you two arguing again."

"Come on, it's not that bad."

I stare him down. "You yelled at an old woman moments ago." I follow Mrs. Perkins out. "He's supposed to be an adult." I take her into the night air. It's cool, clean. We pause at the bottom of the stairs and glance up.

"What a beautiful night." Mrs. Perkins follows the narrow sidewalk. "Thank you, Emma. You're upset with

Tom, but he's worried about us and he's not handling it very well. He's still a good man."

"You're right. You are always right." I follow her to her car and wait for her to settle in. "You up to something? Leaving me out again?"

"Of course not. I wouldn't dare." She starts her car. "I'll see you tomorrow."

As she drives away, I raise a hand and wave.

Tom comes out of the house, joining me on the sidewalk. "Benny wants me to bring the note to him." He shows me the note pinched between his fingers.

"Take it. I don't care anymore."

"Don't care?" He stops in mid-step. "We're okay, right?"

"Sure, I guess." I'm tired and sad, incredibly sad, when I think of him. I'll never figure out where Tom comes from. Why does he hang around? Why do I care? Do I like a man that yells at an old woman, showing her little to no respect? Do I like a man that makes me scared and at the same time excited? I take his hand, running my thumb over his empty palm. "I'm confused, too upset to talk right now. Aunt Alice, Claire, and someone trying to run me over is too much."

"Emma, I lost my head with Millie Perkins. It won't

happen again." Tom lifts my hand to his lips. "I mean it."

He kisses me goodbye.

"Okay," I say as he walks away. I watch his car until it drives around the corner and then go back in the house. Grace makes tea as if she is a programmed machine. I'm not the only one suffering from shell shock.

"You've been taking care of Peter all day. How about I apologize for my earlier behavior by taking care of you?" I lead her to the chair at the kitchen table and settle her in. "Relax for a moment."

I open some cupboards, searching for the things I'll need for tea, and set the table. Grace silently follows my movements, picking at her nail polish.

"You have anything to eat? What I mean is you should eat something and then go to bed yourself."

Grace shakes her head. "I'm not hungry."

"A light snack and rest your eyes." I smile at her. "I promise to stand guard over both of you."

"No, not until I'm sure you believe me." Grace drops her hands into her lap. "I'd never hurt Peter or you. I have a guilty pleasure. To sate it, I sneaked over to the gift shop in the hospital and picked up some chocolate." She smiles weakly. "It helps with stress."

But her hands were empty when she came through

the hospital doors. "You weren't carrying anything when you joined us."

"I ate it right away." She met my eyes. "Like I said it's a guilty pleasure."

Possible, I suppose. "Anyone see you?"

"I cut through the clinic waiting room. I'm not sure if anyone noticed."

"And the receipt?"

"I tossed it." She looks down and starts on another nail. "I didn't know I'd need proof."

"Tomorrow will be a new day." The kettle whistles, and I pour water into the teapot. "I'll pop over and check if anyone remembers you."

I open the fridge searching for a yogurt or another quick snack. Nothing appeals and when I close the door I'm face to face with receipts for Claire's medication, ten thousand dollars for last month's meds and forty thousand for this one. Motive spotlighted for anyone to read.

No wonder Claire was broke and staying away from her kid. This would destitute anyone. She tried to stop Peter. He must have been going through money fast. Six months would equal thousands upon thousands of dollars. The longer Claire stayed alive, the more money it cost the family.

Little squares of bright letters flash into my mind spelling out, "Stop it or I'll kill him."

A chill goes through me. Maybe I'm not as safe as I thought. I found the motive. I'm sure of it. Opportunity, Grace at the hospital. Means. Yes, both strong enough and smart enough to kill Claire and Aunt Alice.

"Need help finding anything?"

I spin on my heel covering the bill with my back. Grace's quiet footsteps let her come up behind without warning. She's so close my skin crawls.

"Looking for a snack. Do you have any cookies?"

"I have a stash." She waits until I step aside before she opens the fridge freezer.

I back away, hitting the island, thinking hard on how I sneak Peter out of here. Everything clicks and my heart's jumping. The cups clink and clatter as my hands shake taking a tray to the table.

"Why don't you sit?" Grace pulls cake slices from the freezer and places them on a plate. "I love frozen cake. It's just so—" Grace notices the change in me. "Oh dear, the accident caught up with you. You're going into shock." She rushes to me, slipping me into a chair like her daughter did hours before.

I'm shaking and wish with all my might not to be

alone with a murderer. Scared, I meet Grace's warm and kind eyes. "I'm sorry. It hit me…first Claire's sudden death, and then Aunt Alice with no one to know."

Tap, tap, tap. One of my fingers twitches on the tabletop. Grace selects flatware, sets them beside our plates, and lifts the lid of the teapot, playing with the teabag with a spoon. She pours milk in her cup, heaps of sugar into mine, and pours a round.

"Sweet tea will help." She gives my cup a quick stir and pushes it toward me.

"Where's Peter?"

"Still resting in our room. He'll sleep until tomorrow."

"An upsetting day for all of us." I nod and sample the tea. It's good.

"Yes. You said something about Alice. What's happened?" Grace sits, draping a napkin across her lap.

I have to try twice to answer her. My voice sticks in my throat. "Dr. Logan told us today that Aunt Alice didn't die of natural causes."

"Everyone said she fell down her loft stairs because of a heart attack. After all this time, how does he know any different?"

"I didn't ask, so I'm not sure. Dr. Logan examined

her. He found something to cause concern." I straighten my cup on its saucer, the china rings as I set it right. This might be my last night alive. "She was murdered."

"I'm sorry, Emma." Grace takes a long drink of tea and sighs. "Let's try some cake. If we pretend to be normal, we may feel more normal."

"Sure, let's try that." I finish my tea.

"It's true then. You and Millie aren't imaging murder everywhere you look." Grace shivers. "Some of it's real."

"Afraid so. No one knows who your car tried to run over. I think when they missed Peter, they went after Claire."

"No." The word was soft. Grace stares for a moment. "Why?"

"Money," I suggest, unable to stop. "Possibly, jealousy."

"I don't understand." Grace tastes her cake. "Oh, delicious. Try some."

I pick up my fork and poke at the chocolate icing. "Peter spends large amounts of money on her." I point at the note on the fridge.

"Yes, but it was only a loan." Grace pours another round.

"I'm sorry. How does a dead woman pay back that kind of money?"

"Peter the banker suggested Claire sign over all her funds, and he would manage them for her. With her insurance and his investments, there will be more than enough money." Claire smiles at me. "So, you see, that can't be a motive."

"Claire's estate will pay all the money back." I sigh, and my hands stop trembling.

"Peter wouldn't make such a decision without both of us agreeing." Grace puts her cup down and leans forward. "You don't understand how a good marriage works, do you?"

"I guess not." Tea leaves in the shape of a chapel flash in my mind. *More to learn, but it's time to focus.* "Did anyone else know about your arrangement?"

"I doubt Peter or Claire discussed it openly." Grace stops eating and sets her fork down.

"Anyone might misunderstand what's going on."

"Misunderstand what?"

"May think Peter still loves Claire." Like I just did. "And would spend his last dime paying for her care and comfort."

Grace bursts out laughing. "He loves both of us.

Three of us, if you count his first wife." Grace takes in my face. "She's never been competition. The poor woman was dying."

I agree with Grace. "But from the outside looking in, it appears completely different." The pieces fall into place. Grace and Peter, happily married, have no secrets.

"How would this person find out about Peter paying Claire's bills?" She quirks an eyebrow. "And why would this someone care about it?"

How did they know? Most townsfolk know half the story. People from the party might have seen the bills posted on the fridge. I know who the killer is, and my stomach churns at the thought of how much I provoked the person. "I gotta go."

"Are we safe?"

I can't help but smile confidently. "Oh yes, the killing is over."

Chapter 25

I'm somewhere between standing with my feet planted securely on the floor and lost inside my head with alarms blaring. The tinkle of Grace's spoon on china wakes me up. I run for the back door, leaving her behind, and hurry across the street to the hospital. The halls and stairwell echo the slap of my shoes. I need to retrieve Claire's things before she finds out the note is gone.

A brunette nurse doodles with a phone tucked between her ear and shoulder. She ignores me, and I catch my breath as I wait, pacing and muttering. She's pixie-like, glancing up at me while she cups the receiver and lowers her voice.

"I will." The nurse giggles, blushing. She puts the phone down. "How may I help?"

"A patient died today, Claire. I've been instructed to pick up her belongings by her daughter." With all my heart and soul, I will her to cooperate. My pent up energy pours from me, the nurse must sense it too.

She blinks. "That's funny. Mrs. Perkins said the same thing not even a half hour ago."

My hands drop to my sides, not believing Mrs. Perkins took Claire's things without telling me. I should have known. She never gives up. *No, she left me out of it, again.*

The nurse's pleasant face turns from pixie to suspicious guard. "Something wrong?"

"No, no, of course not." My brain won't work. "Are you all on your own tonight?" My voice not as friendly or welcoming as I hoped.

"Skeleton crew at this hour." She smiles. "Unless you need something else I have my duties to do."

"Sure. Have a good one." I turn on my heel with that incessant tapping from inside my head driving me mad. "Not now, Aunt Alice. I have no time to play stupid mind games."

"No games." Her voice is like a sigh. "Too proud."

I retrace my steps and gulp the fresh air as I run for my van. Thank the heavens I insisted on getting my own car earlier. I pull my phone from my pocket and punch in Mrs. Perkins number.

It rings, but she doesn't answer.

I drive out of town forcing myself to slow for corners until I hit the highway. Ten minutes out, a herd of deer wander on to the road. I honk my horn and flash my lights, trying to warn them away, but they gather together, blocking the road as they walk to the river.

I try her number again.

"Where is she?" But Aunt Alice doesn't need to tell me.

It's as if a tether links the two of us, she's scared, needs help, and is waiting for me. I've never been as sure of anything before in my life. The killer is with her. My blood runs cold and my tears run hot as I drive through the herd of white-tails, slowing me to a crawl.

***

I slam my ride in park and jump out, running in the dark. I crack my hip on the gate and limp to the backyard. As I near the back door, I slow my pace because the door's ajar. I pull out my phone and try her number. It rings inside, but she won't pick up.

I crept through her house only days before and realize real life doesn't compare to a crime drama. I push the door to open it wider and inch forward with my heart pounding. The door gently taps the fridge and goes still. Not trying the light, I step into the mixed shadows of twilight.

My shoes whisper on the tiles as I look around. I see no clue as to why the door is ajar or why Mrs. Perkins doesn't answer the phone. But something sinister scratches at my last nerve.

"Mrs. Perkins? It's Emma from next door. You okay?"

Silence. I inch toward the knife drawer. It's open and empty. I open the next drawer over, pulling a ladle, slotted spoon, potato masher, and finally a rolling pin.

A small sound carries from deeper in the house, and I'm tempted to call the police. I need the police, but Benny the bully is all that's available. By the time we finished arguing—

I pick up the bulkiest utensil and take a step, following the sound. Not thinking of what might happen, I heft the rolling pin into the air, test it for weight. Armed, ready, here I go.

A small thump like a cat landing on carpet makes me jump. As I step into the dining room I hear muffled voices upstairs. I kick off my shoes and pad to the stairs, eyes toward the second floor.

"Put that away. No one will fall for another accident. Dr. Logan knows about Alice. You're not fooling anyone anymore." Mrs. Perkins is angry. She's stalling.

My heart rises in my throat. She knows I'm here.

"Stop it. Just stop it and let me think," an unfriendly

voice replies.

"They're coming. They're probably surrounding the house right now." Mrs. Perkins' military footfalls move across the ceiling and stop at the far wall.

"Shut it! I mean it. I need time."

Taking one stair at a time, I creep forward with the end of my club shaking like a leaf.

I tighten my grip and glance up at the glittery ceiling. Time to do the sensible thing, I'll call 911. I back up and move to the kitchen. When I pick up the wall phone, the beep-beep-beep from the phone being engaged too long sounds in my ear.

I guess they didn't like me calling a few minutes ago.

A loud thud comes from upstairs. Before I can stop myself, I'm running to the stairs. Another thump and I imagine Mrs. Perkins falling to the ground. I take my first step, gripping at the stair railing for support. My toe catches on the riser, and I push hard on the railing to stop from slamming my face or the rolling pin into the stairs.

Shoulder aching, I rest the rolling pin over my heart. It's pounding through the fabric. I dry my hand on my chest, gaze up. *Don't worry, Mrs. Perkins. I'll save you. I'll save you or die.*

I take the stairs one at a time, listening with all my might for more signs of life. Tears blur my vision, forcing me to let the banister guide my way. At the top of the stairs, I drag my sleeve over my cheeks. A bright crack shines between den door and doorjamb. A shadow passes through it, a whisper of cloth on cloth, a squeak of a chair.

I close my eyes, recalling the wooden guest chair, wobbly and tucked in the corner, the bookcase full to bursting, the desk and adjustable chair, and all the clothes by the window. I raise the rolling pin to my shoulder, readying myself for war.

Quiet steps. Slow steps. Closer and closer I move listening for Mrs. Perkins voice. It sounds muffled and slurred.

Then the other voice, the high pitch of an upset female, speaks, "…Millie…you sound like her. She said anything at the end, trying to save her life. The fool does a reading for me, and she stops in the middle. How obvious? Says she's too tired to continue but I saw it in her eyes. She knew, and I had to…I had to…like I have to with you. I've come too far. No quitting now."

I'm at the door and see nothing but a corner of the room. Mrs. Perkins sits in her adjustable chair. It's tilted back. She can't move. Her feet resting on her desk. The wooden chair gone, but I hear it beyond the door. A squeak comes from the left. She's between me and the window.

I meet bright green eyes. Does Mrs. Perkins see me? Something wrong with her face. It's swollen, and her bottom lip split.

"Alice, cocky, arrogant, underestimated me. I wasn't about to risk her telling someone. I worked too hard breaking Peter and Claire up. Claire and I used to visit, you see. I was her friend—her confidant. A gentle woman. I easily pushed her trusting soul in the direction she needed to go.

"Got her thinking about what dragging a new husband through such loss would do to him. She broke it off. Mom did without for years to put me through school. Not a complaint. She spent all her money on us. Always giving, giving, giving. I told her about the volunteer program at the hospital and how it needed her.

"Peter and Mom met and clicked just as I had hoped. They were happy. Very happy until Dr. Logan pulled strings and Claire found her way into a drug trial. I didn't count on Peter spending all his money on his ex-wife." Marcy sobbed. I knew that sob. It was the sound of a woman breaking deep inside. She had nothing to lose. Everything was already gone.

"Why did I go to all that trouble if Mom would live in poverty? I worked so hard." She sobs again.

"Ingenious. Very smart." Mrs. Perkins swollen lip makes it hard for her to talk. "Claire's gone now. Nothing left to worry about."

"No," Marcy shouts. She walks into my line of sight, the cleaver in her right hand. "When I missed Peter today, I knew there wouldn't be another chance. Not with the two of you in my way. The spending had to stop. It had to." Marcy hiccups, her breath stuttering.

With Marcy's back to me, I gently push the door open an inch. Mrs. Perkins sitting at the desk shakes her head slightly. Marcy wearing her nursing uniform paces out of sight and back again, hair on end. Light glints off of the cleaver's polished surface in her right hand. It catches her face, her eyes wide, and her mouth almost invisible.

I pull my phone from my pocket and almost cry out. The battery is dead. With trembling lips and hand, I replace it in my pocket. Mrs. Perkins pulls her lips into a firm line.

She knows what I will do and braces herself.

I dig in my toes then slowly push the door wider, not taking my eyes off Marcy's back. I take a deep breath, and throw the rolling pin at the window. As Marcy turns toward the noise, I run at her, slamming her into the desk. I knock the wind out of myself, sprawled on the desktop with Marcy twisting below me waving the cleaver's sharp edge near my ear.

Somehow, the cleaver passes without taking a chunk of me. Pulling her forearm in the direction of the cleaver, we spin and fall. The blade hits the floor above my shoulder. I bend my knee, buck my hips, and toss her into the clothes. As quickly as I'm able, I stand, ready to defend myself.

"Mrs. Perkins, leave. Get out." I run at Marcy not knowing how I will stop her, only knowing I must. My hand gets caught in the boa, and I pull hard on it. The whole stand falls, bringing clothes and all on top of us. I find her hair, grab a fist of it, and pull it up and away. Next, I'm slamming her forehead into the floor.

I raise her head to do it again, but a gentle hand lands on my shoulder. "Stand down, Emma." Mrs. Perkins' hand digs in and pulls me away from the stunned nurse and murderer. She kicks the cleaver away from Marcy's hand.

Not yet. I take the blue boa and pull the woman free of the clothes. I tie her arms legs together. Mrs. Perkins stands beside me, her curls mussed, her face bruised. I pull myself to my feet, take her into my arms, and silently thank God she's okay.

I let Mrs. Perkins go once the shaking stops. Aching all over, I step back, and examine her face. "Does it hurt?"

"It certainly does." She traces the bruise, using her fingertips, along her jaw line, and wincing at her split lip. "Never do that again."

"What?" I pace away. "Don't save your life again? You kidding me?"

"Well no. I didn't mean that. I meant…wait a minute. Why did Benny let you come bursting in here alone?" Mrs. Perkins eyes grow wide. "Where is everyone?"

"Everyone?"

"You didn't do this alone, did you?" She huffs, steps around Marcy, and looks out the broken window. "You might have been killed! What's in that head of yours?"

I smile and admit it was a bitter one. "I rescued you. If you hadn't gone off on your own… Not a thought about me. What were you thinking?"

"Show some respect, young lady." She walks over to a small wooden box on her desk, flips the lid, and pulls a telephone handset out of it. Dialing, she mutters, "Youngsters today."

"I wonder where we get it from." I huff.

Blue feathers ruffle with each breath Marcy takes.

"You didn't answer my question. Why did you go to the hospital and alert Marcy?" I cross my arms. "And dump me."

"I wanted to take Claire's things before anyone found out about the note." Her explanation is rather lame. "I didn't know Marcy killed anyone."

"Why didn't you call me? You're doing it all over again, leaving me out of it, and provoking a killer."

Mrs. Perkins waves a hand at me to shut me up. "Katie, that you…would you let Benny know we have the killer tied…Yes, I did. Tied as in tied up…in my den…Is that Tom shouting? Would you put him on?"

She offers me the phone. "He sounds upset. You'd better talk to him. I'm sure he'll have a few things to say to you."

"Yeah, and to you, too." I take it. "We're not done. You're not getting out that easy."

"Emma really. It's this kind of behavior that scares men away." Mrs. Perkins waves the handset at me. "Take it before he sees sense."

I suck in a deep breath, knowing there is no one else I'd rather get heck from, but not now. I want to see his face when he finds out what kind of hero I am. And whether he yells, or hugs, I want that too.

"Hey, tonight's been a bit busy, but I was wondering if you'd like to get together tomorrow for breakfast." I roll my eyes when Mrs. Perkins gives me a thumbs up.

Acknowledgements

I wish to thank the following people for their feedback and support:

Emma, Erika, Erin, Kristine, Leti, Sheryl, and Zahra

Note to my Readers

Thank you for taking the time to read White Light. I hope you enjoyed it.

If you did and you're willing, please share your feelings in a short review. Word of mouth is an author's best friend and it will be much appreciated.

Anna

About Anna

Anna Simpson lives near the Canadian-US border with her family. Although she's lived in several places in British Columbia, her free spirit wasn't able to settle down until she moved back to her hometown.

The woman is easy to find if you know the magic word -- emaginette. Do an internet search and you'll see what I mean. :-)

Anna's Links:

https://emaginette.wordpress.com

http://emaginette.wix.com/emaginette

https://www.facebook.com/ShoutWithEmaginette

https://www.goodreads.com/author/show/6577123.Anna_Simpson

Book Club Questions

1. Do you ever imagine what it would be like to live a non-violent/crime free area? How would it change your day to day life?

2. Is it wrong to hang out with someone that is older or younger? Is adopting a grandparent/grandchild something we all should do?

3. Can arguing actually bring people closer?

4. Ever gone to a fortune teller just for fun? What did you think?

5. Do you think acceptance builds relationships?